Second Line

Second Line

Two Short Novels
of
Love and Cooking
in
New Orleans

Poppy Z. Brite

Small Beer Press
Easthampton, MA

Small Beer Press
150 Pleasant Street #306
Easthampton, MA 01027
smallbeerpress.com
bookmoonbooks.com
info@smallbeerpress.com

Distributed to the trade by Consortium.

Library of Congress Cataloging-in-Publication Data

Brite, Poppy Z.
Second line : two short novels of love and cooking in New Orleans / Poppy Z. Brite.
-- 1st ed.
p. cm.
ISBN 978-1-931520-60-7 (pbk. : alk. paper)
1. New Orleans (La.)--Fiction. I. Brite, Poppy Z. Value of X. II. Brite, Poppy Z.
D*U*C*K. III. Title.
PS3552.R4967S43 2009
813'.54--dc22

2009026607

First edition 2 3 4 5 6 7 8 9

Printed in the USA.
Text set in Minion 11 pt. Titles set in Bernard.

The Value of X

For Jamie Shannon
1961–2001

"The food in Heaven just got a whole lot better."
—Ti Adelaide Martin

1

"Awright," said Mrs. Reilly to her eleventh-grade algebra class, "if Y equals thirty-six, who can tell me what X equals?"

Surveying the class slumped in their desks, she could not blame them for their apathy. Though it was only April, the weather was already hinting at another brutal New Orleans summer. For public schools to be without air conditioning in 1990 was a disgrace, but such things were usual in this little corner of the United States that might be more properly called part of the Third World. Mrs. Reilly suddenly felt hopeless and decided to call on her one dependable student. "Gary?"

But this time there was no answer.

"Gary Stubbs? Are you paying attention?"

Gary Stubbs, who in another couple of years would be known to one and all as G-man, didn't even glance her way. He was a tall, rangy sixteen-year-old with eyes so weak and light-sensitive that he liked to wear dark glasses in class when he could get away with it. Mrs. Reilly did not let him get away with it, and today he wore a regular pair of thick spectacles that only somewhat camouflaged his good looks. Thanks to the clear lenses, she could see where his eyes were aimed. He wasn't looking at Mrs. Reilly or at the blackboard. He appeared to be staring at his best friend, John Rickey, an indifferent math student who sat across the aisle a few rows ahead of him.

"Gary," she said again. Some of the other students laughed, but Gary's gaze never wavered. Magnified behind his glasses, his eyes were soft, almost dreamy. Maybe he wasn't looking at John Rickey at all. Maybe he was just daydreaming about some girl. He looked very much like a boy in love.

Mrs. Reilly walked to his desk and rapped on it with her knuckles. She expected him to jump, but he only blinked rather slowly, then looked up at her. "Sorry, Mrs. R," he said. "I kinda forgot where I was for a minute."

She pointed at the problem on the board. Gary squinted at it, then said, "X equals six."

He really was an excellent student, and Mrs. Reilly decided to let the matter slide. "Try to pay closer attention," she said, returning to the front of the room.

Gary looked at the open algebra textbook in front of him. He wasn't even on the right page—they'd finished with triangles a month ago. Usually he liked math pretty well. Where had his mind been? No, scratch that; he knew where it had been. He flipped to the next chapter and tried to focus on the blackboard. His face felt hot. In another month this classroom would be a furnace. Now it was just warm, tropical … languorous. He found his gaze returning to Rickey's profile, to his straight nose and strong chin, to the longish light brown hair at the back of his neck. He imagined running his fingers through that hair, imagined putting his mouth there, and he shuddered a little. It was so bad. Every day he sat here and had these thoughts, and every day he hung out with Rickey for hours and hours after school and tried not to show any sign that he was having them. He couldn't quite believe that Rickey would *hate* him if he knew, but that was only because he couldn't conceive of Rickey ever hating him. They'd been best friends since fourth grade. Why was he thinking such things now?

Mrs. Reilly was writing on the blackboard, her back to the class. Rickey turned to look at his friend. Gary wasn't sure whether the thoughts he'd been having could be seen on his face. He was afraid they could, because Rickey's eyes widened as they met his. Rickey didn't look mad, though, only a bit puzzled. Then he smiled. It was a gorgeous, heart-lifting smile, and Gary knew he wasn't the only one who thought so; adults were always remarking on what a beautiful smile Rickey had. It transformed his already handsome face and lit up his blue-green eyes. You couldn't help smiling back, and Gary did.

Rickey raised one eyebrow. With the semi-telepathy they'd developed from spending so much time together over the years, Gary understood its message: *What's with you today?*

He shrugged, hooked a finger into the collar of his shirt: *Don't know. Hot in here.*

Rickey mimed a scrubbing motion, one hand against the other: *You want to go wash dishes later?* They didn't have regular jobs, but the owner of a greasy-spoon diner near the school would sometimes pay them a few bucks an hour to work off the clock.

Gary made a little seesawing motion with his hand: *Maybe.*

"John Rickey!" said Mrs. Reilly, and Rickey swiveled back around in his seat. He couldn't get away with woolgathering like Gary could; he never knew the value of X.

"Sorry, kids," said Sal Keller. "I ain't got no work for you today." Sal had owned the Feed-U Diner in the heart of the Lower Ninth Ward for twenty-three years, and had been cooking there for seven years before that. In all this time, no one could remember seeing him without his dirty white apron or the cigar (currently unlit) that jutted out of his stubble-ringed mouth. He spoke in a gritty baritone that even the bums who frequented the Feed-U didn't dare argue with.

"We'll check back tomorrow," Rickey said.

"You do that," Sal agreed. He sounded sarcastic, but that was pretty much his normal tone of voice. "Probably I'll letcha take over the grill tomorrow."

"Really?" said Rickey eagerly. He was always bugging Sal to give him a crack at the grill.

"Hell, no. Young kid like you, be liable to burn the burgers, bust the yolks on the sunny-side-up, God knows what. Working the grill takes a talent."

"I got a talent."

"You got a talent for scrubbing grease out my pots. Come back by tomorrow—if I don't hear no more of this smart talk, I might have some work for you."

They left the diner, rode the city bus down St. Claude Avenue, and walked to Rickey's house near the corner of Tricou and Royal Streets. Rickey's mother had left a long list of chores under the sugar bowl. The list ended with the words "Fix Supper"—she was a horrible cook, and Rickey was getting to be a pretty good one. Gary offered to help with the chores, but when Rickey told him not to worry about it, he didn't insist. Truth be told, he wanted to get off on his own and think about things.

His house was only a few blocks away from Rickey's, over on Delery near the Jackson Barracks prison complex, so he took a roundabout way home. There was never much chance of being alone in the Stubbs household. Gary was the youngest of six children. The older ones had moved out, but last year his second-oldest sister had left her husband and moved back home with her two little kids. It was basically a happy place, but it was kind of a madhouse.

Rickey was an only child whose parents had divorced years ago, so now it was just Rickey and his mom living in the house on Tricou. Gary had always been glad of the refuge. He still was, but lately he felt a little weird at Rickey's place. Hanging out in Rickey's room, sitting on Rickey's bed, made it almost impossible to control these thoughts he'd been having. The last couple of times Rickey had invited him to sleep over, Gary had said no. He didn't want to hurt Rickey's feelings, but he'd gotten to the point where he could no longer stand sleeping on a pile of quilts on the floor, listening to Rickey's breathing, wondering if Rickey was really asleep, wondering what would happen if he just crawled into bed—

Well, this wasn't helping. He shook his head and quickened his pace on the uneven sidewalk. He needed to keep a better eye on his surroundings anyway. The Ninth Ward wasn't as dangerous as people elsewhere in the city believed it to be, but when it started to get dark, you had to watch your back. Particularly if you were a scrawny white kid with Coke-bottle glasses, you had to watch your back.

He glanced at the shabby old houses around him, Victorian gingerbread cottages, camelbacks, doubles. Some were decorated with rusting wrought ironwork, some with Christmas lights even though it was April. One house he'd admired since he was very small had shards of colored tile pressed into the cement stoop, forming an intricate design. People who didn't live here only seemed able to see the trash on the street and the possibility that somebody might ride up on a bike, smash your head open, and steal your wallet. They felt safe in their big Uptown houses and Metairie condo-warrens, but Gary thought his neighborhood was a lot more interesting than Metairie, not to mention friendlier. Everyone here smiled and spoke to you. He'd never seen strangers smiling at each other in the suburbs.

He wouldn't mind living Uptown, though, someday. He and Rickey could get one of those little shotgun houses near the river; the rent was cheap and they'd only need a one-bedroom place …

Damn. The thing just kept sneaking up on him. Thinking about it rationally didn't help; giving it free rein always exhausted him; trying not to think about it was about as effective as willing himself to have 20/20 vision. So what was he supposed to do?

He'd always known, in a rather vague and purposeless way, that he liked boys. He'd learned to hide it early on, too: growing up in a tough neighborhood, in a Catholic family, you just didn't tell anybody that you had a crush on Han Solo or Michael Jordan. He'd even hidden it from Rickey, from whom he'd never hidden anything else. Every kid they knew thought fags were gross; how could he dare to think Rickey might be any different? The height of devastating wit was to accuse another kid of going to a gaybar in the French Quarter—that was how they said it, *gaybar*, as if it were one word. Insults like *homo*, *queer*, and the strangely popular *doughnut-puncher* had little to do with the perceived sexual habits of the insulted; they worked because that was the worst thing a boy could be. Rickey never said shit like that, but then Rickey had a smart mouth and seldom stooped to garden-variety epithets.

Thinking about it before, when he had done so at all, Gary had told himself he would deal with his sexuality at some unspecified time in the years ahead. His peaceful soul counseled him to watch and wait. He had no taste for conflict; Rickey was the shit-disturber of the pair. Once he got out of school and didn't have to face the same bunch of people every day, he would figure out what to do. He might even go to one of those gaybars—not necessarily looking for anything, just to see what went on there. When he was still only a theoretical queer, he hadn't given that much thought to his future.

But his theoretical days were gone—forever, he was pretty sure. There was that line you could only cross once, the line between trying to imagine a thing—in this case, a touch that would thrill every nerve in your body—and actually feeling it. Gary knew it was laughable that he should feel he had crossed that line, because nothing out of the ordinary had even happened. Nevertheless, he was very conscious of the moment he had crossed it.

The thing had happened after they finished work at the Feed-U one day. They had gotten off the bus and were sprinting toward Rickey's house, excited because of the money in their pockets or maybe just galvanized by one of the last cool spring evenings before another long summer set in. When their feet hit the grass of a little corner park (really just a well-kept vacant lot) near Rickey's house, Rickey ran up behind Gary and clamped an arm around his neck, pretending to throttle him. It was just horsing around, something they'd done a million times before. Being a little taller, Gary usually leaned forward, lifting Rickey's feet off the ground until Rickey let go. This time a shock went through him, a powerful wave that was more than mere sensation but too primitive to be called emotion. It was as if two things, previously incompatible, had meshed to form a perfect design: he felt Rickey's familiar, playful touch, but all at once he was also conscious of *another body* touching his, a smooth, strong, warm-skinned body that had him securely in its arms, and he didn't want it to let go.

The feeling ended up somewhere in the pit of his stomach, twisting there in a way that was sort of pleasurable but intense enough to edge toward pain. Instead of leaning forward and pulling Rickey's feet off the ground, he pretended to stumble and fall, dragging them both down but managing to hide his sudden, appalling boner.

"Dude!" Rickey had said, climbing off him and trying to help him up. "Sorry about that. You OK?"

"Just lemme lay here a second," Gary had mumbled into the hot grass, wondering if he'd ever be able to get up without giving the whole neighborhood an eyeful of his tented pants.

He'd thought maybe it was just one of those hormone things. His mother was always cracking jokes about hormones, about how foolish they would make him act once he started liking girls. In the past year or so these jokes had taken on a slightly desperate quality. Gary didn't understand exactly what hormones were, but he gathered that they had to do with sex. Maybe they would have caused him to feel that way if any guy touched him, and he'd just felt it with Rickey because he was around Rickey more than anybody else. But he couldn't convince himself. He felt that way the next time Rickey jumped on his back. He felt it when Rickey slung a casual arm around his shoulders as they ambled through the grocery store, one of the places they liked to go to escape the afternoon heat. He felt sad all the time. Eventually, certain that he would betray himself, he began shying away from Rickey's touch. He did this until he saw the puzzled hurt in Rickey's eyes, and he couldn't stand that, so he started forcing himself to think of basketball statistics every time Rickey's elbow so much as brushed his. Pete Maravich had had a career high of 68 points playing against the New York Knicks. Karl Malone had averaged 27.7 points per game last season. That kind of thing.

It worked, sort of. At any rate, he didn't have to fling himself to the ground again. But now he spent countless hours wondering if the things he thought about before he went to sleep at night, when basketball stats were far from his mind, could ever come true. Was he crazy to think, sometimes, that Rickey might want to be with him? Was anything really there, or was it just wishful thinking?

Only negatives gave him hope. Rickey didn't talk about fags, homos, or doughnut-punchers. Rickey had never had a girlfriend even though he was unquestionably a good-looking kid. That might have been because most of the girls they went to school with weren't interested in white boys, but Gary wondered. Unlike the other boys they knew, who were always bullshitting about pussy they'd had or pussy they'd like to have, Rickey didn't talk about girls. He didn't talk about boys either, but of course you couldn't do that even if you wanted to.

Gary rounded the corner of his block and saw his father sitting on the stoop. That was nothing unusual; only a couple of rooms in their big old clapboard house were air-conditioned, and the family often sat outside as twilight fell. It wasn't the safest habit in the world, but as Elmer Stubbs was fond of saying, you couldn't let the criminals control your life.

"Hey, Daddy," he said.

"Hey, Gary. How you doing? Y'all worked at the diner today?"

"Nuh-uh. Sal didn't have anything for us to do."

"Where you been, then?"

"Just over by Rickey's."

"You seen his momma?"

"She wasn't home yet."

"She's usually home when y'all over there, ain't she?"

"Not always," said Gary, wondering at all the questions. "You know she does the books for Lemoyne's Restaurant. She gets home around six most days, I guess."

"Huh," said Elmer, and leaned back on the stoop to light a cigarette. The flaring lighter illuminated his pale blue Irish eyes and picked out reddish highlights in his close-cropped brown hair. For a New Orleanian, Elmer Stubbs was a skinny man. He had wed Mary Rose Bonano, a girl from one of the city's old Sicilian families, and their first five children had stocky builds, glossy black hair, and a touch of olive in their complexions. Gary looked a lot like his father; all he'd gotten from the Bonanos was his dark eyes.

"How was work?" Gary asked. Elmer managed the shipping department of Tante Lou's Confections, a candy factory near Bayou St. John.

"Aw, the usual shit. Some squirrel calls up from New York City, says, 'Hey, Elmer, I need another case of those PRAY-lines—'"

"He said PRAY-lines?" At this point in his life, Gary had not had much contact with tourists, and this pronunciation was as foreign to his ears as Arabic.

"Sure he said PRAY-lines. What, you think that's how *I* say it all of a sudden? I say PRAH-lines, like a normal person. Anyway, this squirrel, he goes, 'I need another case of those PRAY-lines but can you make 'em with macadamia nuts instead of pecans this time? We're having a luau party and we think that would be really special.'"

"Jeez," said Gary. "So did you tell him you'd do it?" He knew the answer, but he wanted to keep his father talking about the annoying customer, maybe get him started on customers in general, or his co-workers, or something. Anything would be preferable to another round of questions about whether Rickey's mother was usually home when they were at Rickey's house. He hadn't liked that at all. It gave him an uneasy feeling in his gut, rather like the feeling he got whenever Rickey touched him, but not as pleasant.

Elmer shot the shit with his son for a few more minutes, then said, "Your sister's making spaghettis. You better go on in, see if she needs any help." As Gary got up from the stoop, his father caught hold of his wrist and looked up at him. Even in the fading light, Gary could see that Elmer's eyes were very clear, almost naked-looking. "Son?" he said.

"What, Daddy?"

"You and Rickey don't go messing around in the French Quarters, do you?"

Oh, shit. "Well," said Gary, trying to sound as if he had no idea why his father would ask him such a thing. "I mean, we've *been* to the Quarter, sure, but we don't go a *lot*. It's pretty far."

"Good. Y'all don't need to be going up there. Your momma doesn't want you to. It's ... it's dangerous."

His father's eyes had been locked on his. Now Elmer looked away. Feeling released, Gary went into the house and walked down the long hall to the first-floor bathroom. Only when he got to the sink and turned on the water to wash up did he realize that his hands were shaking.

It didn't necessarily mean anything, all those questions. Nobody's parents wanted them to go to the Quarter. Black kids weren't supposed to go because their parents thought they'd get in trouble with the police, who would assume they were there to pick tourists' pockets. Girls weren't supposed to go because their morals would be corrupted, or something. It didn't necessarily mean his folks thought he had been going to gaybars. But when you'd grown up in the Ninth Ward and your father tried to tell you the French Quarter was dangerous, what else were you supposed to make of it?

He briefly considered calling Rickey up and telling him about the conversation. "I think my parents think I'm a homo," he would say. And then Rickey might say, "Well, are you?" And ... what then?

Gary looked down and saw that the bar of soap had turned to mush in his hands. He rinsed it off and went to help his sister finish making dinner. She never put enough seasoning in the red gravy, and it wouldn't be any good unless he got to it pretty soon.

For Rickey, the realization had been somewhat easier. It was not in him to believe he could be completely wrong about anything, and he knew with a clear adolescent fervor that there was nothing wrong in how he felt about Gary.

It was hard to know exactly how to act on his feelings, though. He knew a little more about sex than Gary did—not having been raised Catholic, he had no compunctions about pornography or masturbation—and he had heard about some boys who had gotten drunk and jerked each other off. That much, apparently, could happen. But what if you wanted a lot more than that? Not just in the way of sex, but actual love? There were books about how to be gay; he'd seen them in stores and libraries. Some of them even had diagrams. But there weren't any diagrams about how to fall in love with your best friend and not fuck everything up.

Once or twice he'd almost said something to Gary, but he always stopped at the last possible second, thrown off by a small perverse voice in his head. *What if you're just kidding yourself?* the voice said. *You think he feels the same way you do, but what if you're wrong?*

He had convinced himself of things before, only to find out that they weren't true at all and he'd just believed in them because he wanted them so badly. The thing he kept flashing back to—it was so stupid that Rickey cringed whenever he thought of it—was the time he had convinced himself it was Christmas in March. Five years old, and he'd woken up in the middle of the night with that Christmas feeling, wondering how he had missed all the holiday preparations and decorations but purely certain that it must have just slipped by him. His mother had found him in the living room at the crack of dawn, glassy-eyed but determined that the tree, the stockings, and the heaps of presents would be making their appearance at any moment. Only when she showed him the calendar and reminded him of the recent passage of Mardi Gras did Rickey believe he was wrong, and even then he had been one pissed-off kid, sure he'd been gypped somehow.

He was pretty sure this was different. After all, he wasn't five years old any more. On the other hand, this was a lot more important than Christmas. So beneath his natural confidence was the fear that he might just be kidding himself. He didn't *really* believe it, but he believed it enough to keep quiet; saying anything to Gary would be the biggest risk he'd ever taken, and he wasn't sure he was ready for that. Had it been anyone else, Rickey was certain that he would have already made his move, gotten shot down or gotten some action, and dealt with it either way. Sometimes he wished he *had* fallen for someone besides his oldest friend. He'd even tried to think about other people, but it didn't work.

Then today he had turned around in math class and seen the look on Gary's face, a look he'd never seen there before, a look he could interpret in only one way. It wasn't the look itself that kicked him in the ass, exactly. It was the thought that, if he didn't do something, Gary might eventually look at another person that way. This was an idea Rickey could not stand, not under any circumstances. He still wasn't sure exactly what he was going to do, but he figured he would recognize his chance when it came to him.

He had finished all the other chores and was chopping onions and celery for a chicken dish when his mother got home. She'd given her hair a fresh color rinse the previous night, bringing it up to a wholly artificial, almost fluorescent orange, and her eyes were nearly as bright as the rhinestones that decorated the upswept corners of her glasses. "Johnnie, guess what!" she said.

Rickey's mother had dropped her husband's name years ago, and now went by her maiden name, Brenda Crabtree. Furthermore, she insisted on addressing her son as Johnnie. He was resigned to this but not especially pleased by it. Everyone else had been calling him Rickey since the day he'd started kindergarten and found himself in a class with four other boys named John.

"What?" said Rickey, using the dull side of his knife to scrape the chopped vegetables into a skillet.

"Claude invited me to spend the weekend at Grand Isle. He and his brother got them a beach house out there." Claude was her new boyfriend, a nice retired man who seemed to have a little money.

"That's nice, Momma. You gonna go?"

"I sure would like to, babe. I ain't been out of New Orleans in years. But I hate to leave you all by yourself. You think you could stay by Gary's for the weekend?"

"You know how crowded their house is," Rickey said casually. "Why don't I ask him to stay over here? We're old enough to stay by ourselves."

"Well, I don't know ..."

"Sure," said Rickey, trying to sound as if he didn't care one way or the other. "We'll be here to watch the house, and I'll have it all nice and clean when you get back."

There might be a little more discussion of the matter before his mother gave in, but seeing the look on her face, Rickey already knew he had won. She loathed housework, and by promising to do it, he had always been able to get almost anything he wanted.

2

On Saturday, Gary told Rickey he couldn't work at the diner until afternoon because his mother wanted him to go to the morning Mass with her. Rickey had always been slightly unnerved by his friend's Catholicism. Gary suspected that Rickey's father, a chiropractor who now lived in California, had fed him a lot of misinformation about Catholics. Rickey had seen his father only a few times in the past ten years, but he clung stubbornly to some of the man's attitudes. So he wouldn't ask a lot of troublesome questions about this excuse. Gary didn't like lying, especially to Rickey, but it wasn't precisely a lie. He really was going to church.

He had been baptized, of course, and taken to Mass twice a week until he was thirteen, just like his brothers and sisters. All the Stubbs children—Gary, Carl, Rosalie, Henry, Little Elmer, and Mary Louise—had been required to make their First Communions, to be confirmed, and to attend Mass until they were thirteen. After that, their parents reasoned, school started getting difficult and the kids needed more sleep. That was the official parental party line, anyway. Their eldest son (at thirty-two and six-foot-three, he was still known to his family as Little Elmer, and probably would be long after Big Elmer had gone to his reward) often put forth the opinion that their parents didn't relish the task of dragging teenagers to Mass and had come up with the school thing as a virtuous-sounding excuse.

Since he'd turned thirteen, Gary had only been to church on the major holidays and hadn't made confession at all. He didn't think he believed in all that stuff any more, not really. But he was going to do it today. He wasn't even sure why, but he was going to do it.

Of course he didn't go to his parish church. He got up early and took the bus way the hell out to Chalmette, to a church called St. Martin of Tours. He'd once known some kids who went there, so he was vaguely familiar with it, but it seemed remote enough to be safe. It never occurred to him that life might suddenly get easier if he caught the bus going the other way, up to the Faubourg Marigny. He knew there were queers in the French Quarter because people snickered about them, but he knew nothing of the large, wealthy gay contingent that had gentrified the Marigny, and certainly he had no idea there were gay-friendly churches there.

St. Martin of Tours was a lot newer than the one his family attended. It smelled different, like floor polish and cleanser instead of incense and old wood. No one was waiting at the confessional. Gary dropped to the dusty kneeler before the screen and crossed himself. He was a little surprised at how easily the motions came back to him, but he supposed if you had done something several times a week for several years, you could probably do it in your sleep.

Hearing the priest's voice mutter a welcome, he said, "Bless me, Father, for I have sinned. It has been, uh, three years since my last confession."

"Go ahead."

He wanted to get to the important matter right away, but nerves and force of habit made him start rattling off a list. "I stole from my parents' liquor cabinet four times. I stole from my friend's mother's liquor cabinet, uh, probably about ten times. When my friend was there, I mean. I didn't just open it up and *swipe* something."

"There's no difference between the two," said the priest. "No point in making that distinction." He had the kind of gravelly New Orleans accent that made Gary's father sound like Sir Laurence Olivier: *no pernt in makin' dat distinction.*

"Sorry."

"Go ahead."

"I painted a word on a pole last Halloween."

"What kinda word?" *Woid*, said the priest.

"A curse word."

"Blasphemous?"

"I don't think so," said Gary. The word had been **FUCK**, followed by **YOU**, and he wasn't sure for whom he had intended it. Anyway, Rickey and the other kids with him had written much worse things. "I guess I've taken the Lord's name in vain, though. I don't know how many times."

"Go ahead."

"I, um ... I ..." His heart felt like a little jackhammer in his chest. He was certain the priest could hear it through the screen. "I think I'm in love with my best friend," he said, then added quickly, "He's a guy."

Gary heard the priest shifting on the other side of the confessional. The horrible thought came to him that perhaps the priest would be turned on by this admission—he'd heard things about priests—and he tried to put it out of his mind.

"You have sexual feelings for your friend?" the priest said at last.

"Uh, yeah."

"Have you acted on these feelings?"

"No." *Not yet*, he thought, but managed to keep from speaking the words.

"Have you had a homosexual experience with somebody else?"

"I've never had any kind of sexual experience with anybody," Gary said truthfully.

"Well, then you haven't sinned."

"I haven't?"

"Thoughts are not mortal sins," the priest intoned. "Only actions are sinful. We'll get to that in a minute. Listen to me. The Book of Genesis teaches that God created humans in His own image. The male and female represent the inner unity of God, and their sexual union is a gift from Him to us. When a man and a woman unite in marriage to create new life, they repay that gift. You understand?"

"But in the Book of Genesis ..."

"Hang on, I'm getting to that. The gift of unity between a man and a woman was marred by original sin. The sin of Adam and Eve. That's what you were gonna ask about, right?"

"I guess."

"Original sin introduced lust into the world. Homosexuality is nothing but an example of lust. You can't really be in love with your friend, see?"

"No," said Gary. "No, I don't see."

"It's not possible," the priest said heavily. "You can love your daddy. You can love your brother. But romantic love cannot exist between two men. Or two women. That's nothing but lust caused by original sin."

"But how do you know?"

"I know because God knows." And there it was, the Great Unanswerable. He'd heard versions of it from his mother a thousand times, though not on this particular subject. Even if he'd wanted to argue with a priest, there was nothing to say to that.

"So what do I do now?" he asked.

"You pray to God to take away these feelings you think you got for your friend. Pray for Him to help you like some nice li'l girl. Ask her out on a date. In a few years you'll get married and forget you ever had this problem."

"What if I can't?"

"What you mean?"

"Well," said Gary, trying to collect his thoughts. "I mean, the Church believes that homos … that homosexuals exist, right? Not that it's OK, but that some people really are like that, and they can't just convert?"

"We believe in intrinsic moral evil. Homosexuals have a disorder that gives them a strong tendency to commit evil. That doesn't mean they *gotta* commit evil."

"So what do they … what do I …"

"Slow down, son. What are you trying to ask me?"

"What if I'm one of them?" said Gary. "What if I have that …" He couldn't make himself say *disorder*. "That tendency? What if I can't just forget about it and marry a girl like you said? What do I do?"

"Ah," said the priest. "Well, in that case, you strive for a chaste life."

"Chaste?"

"Virginal. Pure."

Gary knew what the word meant. He just couldn't quite get his mind around it. "You mean," he said. "You mean, I can't have sex with *anybody ever*?"

"Well, that would be the scenario, yes," the priest said rather dryly.

Gary tried to swallow and heard a click in his throat. His face and his hands felt numb. He'd believed his heart was audible in the little enclosure; now it seemed to have stopped altogether. "OK," he said. "I mean, I guess that's all." He made his Act of Contrition and waited for his penance.

"Say Ten Hail Marys and ten Our Fathers," the priest told him. "Go now and sin no more. And son?"

"Y—" There still seemed to be something stuck in his throat. Gary stopped, took a deep breath. "Yes, Father?"

"You'll get past this," the priest told him. "It'll be all right if you just pray on it. And listen, there's some doughnuts down in the Sunday School room if you want one."

Gary left the confessional and went to a pew near the back of the church. He took a rosary from his pocket, a small white one his mother had given him for his first Communion. "Hail Mary, full of grace, the Lord is with thee," he whispered, fingering the first bead. "Blessed art thou among women and blessed is the fruit of thy womb, Jesus. Holy Mary, Mother of God, pray for us sinners now and at the hour of our death. Amen. Hail Mary, full of grace ..."

Maybe it would have been better to start with the Our Fathers. He got through five prayers before he realized he couldn't bear to say *fruit of thy womb* one more time. It reminded him too much of what the priest had said about a man and a woman uniting to create life, of the priest's advice to forget Rickey and marry some girl, which Gary could only think would be throwing away two lives. Maybe three, if Rickey felt anything like he did.

Gary stood up, shoved the rosary back into his pocket, and walked out of the church with five Hail Marys and ten Our Fathers left unsaid. Though it was a long bus ride back to the Ninth Ward, the neglected prayers didn't bother him at all.

Sal Keller was tired of hearing Rickey go on about working the grill. "OK," he'd said when Rickey showed up that morning. "You wanna learn about cooking? The place is gonna be dead all afternoon. Good time to change the oil in the fryer. You do that, then maybe we'll talk about the grill."

Rickey had no idea that changing the fryer oil was the most despised job in any restaurant, though he began to figure it out as he went along. He drained the hot, nasty oil into a series of plastic buckets and carried it back to the garbage-reeking alley behind the diner, where he tipped it into a fifty-five-gallon drum. Occasionally the oil would spatter up onto his hands and forearms, making little burn spots, and once a rat ran across his foot. Still, he was happy to be doing something besides washing dishes. If he did this whole job perfectly, maybe Sal would let him cook tomorrow.

When the old oil was completely drained, Rickey peered cautiously into the bottom of the fryer. It was covered with a layer of cremated food silt at least two inches deep. He thought there might be some way to remove the whole oil reservoir and just dump the silt, but he couldn't figure out how to do it. Sal was busy with paperwork in the office, and Rickey hated asking him questions anyway: Sal could spend fifteen or twenty minutes telling you how he wanted the toilet paper hung up in the restroom.

Rickey scooped the bulk of the crud from the fryer with a long metal spoon, then chased down the smaller particles with paper towels. This shit had been swimming around in the same oil that cooked people's food, he thought as he shoveled it into the trashcan. It made him feel a little sick, but not too much so; he'd already seen worse things at the Feed-U. He had nearly finished the job when the little bell over the door jingled and Gary came in.

"Dude," said Gary, eyeing Rickey's grease-blackened apron and burn-speckled hands. "I see you're really moving up in the restaurant world."

"Yeah. Sal said if I did this, we'd talk about me working the grill."

"Sounds like a deal. Probably you'll be the head cook by next week."

"Fuck you. How was Mass?"

"Aw, you don't wanna know."

"That's true."

"You know what?"

Something in Gary's voice made Rickey look up from his latest wad of cruddy paper towels. "What?"

"Screw the Church," said Gary. "I mean, just screw it. It's stupid. It sucks. I don't want to be Catholic any more."

"Damn, dude. I mean, I been saying all that for years, but … damn. What brought this on?"

"Maybe I'll tell you some other time."

"You gonna tell your mom?"

"Are you kidding? I'm not telling her shit. I'm not telling any of them shit."

Rickey turned away from the fryer and watched as Gary took an apron from the row of pegs that held them, slipped it over his head, and tied it behind his back. Gary was wearing shades as usual, but behind their dark lenses, Rickey could see a certain whiteness around his eyes. That was a rare thing to see, because it usually meant Gary was really angry. "You're not mad at me, are you?" Rickey said.

"What?" Gary finished tying the apron and looked around at him. "No. No, course I'm not mad at you."

"Well, do you want to stay at my house next weekend?"

"Huh?"

"My mom's going out of town," Rickey said patiently. "She doesn't want me staying by myself. You want to sleep over?"

Gary's lips moved wordlessly, as if trying out responses. *He's gonna say no,* Rickey thought; *he's freaked out about something, maybe the same thing that's been freaking him out for a while now, and he's just gonna turn me down flat.* But then Gary reached up and took off his shades. The angry white rings were gone from around his eyes, and he was smiling, the first really happy smile Rickey had seen on his face in a long time.

"Yeah," he said. "I'd like that."

They stared at each other, the air between them almost seeming to crackle a little. Rickey opened his mouth to say something else, but just then Sal came out of the back brandishing a sheaf of papers. "Goddamn meat guys gonna dig my grave for me. Rickey, you done with that fryer yet? We ain't got all day, you know, people gonna be ordering french fries later on and what I'm gonna tell 'em? 'Sorry, you can't have no fries, cap—this goddamn lazy kid I got in here's been standing around with his thumb up his ass'?"

"I'm done, Sal. Look, I just gotta put the new oil in and get it heating up."

"Well, do it, then. Hey, Gary, where y'at? I got a buncha burnt-up pots in the back with your name on 'em."

"Right away, Sal," said Gary, and let his arm brush Rickey's as he headed for the kitchen.

3

So Rickey wanted him to sleep over, not just for one night, but for the whole weekend. And so he had brushed Rickey's arm in the diner. But by the time Friday came, Gary had convinced himself all over again that he was the only sixteen-year-old homo in the world and that Rickey had no idea how he felt. Probably if he did know, Rickey would never have asked him over.

He was useless that whole day. His father spoke to him three times over breakfast before Gary heard him. He looked at a word problem in Mrs. Reilly's class—something about how fast Jack could get to Baton Rouge if he took a train going twice as fast as Betty's car—and came very close to saying *Who the hell cares?* He saw Rickey at lunch, but they sat with a bunch of their friends who only wanted to talk about whether or not the Lakers could win a third NBA championship. Gary didn't like the Lakers that much, since they were always beating the crap out of his favorite player, Karl Malone. He kept quiet. Rickey looked over at him a few times, and Gary just smiled. He actually felt pretty happy in spite of all his worrying, though he couldn't imagine why.

They'd gone by the Feed-U a few times since Saturday, but Rickey was pissed because Sal still wouldn't let him on the grill. They didn't go today, but rode the bus to Gary's house so he could pick up his toothbrush and a few clothes, then walked over to Rickey's. Brenda had already left for Grand Isle, and the house was warm and still in the lengthening afternoon shadows.

"You want to help me make something for dinner?" said Rickey, parking himself at the kitchen table.

"Sure. What do you want to make?"

"I don't know. Let's pick something out the cookbook, then go over to the Schwegmann's to get the stuff."

Gary found a cookbook lying on the kitchen counter and handed it to Rickey. Seeing Justin Wilson in his red suspenders on the cover, Rickey winced. "I hate this one. Get me Julia Child—on the shelf over by the toaster. That's the only halfway-decent cookbook my mom owns."

"What's the matter with Justin Wilson?"

"Dude, none of those recipes work worth a shit. I *gar-on-tee*."

Rickey opened the Julia Child book, which looked considerably more well-thumbed than any of Brenda's other cookbooks. Gary pulled up a chair next to Rickey's and leaned over to see the pages as Rickey flipped through them. Some of the recipes had notations and modifications in Rickey's handwriting. "You really like cooking, don't you?" he asked.

Rickey looked up from the book. "Yeah. You know my mom can't cook—that's why I started doing it. But then I got really interested. I mean, you live in New Orleans, you spend half your life thinking about food. But there's so much we don't know. Like, look at this here. What the fuck is a parsnip?"

"You got me."

"I think it's something like a carrot, but what does it taste like? How come I never tasted one? I don't know. That kinda stuff just interests me. You think it's dumb?"

"No, it's not dumb at all. I like it too, but my mom and my sisters taught me to cook a long time ago. I just think it's cool you taught yourself."

"I'm *trying* to teach myself," said Rickey. "I don't know anything yet, really."

Gary thought about that as they got into Brenda's old Plymouth and headed for the grocery store. He might have learned to cook years and years before Rickey, but he was quite sure that Rickey would soon be better at it. When Rickey really got interested in something, he was driven. That was pretty much the first thing Gary had ever learned about him, when they were partnered for Career Day in fourth grade and Rickey had decided to fashion an alarmingly realistic false arm that could be ripped from Gary's body during a demonstration on the chiropractic arts. They'd gotten in a fair amount of trouble, especially when the "blood" (red hair dye shoplifted from the K&B drugstore) wouldn't come out of the classroom carpet, but they had been fast friends from then on.

Rickey had come up with the idea of the arm, masterminded the K&B raid, and figured out how to set the dye packets into the Play-Doh; Gary hadn't had to do much more than stand there and get dismembered. Probably that had set the tone for their whole friendship. Rickey was capable of applying himself to things with an intensity Gary had never seen in anyone else. *Wish he'd apply himself like that to me,* he thought, a little shocked at himself. He wound down the Plymouth's passenger window and took a deep breath of Ninth Ward air, which smelled of chemicals from the Industrial Canal and burnt coffee beans from the Luzianne plant miles away.

They bought a large eggplant, a bunch of scallions, a carton of heavy cream, a block of Swiss cheese, a container of shredded Parmesan, and a pair of Pet-Ritz pie shells. "We ought to make our own crust," said Rickey, eyeing the plastic package skeptically.

"Dude, how hungry are you?"

"Pretty hungry."

"You really feel like rolling out pastry?"

"I guess not. But we gotta try it next time."

Back home, they changed out of their school clothes into T-shirts and boxer shorts, since it would be getting hot in the kitchen. Gary peeled and sliced the eggplant, then salted the slices to draw out excess water. He'd never made a quiche, but he had a long and comfortable acquaintance with eggplant. Rickey mixed a spoonful each of mustard and mayonnaise and spread this mixture inside the pie shell before browning it in the oven. "The recipe doesn't say to do that," Gary told him.

"I know."

"So who told you to?"

"I thought of it myself." Rickey shrugged. "I done it before. It's good."

"You made quiches before?"

"Sure. My mom loves 'em."

"You're way ahead of me."

"Not really. I made a lasagna last week that came out terrible. You made lasagna last time I ate by your house, and it kicked ass."

"Aw, that's just because I'm half Italian. It's genetic or something."

Gary was standing at the stove sauteeing the diced eggplant in olive oil. He felt Rickey's arm slip around his waist and Rickey's chest press against his back. "You really shouldn't do that," Rickey said. "Diss yourself like that, I mean. So you learned to cook from your family. So what? I kinda wish I'd learned that way too."

Rickey held onto him a second longer, patted him on the ass so quickly that Gary scarcely believed it had happened, and turned away to get the eggs out of the icebox. Gary stared down at the sizzling cubes of eggplant, at the wooden spoon in the skillet, at his own hand holding the other end of the spoon. Only when he smelled the garlic beginning to scorch was he able to remember how it all went together and start stirring again.

They ate most of the quiche, then opened the window and sat at the table for a while, allowing the heat to air out of the kitchen. Maybe it was just the effect of the food in his stomach after not eating all day, but Gary felt hyperalert, as if his senses had been enhanced somehow. The colors of the greasy old wallpaper seemed newly vivid, the pattern in the worn linoleum more intricate than usual. It felt a little like the few times he'd smoked pot. He'd forgotten to tell the priest about that, he realized. Well, to hell with it. He was never going to tell a priest anything again.

Maybe he should tell Rickey what had happened at the church, though. If the time had come to talk about this whole thing, maybe that would be a good place to start. He was thinking about how to phrase it when Rickey said, "You wanna go in my room?"

Rickey's bedroom was at the back of the house, a cramped chamber barely large enough to hold a twin bed, a chifforobe, and a child's desk that Rickey had outgrown but still used. The room was so tiny that Brenda had once offered to trade with him on the grounds that a growing boy shouldn't be cooped up in such a space, but Rickey said he felt comfortable here. Gary sat on the floor with his back against the bed, as was his usual habit. It was dim in the little room, so he took off his shades and placed them on Rickey's nightstand.

Rickey shut the door and turned to him. "Look, I gotta talk to you."

"OK."

Rickey sat down next to Gary, pulled his knees up to his chest, wrapped his arms around them, shook his head so that his hair fell in his face. All in all, he looked about as nervous as Gary had ever seen him. "I was just wondering ..." he said, then stopped and stood up. "Oh hell. I gotta pee."

He crossed the hall to the bathroom, stayed in there for what seemed like a long time, and came back smelling of toothpaste. Gary had already brushed his teeth right after dinner, not because he really thought anything was going to happen, but just in case it did. Lately, whenever he was around Rickey, he felt like brushing his teeth every five minutes. Maybe it was one of the symptoms of love.

"OK, um," said Rickey, and fell silent.

"What is it?" Gary was starting to get a little concerned. He couldn't remember ever seeing Rickey at a loss for words before.

"C'mon. You know what it is."

"Well ..."

"You been acting weird around me for a while now. At first I thought I might've pissed you off, but I couldn't think how. Then I thought maybe you were just sick of me."

"Rickey—"

"You hear about friends, like, *outgrowing* each other. I was scared it'd happen to us. That would really suck."

"No kidding."

"So I was worried. But then I turned around in math class last week and I saw the way you were looking at me."

"Oh, God." Gary hid his face in his hands. He hadn't seen that coming. "I'm sorry, awright? I'm sorry."

"Now, see, that's the kinda thing you need to stop doing. What are you sorry for?"

"I don't know. You're confusing the hell out of me."

"Dude. What's so confusing? I invited you over here for the whole weekend. I grabbed your ass at the stove, not that you even noticed. I—"

"Wait a minute. What do you mean, I didn't notice? I almost passed out in the fucking eggplant."

"Well, you could've said something."

"What was I supposed to say?"

"I don't know what the fuck you were supposed to SAY!" Rickey yelled. "I don't know how to do this either, OK?"

"Do what?" said Gary, almost sobbing. "What do you want to *do*?"

"What the hell do you *think*?"

"I DON'T KNOW!" Gary was so frustrated that he reached out and smacked Rickey on the shoulder, though not very hard. "Look. I'm sorry, but if you're trying to tell me what I think you might be trying to tell me, you're just gonna have to come right out and say it, cause I'm not gonna dare to believe it otherwise."

"Fair enough. Let's start over." Rickey made a little erasing gesture in the air. "OK. So can I kiss you?"

Gary didn't trust himself to speak. He met Rickey's eyes, which were very wide, very blue, a little angry, a little scared. Seeing that Rickey meant it, he made himself nod, and Rickey leaned over and kissed him. The feeling of Rickey's mouth on his drove all other thoughts from his head. Their families and the entire junior class of Frederick Douglass High could have paraded through the room right now and Gary wouldn't have noticed. He leaned into Rickey's arms and inhaled the kiss like a drowning man suddenly thrust into a chamber full of pure, sweet oxygen.

"Wow," said Rickey when they stopped to catch their breath. "That was even nicer than I thought it would be."

"You mean you been thinking about this?"

"Sure, haven't you?"

"Well, yeah, but ..."

"But what?"

"I don't know. I guess I just never thought that when I was laying in bed at night thinking about you, you might be thinking about me too."

"Well, I was. I have been for a while now." Rickey ran his hand down Gary's back, then up under the hem of his T-shirt. "So you lay in bed and think about me, huh? Doing stuff a nice Catholic boy's not supposed to do?"

"I don't know," said Gary, distracted by the touch of Rickey's fingers on his bare skin.

"I do," Rickey said. "I done it too. But this is about a million times better."

They started kissing again. Gary had been worried that he wouldn't know what to do, but it didn't seem to be a problem; everything was right. He put his hands under Rickey's shirt, felt Rickey's skin shiver into goosebumps. *I made that happen*, he thought, awed by the concept of another person's body responding to his touch.

"Lemme just take this off," said Rickey, and pulled the shirt over his head. "Why don't you take yours off too?"

Free of the bothersome clothing, they embraced again, and the full-body contact literally took their breath away for a moment. Gary could feel Rickey's heart hammering against his own. "I love you," he said before he even knew he was going to speak.

"I love you too," said Rickey, unperturbed. "Always have, always will. Listen, you wanna keep doing this on the floor, or you wanna get in bed?"

Somehow they managed to crawl up onto the bed without really letting go of each other. Gary's mind registered the fact that he was actually in Rickey's bed, where he had so often dreamed of being. Then Rickey rolled on top of him and started kissing his neck, and he realized he wouldn't have cared if he were on a glacier in Siberia as long as he could keep feeling this way.

"You like that?" said Rickey, rubbing against him. "Does that feel good?"

"Yeah … it feels too good. I think I'm gonna come."

"Oh my God … me too."

They clung to each other, trying to ride out the waves of pleasure.

Then they looked at each other and started to laugh. "Couldn't even take off our underwear first," said Gary. "Shit."

"That's OK," Rickey said. "We got the first time out the way. Now we can go slower."

Rickey had promised Brenda that he would clean the house in exchange for being allowed to have Gary over all weekend, so on Saturday afternoon they washed the dishes, wiped down the kitchen counters, took out the trash, and tried to sweep the floors. They didn't get very far with the sweeping. Gary had the good broom and was working in the front room. Rickey, who was using the crappy broom in the kitchen, couldn't stop thinking about everything that had happened the night before. He got bored with sweeping, threw the broom in the corner, went into the front room, and pulled Gary down on the couch. "Dude, not *here*," Gary said as Rickey nuzzled his ear.

"Why not?"

"Well, I mean, if your mom walked in right now she'd see us."

"She's in Grand Isle."

"Still . . ."

"Then let's go in my room."

"Shouldn't we at least finish sweeping?"

"To hell with it. Leave the damn dust bunnies."

"OK."

"That's what I like about you," said Rickey. "You're easy."

"Fuck you. I am not."

"For me you are."

"Well, that's different."

Later, as evening stole into the house, they lay in bed talking about how their lives were going to change from now on, and also about ways in which *nothing* could appear to be different. They hadn't wanted to bring up the subject before, but they knew that tomorrow night they would be back in their separate beds, and the thought chilled them a little. Their two houses, which had seemed so close for the past seven years, now seemed disturbingly far apart.

"Maybe we should just move out," Gary suggested. "We could quit school and get jobs in a restaurant or something."

"I can't do that. Your folks have all those other kids. Plus they got each other. I can't leave my mom alone."

"You're not gonna live here forever, are you?"

"No, but she's counting on me being here a couple more years, anyway. What's the problem? We sleep over all the time. They're not gonna know anything."

"I think maybe mine already do," Gary said, and told Rickey about the conversation he'd had with his father on the stoop.

"Huh," said Rickey. "Well, they don't know anything for sure. They're probably just worried because you don't have a girlfriend. My mom talks about that stuff too."

"So what are we supposed to do about it?"

"Maybe we could meet some lesbians whose parents are worried because they don't have boyfriends. We could be each other's cover story, like."

"Sure, Rickey. Where we're gonna meet lesbians? And what makes you think they'd hang out with us anyway? And even if they did, our parents aren't retards. They'd figure it out eventually. Jeez, it all sounds like some kinda queer episode of 'I Love Lucy.'"

"It was just an idea."

"I know," said Gary. "But I don't want to pretend we have girlfriends and shit. I don't want to act like we're not together. I know we have to at school, just so we won't get killed. But I don't want to lie to my family about who I am."

"Neither do I. But I don't want them to try and separate us, either."

"You think they could separate us?"

"I think they're our parents, that's all. They got the money, they got the power, and they think they know what's best for us."

"What money?"

"My dad's got money," said Rickey. "What if he tried to make me go live with him in California or something?"

"You always say he doesn't want you."

"He doesn't. But what if my mom convinced him you were turning me into a homo? Maybe he'd rather have a normal kid living with him than a queer kid in New Orleans."

"That's so fucked up."

"I know it." Rickey pulled the covers up over them. There was a smell on his sheets that had never been there before, a heady mixture of come and sweat and probably even a few tears. He wished he could leave the sheets on the bed for a while—it would be nice to breathe in that smell when he was lying here by himself—but he knew he'd better get them in the wash before his mother came home.

"Just don't go," Gary said. "Whatever else happens, please just don't go."

"I'm not going anywhere, G. Look, we'll be eighteen before too much longer. Then they can't make us do anything. It's not that long to wait."

"It seems pretty long."

"We'll get through it."

"I guess."

"Dude, are you OK?" Rickey propped himself up on his elbow and tried to get a look at Gary in the dim light from the window. "I mean, I know things are gonna be rough for us sometimes, but aren't you glad this happened?"

"Oh my God, yes." Gary rolled over and buried his face in Rickey's chest. "Course I'm glad. I'm scared shitless of what's gonna happen next, but I'm really, really happy. If I say anything else that sounds like I'm not, just smack me a couple times, OK?"

"That could be fun," Rickey said. "But I don't think I'll start smacking you yet. I got some better ideas."

4

School on Monday was bizarre in its very normalcy. After the weekend Rickey and Gary had spent together, it seemed strange to sit at an uncomfortable particleboard desk listening to a teacher drone on, strange to breathe the cheese-pizza-and-boiled-vegetable air of the cafeteria, and very strange indeed to dress out for gym in the locker room. Gary had always found the whole locker room experience unnerving but rather bracing. Rickey had never given a damn about it either way. Today, though, there was an undeniable oddness to being in a roomful of naked boys. Fortunately, they had different gym periods.

They hardly even saw each other until lunchtime, and then they sat with their usual table of friends; anything else would have looked weird. They definitely didn't want to look weird today. "What up, G," Calvin Brody said to Gary as they sat down with their trays. Calvin was Gary's second-best friend, mainly because they were both crazy about basketball. "You seen the L.A.–Utah game Saturday night?"

"Nuh-uh," said Gary, looking stricken for a moment. "I, uh, I forgot about it."

"Say *what*?" said Terrell Washington, a runty kid with a high voice. "I heard a lotta messed-up shit in my life, but I ain't never heard of Gary missing no Utah Jazz game when Karl Malone was playing."

"Shut up, Terrell," said Calvin. "It's not his fault if his momma made him go to church or something."

"I didn't go to church," said Gary. "I'm never going to church any more." It came out too loud, and he hadn't even meant to say it. He looked over at Rickey, who raised his eyebrows and shrugged.

"Damn!" said Terrell. "You told your momma?"

"I don't have to tell her. I'm almost seventeen. I can do what I want."

"Tell it to *my* momma," said Calvin. "She says as long as I live under her roof, I be going to her church every Sunday. Say, G, the ladies at your church, do they wear a bunch of crazy-ass hats?"

"Not really," said Gary, grateful that Calvin had changed the subject. "Some of the real old ladies wear hats, but I wouldn't call them crazy-ass hats."

"What's a crazy-ass hat?" said Rickey.

"You know," said Calvin, "like with fake birds and shit. Last week this one lady, Mrs. Ettajay Thomas, she wore one looked just like a big old pink Superdome."

"Her name is not Étagère," said Rickey. "You're shitting us. That's a piece of furniture."

"She spells it E-T-T-A-J-A-Y, but it's pronounced just like the furniture."

"Who cares?" said Terrell. "Back it up a minute. So, Gary, if your momma ain't made you go to church, then what was so important that you missed the game?"

"Mind your own business," said Calvin, but he looked curious too.

"We had to go to a wedding," said Rickey. It was the first thing he could think of.

"Well, then you *were* in church."

"No, it was a friend of my mom's. She's not religious. She got married in, uh, in a restaurant."

"In a restaurant!" said Terrell. "That's fucked up."

"Well, she works there. With my mom."

It turned out to be a good answer; Calvin and Terrell didn't want to hear anything else about a wedding. They began giving Gary a play-by-play description of the basketball game. Rickey toyed with his breaded veal patty, mildly interested in the conversation. He liked hoops OK, but not as much as Gary did. Without warning, the thought *I was born to suck dick* popped into his head. Instead of pushing it away, he turned it over and over in his mind, considering. He had started to think he might be born to cook. Until this past weekend, it was the only thing he had believed himself to be really good at. But even cooking hadn't made him this happy, at least not yet.

He zoned out for a while and didn't realize anyone was speaking to him until Calvin reached over and knocked gently on his forehead. "Hello? Anybody in there?"

"Huh?" said Rickey, returning to the odorous reality of the cafeteria.

"I asked do you want your roll."

"Oh." Rickey looked down at his tray. He'd hardly eaten anything. "No, you can have it."

Calvin grabbed the spongy, margarine-soaked roll and finished it off in three bites. He bought a hot lunch and two cartons of milk every day, but even so, he was always hungry and had a habit of scrounging stuff off other kids. Rickey, a fairly picky eater, was one of his favorite lunch companions.

They left Calvin and Terrell in the cafeteria and walked together to Gary's next class, a chemistry lab. Rickey's next period was English, and the teacher liked him because he read an unassigned book every now and then, so he could afford to be a couple of minutes late. They stood outside the door of the chem lab staring at each other. Kids milled around them, slamming lockers, shouting, cutting loose in their few remaining minutes of lunchtime freedom. Boyfriends and girlfriends walked through the hall intertwined, kissed each other goodbye before entering their classes. Rickey wanted to kiss Gary. He leaned against the wall and put his hands behind his back.

"You OK?" said Gary.

"I guess. I mean … you know." Rickey found himself thinking about something Gary had said over the weekend:

Maybe we should just move out … quit school and get jobs in a restaurant or something … He knew they weren't actually going to do it, but a spot just below his heart ached a little as he tried to imagine living a life with Gary where they could go home together, wake up in the morning together, and not have to pretend about anything.

"Yeah," said Gary. "I know."

"How about you? Are you OK?"

Gary smiled. It was a sweet, sunny smile, but there was also something a little crazy in it, something Rickey had never seen there before. "I'm doing great," he said. "See you later, huh?"

The bell signaling the end of lunchtime rang as Gary went into his class, but Rickey stayed leaning against the wall. *That was lust,* he realized, *the way he was smiling at me, sheer, unadulterated lust.* He'd get to his own class in a minute. Right now his knees felt a little weak. He wondered how in the world he was going to make it through Mrs. Reilly's class later. Gary's presence would be comforting, but he was certain that today it would render him incapable of math.

"You even believe this shit?" Sal Keller asked rhetorically. His tone of disbelief was so complete that it verged upon awe. "They screwed me on my bun order. This dame at the company says they got no record of my order. I been ordering buns from these people three times a week for eight years, but they got no record of my order and they can't do nothing about it till tomorrow."

"You act like you're stunned or something," said Rickey. "They just did this same thing to you two weeks ago."

"Tell me about it," said Sal, scowling at the half-crumpled invoice in his hand. "Fool me once, shame on you. Fool me twice, shame on me. Ain't that right?"

"It sure is," said Gary, who was sitting at one of the diner's tables filling ketchup bottles. "So you gonna switch companies, right, Sal?"

"Aw, I don't know ..."

"You know he's not," said Rickey. "They sell him those crappy buns for fifteen percent less than anybody else in town will."

"Yeah?" said Sal, bristling. "How you know that, Mr. Smarty?"

"Royce told me." Royce was the nighttime cook at the Feed-U.

"Well, that was very educational of Royce. Royce got him a big mouth. Now how's about you take a ride over to the Schwegmann's and get me some hamburger buns?"

"Sure," said Rickey. He grabbed Sal's car keys from behind the register and stopped by Gary's table. "You wanna come with me?"

"No, he ain't going with you!" Sal roared. "I got pots for him to wash if he ever gets done with them ketchup bottles. Y'all both moving slow as three-legged racehorses today."

"Sorry, Sal," said Rickey. He allowed himself to reach out and squeeze Gary's shoulder very briefly before turning away from the table. They could never do anything like that at school, but maybe in the restaurant they could have a tiny bit of leeway. Not freedom, just leeway. Gary looked up and gave him that same weird, sweet smile, and Rickey knew he'd better get out of there before they both dreamed up some excuse why they couldn't finish work that afternoon.

5

The school year ended without incident. When one of the day cooks at the Feed-U quit, Sal hired Rickey and Gary to work full time all summer and started training them both as cooks. They picked it up fast, and soon either one of them could handle it by himself for most of the day, but what they liked best was working together during the rushes. Usually Rickey would work the grill while Gary dropped fries and made sandwich setups, dressing the bread with lettuce, tomato, and mayonnaise before the burgers and other fillings went on it. They learned each other's habits and rhythms, anticipated each other's moves, and worked much better together than with Sal or any of the other cooks. Sal, who knew a useful thing when he saw it, almost always scheduled the two of them for the weekend breakfast/lunch shifts.

So they got good at that, and in their off-hours, when they could find a little privacy, they got good at making each other feel absolutely amazing. But after that first weekend together, they never, ever seemed to have enough time. Time and privacy became like some fantasy gourmet dinner: they talked about it, they dreamed about it, but they still had to find their day-to-day sustenance where and when they could.

Gary turned seventeen at the end of June. Rickey and Brenda celebrated with him and his folks at an Italian restaurant where you could tell the waitress "Feed us" and the kitchen would keep sending out dishes until you surrendered. Stubbs family legend had it that Elmer had proposed to Mary Rose over just such a dinner, and they had all been very big on the place ever since. Somewhere between the stuffed artichokes and the chicken cacciatore, Rickey looked across the table at Gary and mouthed the words *One more year.* Rickey would not be seventeen until September, but this day still felt like a milestone, as did every occasion that made their eighteenth birthdays seem within reach.

Mary Rose poured herself more red wine, then reached over and refilled Brenda's glass. "My last baby's gonna be all grown up soon," she said. "I just know he's gonna meet some girl one of these days and leave me all alone."

"Eh, la, la," said Brenda tipsily. "You ain't never gonna be alone. You got Elmer and you already got some grandbabies. What I'm gonna do when my boy gets married?"

"Don't worry, Brenda. You'll get you some grandbabies one of these days."

"Not too soon, I hope!" Brenda gave a shrill giggle. "I don't guess I got nothing to worry about, though. Johnnie ain't even got him a girlfriend yet."

Rickey rolled his eyes, but kept silent and sipped his wine. He didn't care for the taste of it—he was already an avowed liquor drinker—but he liked the buzz he was getting now that he was on his second glass, and Gary appeared to be putting it away too.

"I think maybe Gary done met some li'l girl," said Mary Rose. "He got his head in the clouds all the time lately."

"Hush, Momma," said Gary's sister Rosalie. "Leave him alone awready."

"Aw, look, now I embarrassed him," said Mary Rose as Gary pushed his chair back and left the table.

"Course you embarrassed him," said Rosalie. "You live to embarrass your kids."

"And you'll do the same to yours when they old enough, babe."

"Excuse me," said Rickey. He got up and followed Gary to the restroom. It was one of those single-room, one-person-at-a-time deals, but he knew Gary was in there, so he knocked on the door. Gary let him in and locked the door behind him.

"You OK?" said Rickey.

"Yeah." Gary sighed. "I just can't listen to that right now. Not tonight. Not when we only got one more year to go."

"I know what you mean."

"I love them, but sometimes I feel like I hate them too."

"I know *exactly* what you mean."

"I'm just gonna stay in here for a few minutes and let them get on some other subject."

"Well, I'll stay with you." Rickey stepped closer to Gary, pushed him gently back against the wall, and gave him a long, deep kiss.

"Dude," said Gary, breaking it off, "what the hell are you doing?"

"It's your birthday and I hadn't even got to kiss you yet."

"OK, so now you kissed me. Let's get out of here."

"You just said you wanted to stay for a few minutes."

"What if somebody's waiting to use the toilet?"

"They can use the handicapped one," said Rickey. "Shut up. Don't argue with me."

"Nice way you got of talking to me on my birthday."

"Well, c'mon, G. Live it up a little." Rickey kissed the side of Gary's throat, his jawline, the velvetsoft skin just below his ear. When he felt Gary shiver in his arms, he knew he was home free. He knelt on the hard tile floor and undid Gary's belt.

"You're *crazy*," said Gary.

"Maybe so, but you like it. Look, you got a boner."

"Course I got a boner, you only been kissing me and … oh … damn, Rickey."

"I been practicing that with my toothbrush," said Rickey, pausing to take a couple of deep breaths. "I swear I got no gag reflex left at all."

Gary put his hands on Rickey's head and leaned against the wall, locking his knees so they wouldn't buckle. Usually he tried not to come too fast, wanting it to last as long as possible, but the restroom seemed dangerous and Rickey's toothbrush technique felt insanely good. He closed his eyes and let it happen, feeling as if his brain had left his skull and was being sucked out through his dick.

By the time they got back to the table, their parents seemed to have abandoned the ever-popular girlfriend topic in favor of discussing the food. "This here is the best veal I ever had," said Elmer, ladling up some chops in red sauce. "They outdone themselves again."

"Well, I don't know," said Mary Rose. "I think the veal was a little better when we came for our anniversary."

"I think *yours* is better, Momma," said Rosalie.

"Y'all both nuts," said Elmer. "These veal chops are ..." He searched for the right word. "Stupendous."

"They nice," Brenda agreed. "You want some, Johnnie?"

"No thanks," said Rickey. "I feel really full all of a sudden. I don't think I can swallow another mouthful." Gary nearly choked on his wine. Rickey licked his lips and smiled to himself.

Rickey was going to sleep over at Gary's house that night, but after they dropped Brenda off and got back to Delery Street, Elmer told them they could borrow the car if they wanted to. "I know y'all probably want to do some celebrating on your own," he said. "Just be careful."

"Your dad's all right," said Rickey as they climbed back into Elmer's rusty old station wagon.

"They're both all right," said Gary. "They worry, that's all."

"Yeah, but your mom worries too much about what Jesus would think."

"Don't get started on that. Where you want to go?"

"Let's go to the French Quarter," said Rickey. "Let's go to a *gaybar*."

"Dude, you got no fear tonight, do you?"

"I just want to go somewhere with you and not have to pretend. You know?"

"Sure."

"So you up for it?"

"I guess," said Gary, starting the car.

They parked on one of the side streets in the lower Quarter and walked up to the area of Bourbon Street known as the Pink Triangle. Upper Bourbon was for the tourists, and the lower part of the street was mostly residential, but between St. Ann and Ursulines was the largest concentration of gay bars, dance clubs, and other businesses in the city. They had passed through this area over the years, never daring to look too close or appear too interested. Back then it had seemed intimidating, even scary. Now that they were here openly and together, it felt like a playground, if a rather rank-smelling one.

They went into a small grotto-like bar called the Hand of Glory. The green malt liquor sign, the low lighting, and the bunches of dusty plastic grapes hanging from the ceiling gave the place an unfashionable, cozy feel. Rickey got them a couple of drinks and they sat at a table watching the crowd. There were men dancing together to the music on the jukebox, men with their arms around each other, a pair of men kissing in a shadowy corner. A few people passing by their table smiled at them, but nobody bothered them. After a few minutes, Gary moved his chair closer to Rickey's. Rickey reached over and took Gary's hand. They looked at each other, then looked down at their two hands intertwined on the table, right out there in public where anybody could see. Somehow it felt even more intimate than what they had done in the bathroom at the restaurant.

Toward dawn, Elmer Stubbs heard Gary and Rickey come in. He lay in bed listening to their quiet footsteps on the stairs, to water rushing through the pipes, to Mary Rose's faint snoring beside him. By the time everything was quiet again, the squares of the window had become faintly visible in the room's darkness, indigo against black velvet. Elmer sat up and swung his legs over the edge of the bed. As silently as possible, he opened the drawer of his nightstand and felt for the key he had stashed in there. It was a skeleton key that unlocked every interior door in the house.

Elmer walked carefully down the hall, keeping his bare feet on the runner, avoiding the spots that creaked. He paused outside Gary's bedroom door and stood listening. There seemed to be no sound at all in the house, not even a hum from the loud old refrigerator down in the kitchen or a whimper from one of Rosalie's sleeping toddlers. He put his hand around the doorknob, hesitated, then tried it. The door was locked.

That alone was nearly enough to make him turn away without using the key. As of today, his youngest child was one year shy of legal adulthood. If Gary had some reason to lock his door, Elmer was inclined to leave it locked. But he had promised Mary Rose that he would check on the boys. "Just *look* at them, Elmer," she'd said, almost in tears. "Just go look in there real quiet."

"Hon, there's not gonna be anything to look at. Rickey's sleeping over. He's slept here a million times. What you want me to *look* at?"

"I want to know *where* they sleeping," she said, and refused to elaborate.

So Elmer slid the skeleton key into the hole at the bottom of the brass knob plate. The tumblers made a loud clunking sound, and Elmer froze for several seconds before twisting the knob to the right and easing the door open.

Gary's room was at the front of the house, and at night the streetlight shone right in. Elmer could clearly see the rumpled sleeping bag on the floor. It was empty. His gaze moved to the bed beneath the window. Gary lay curled on his side facing the door, covers pulled up to his chest, apparently asleep. Rickey was on the other side of the bed, nearer to the wall. His face was in shadow and Elmer couldn't tell whether he was asleep or not. His left arm was on top of the covers, draped across Gary's hip, his hand dangling there casually, familiarly.

Elmer closed his eyes and leaned his head against the doorframe. If Rickey had been sleeping on the outside, he could have told himself that maybe Rickey got in the bed after Gary was already asleep. As much as he had always liked Rickey, he still would have been happy to grasp at that particular straw. But as it was, he could tell himself no such thing. Obviously they had crawled into bed together. That didn't really tell Elmer anything; it only raised more questions. *Why* were they in bed together? Were they just drunk and distracted, or was this something they'd been doing? And for how long? And what did it mean to them?

He and Mary Rose had gone over to Brenda's one Sunday afternoon a few weeks ago. Gary and Rickey were working at the diner, and the parents had planned the meeting accordingly. Brenda poured tiny glasses of her beloved Tia Maria, and they talked for what felt like hours about any silly subject that came to mind, no one really wanting to bring up the reason they'd convened. Finally a silence fell in the room, and Brenda stared into her glass and said, "I just think maybe they spending too much time together."

"They're best friends," said Elmer. "They been best friends since they was nine. We can't fault them for that."

"Brenda," said Mary Rose, then trailed off.

"What?"

Mary Rose picked up a magazine and fanned herself with it, seeming to gather her thoughts. Finally she said, "If something … unnatural is going on, wouldn't you rather know about it while they still young and we can do something about it?"

"Well, sure, babe. But if we do find out something, God forbid, what we gonna do?"

"They got places we could send them."

"We ain't sending Gary to no *place*," said Elmer. "Whatever's going on, we deal with it ourselves. Brenda, I can't tell you what to do with your boy, but I sure wouldn't do nothing like that."

"What they do in those places, anyway?" asked Brenda.

"They brainwash people," said Elmer. "And I heard most of the time it doesn't even work. It just messes 'em up worse."

"But Elmer …" Mary Rose fanned herself furiously. "If they trying to *help* the kids, to make them normal …"

"Listen." Elmer stared at the women, feeling outnumbered. "I don't like the idea of having abnormal kids any better than y'all do. But it seems to me that sending your child to that kinda place is about the same as telling him you don't love him."

"I'm not sure I *could* love a gay child," said Mary Rose.

"Oh, honey!" Brenda's lips made a perfect O, and her hand flew up to cover it. "You don't mean that!"

"I don't know if I do or not," said Mary Rose. "And I don't want to find out."

"I just want whatever's best for Johnnie," Brenda said. "If there *is* something wrong, I'm afraid maybe it's my fault cause he ain't grown up with a man around."

"Then what's our excuse?" said Elmer, irritated.

"I didn't mean …"

"Let's not argue," said Mary Rose. "We gotta stick together on this. We gotta present a united front."

"I guess so," Brenda murmured sadly.

Despite all this talk, they hadn't really come up with any kind of plan. They all agreed that the boys had been good for each other: Elmer and Mary Rose felt that as the youngest of six kids, Gary had sometimes gotten rather lost in the shuffle of the family, and Rickey's friendship was one thing he'd never had to share with his brothers and sisters. Brenda said Rickey had been calmer since he met Gary, though if they'd only known the calm version of Rickey, Elmer had to wonder just what he'd been like before. At any rate, they didn't want to split up the boys if there was an alternative, and nobody could think of an alternative, so the meeting had adjourned with nothing decided.

Meeting in secret, talking about sending their kids to a "place," lurking in the hallway outside his son's room before dawn—Elmer found himself thinking that perhaps all this was as wrong as whatever Gary and Rickey had been doing. He pulled the door shut, relocked it, and padded back down the hall.

As he slid into bed, Mary Rose raised her head from the pillow. "Well?" she said.

"They ain't doing nothing. Rickey's on the floor, Gary's in bed, and they both sound asleep, just like we ought to be."

He wondered why he had lied, and told himself it was because he still couldn't be sure of anything. The boys' sleeping together might be a one-time thing. It might mean nothing at all. He wasn't quite ready to admit to himself that he had also lied because he was scared of what Mary Rose and Brenda might do.

Rickey lay absolutely still for several minutes after the door closed. He hadn't been able to see the face of the person looking in at them, just the vague silhouette of a head and upper body, but he was sure it had been Elmer. That was better than if it had been Mary Rose, but it was still pretty bad.

His head was still swimming from all the alcohol. He tried to collect his thoughts, but it was difficult. Gary was asleep; that much Rickey could tell from his deep breathing. Should Rickey wake him up and tell him what he'd just seen? No, that would be a really shitty postscript to his birthday celebration. Should he tell Gary about it in the morning, then? He didn't know.

Rickey scooted across the bed and fitted himself spoonlike against the curve of Gary's back. Something would change now; he was sure of it. He felt a sense of dread so deep it seemed unreal. Earlier tonight, one year hadn't seemed all that long. But if their parents managed to separate them, Rickey knew that a year could seem like a lifetime.

In the morning, he decided not to tell Gary. Maybe Elmer had just looked into the room to make sure they'd gotten home safely. Maybe he hadn't even been able to tell that they were in bed together. It had been pretty dark. If Gary thought his parents already knew about him and Rickey, it would eat away at him, and he might feel compelled to say something to them, and then maybe he and Rickey wouldn't be able to see each other any more. For sure they wouldn't be allowed to have sleepovers.

Elmer had already gone to work by the time they got up, and Mary Rose fixed them French toast and bacon just as she always had when Rickey slept over. Maybe nothing would change after all. Though it went against everything in his nature, Rickey forced himself to leave the matter alone.

As they were finishing breakfast, one of Rosalie's kids came in from the yard. Tommy was a slat-ribbed five-year-old with shiny hair the color of black coffee, and just now he looked as though he had been rubbing handfuls of dirt all over himself. "I ain't had no lunch," he said.

"Grammar!" said Mary Rose. "You *haven't had any* lunch."

"But, Maw-Maw, *you* say 'ain't.'"

Rickey and Gary knew from long experience what Mary Rose's reply would be. "Do as I say," they chorused along with her, "not as I do."

She turned to glare at them. "Hush up, smart-asses."

"Smart-asses, smart-asses," Tommy sang, subsiding when he felt Mary Rose's eye upon him.

"What y'all been doing out there to get so dirty?" Mary Rose asked as she fixed him a peanut butter fold-over.

"Playing Saints."

"Saints!" said Gary. "Saints *football*?" Tommy nodded gravely. "Well, what you want to do that for? Wouldn't you rather be on a winning team?"

"Yeah," said Rickey. "Why don'tcha play Broncos and Redskins?"

"Don't wanna."

"You two hush up," said Mary Rose. "Let the boy have a little pride in his city."

"He can have pride in his city," said Rickey. "Just not in his city's football team."

Mary Rose pointed a spatula at Rickey. "You got a big mouth, mister. I ever told you that?"

"Only about a million times," Rickey said amiably. "A few more strips of bacon might shut me up."

"Maw-Maw," said Tommy.

"What, baby?"

"I heard Paw-Paw walking in the hall last night."

"What you mean?"

"He was walking up and down. He walked past my room, and then he stopped by the end of the hall, and then he walked back again."

"How you know it was Paw-Paw?" Gary asked.

"His feets are heavy," Tommy said as if stating a painfully obvious fact.

"He was probably just going to the bathroom," said Mary Rose.

"But the bathroom ain't down by the end of the hall."

"Tommy! I just *told* you—*grammar!*"

"But Maw-Maw—"

"Forget it," Mary Rose said in a voice that signaled the last word on the subject. "Here's your sandwich. Go on back out and play—Maw-Maw's got a headache."

"What's he talking about?" Gary said when Tommy had left the kitchen. "Was Daddy up late last night? Is something wrong?"

"Not that I know of, babe," said Mary Rose. She was at the stove frying more bacon, her back to them. "Why? You heard something?"

"No. I just wondered."

"Well, I got no idea what he's talking about." Mary Rose turned to face her son. Her dark eyes had a tragic look, but then they frequently did. "You know how it is," she said. "Kids and their imaginations."

6

Rickey and Gary still didn't spend a lot of time in the French Quarter—even at the relatively low-key Hand of Glory, the bar scene was predatory enough to make them uncomfortable, and more than once they'd been approached by older men offering them money to take part in a threesome or some equally unsavory thing. But during that summer, they went to the Quarter more often than they ever had before. As Rickey had said before their first visit to the Hand of Glory, it was nice to go somewhere they didn't have to pretend.

One night in October, just after they had started their senior year at Frederick Douglass, they left the Hand of Glory and went in search of something to eat. Late-night dining options were limited in New Orleans: a couple of loud, queeny diners in the Quarter, a couple of quiet, sleazy diners farther uptown, and the Shoney's over on Decatur about covered it. "This city needs a good restaurant that's open until two in the morning at least," Rickey said. "A place like that would just clean up."

"There's an all-night place on Burgundy that almost looks like a real restaurant," said Gary. "We walked past it last time we were down here."

"I don't remember that."

"You were drunk."

They walked over to Burgundy Street and found the place, a rather precious-looking little property called the Jolly Corner. Inside, it seemed a study in small incongruities. Fresh flowers were carefully arranged on each table, but the menus were greasy. The waiter was impeccably groomed except for damp patches of filth on his trouser knees. The chalkboard listed ambitious but risky-sounding dinner specials like Chinese Apricot Pork and Pasta Fazool. Gary ordered a cheeseburger and Rickey got a Western omelet.

They had nearly finished eating when a huge crash sounded

from the kitchen. The cook came storming out, closely followed by a fiftyish man who appeared to be some sort of manager. The manager tried to grab the cook's arm, but the cook shook him off. "You ain't NEVER gonna talk to me like that again," said the cook, "and if you try one more time, I'm gonna shut that bitch mouth for you."

"LaMonty, please, get back in the kitchen. I promise I won't speak that way to you again."

"I know you won't, Marlon, you BITCH. Because I QUIT."

Two men in a far corner broke into applause. Marlon turned and glared at them. "Sorry," said one of the men. "I couldn't help myself when he said he was quitting. I tried the pork special."

"WELL," said LaMonty. "I see I'm not appreciated around here anyway."

"No, dear," said the man's dining companion. "I'm afraid you're really not."

"That DOES it. I'm LEAVING."

"I'll need your jacket," said Marlon.

"What?"

"Your jacket, Mary. It belongs to the restaurant."

The cook's eyes seemed capable of burning holes in the floral wallpaper as he unbuttoned his double-breasted white jacket. Above his houndstooth check pants, his bare chest was as broad and chiseled as some great teak sculpture. "I'd rather walk down Bourbon Street STARK NAKED," he hissed, "than spend another SECOND wearing anything from this DUMP." He flung the jacket at Marlon and slammed out of the restaurant. Several of the patrons nodded appreciatively, though whether at the dramatic exit or the cook's physique, Rickey and Gary couldn't tell.

Marlon folded the chef jacket over his arm and went into the kitchen. A few minutes later he came back out carrying a used-looking sign that said **COOK WANTED**. As he was taping it to the window, another cook came flouncing out of the kitchen. This one was slight and blonde, and looked as if he had been crying. "I can't believe what you did to LaMonty," he said. "I'm quitting too."

"Oh, for God's sake, Timmy. Not again. You talk me into hiring these big useless hunks, and the minute I say boo to them, you're out the fucking door. Well, not this time. You quit again, you stay gone."

"Fine."

"Your jacket, please."

The little blonde cook was wearing a pale pink T-shirt underneath his chef jacket, and the patrons didn't seem as interested in his exit as they had been in LaMonty's. Marlon took the sign out of the window and altered it to read **COOKS WANTED.** Gary felt Rickey kick him under the table. "You gotta be kidding," he said.

"They get to make *dinner specials*."

"But, Rickey, this would be a terrible place to work."

"How do you know?"

"Did that scene just now inspire confidence in you?"

"We gotta start somewhere. This place might be desperate enough to hire us. I'm sick of making burgers and eggs."

"They got burgers and eggs on the menu here."

"Yeah, but *dinner specials!*"

Gary reached across the table and took a bite of Rickey's half-eaten omelet. There was no use in arguing; he knew Rickey could see himself whipping up wonderful Jolly Corner dinner specials with absolute creative control, and why rob him of that vision? In the event they were actually hired, he would learn the truth soon enough. "If you want to," said Gary. "But I don't see how we can go to school during the day and work here all night."

"Fuck school. All we gotta do is get, like, C's. If we can keep C averages, I bet our folks'll let us work here."

"You talk like we already got the job."

Rickey poked at his omelet. "Why shouldn't we?" he said. "I know we can cook better than this."

Marlon turned out to be the owner of the Jolly Corner, and he was almost pathetically eager to hire them. He had been through a long succession of older cooks whose experience varied, but whose intractability had been constant. In Rickey and Gary he saw a pair of eager workers who could be controlled, at least for a while.

Brenda was easily persuaded to let Rickey take the job as long as his grades stayed acceptable. She'd been no scholar herself, and Rickey got the idea that "acceptable" meant "not flunking." Brenda had been working in the restaurant business for a decade. Though she was in the office rather than the kitchen, she'd known enough cooks to understand that for some people the work was in their blood. She seemed to realize that it was this way for her son.

Gary's parents absolutely refused to let him work at the Jolly Corner. They'd never had any problem with the Feed-U, but they wouldn't even discuss this; they just said no. Of course Gary knew it was because the place was in the French Quarter. Maybe they'd even driven past it and gotten a look at the clientele, or called the place and talked to Marlon. His piping, slightly babyish voice wouldn't have reassured them any.

Gary did not dare argue the matter with his parents. He already spent too much time worrying that they knew more than they let on about him and Rickey. As long as they left that alone, he was afraid to pitch any major battles, especially ones having anything to do with the French Quarter. Anyway, Rickey had wanted the job more than he had. Gary would be happy to stay at the Feed-U; they had a lot of fun there.

So he was pretty much blindsided when Rickey said he was going to take the job anyway.

"Dude," said Rickey, "I have to do it. You gotta understand that. I *have* to." They were sitting in a sunny clearing near the Mississippi River. Behind Holy Cross, the private school for rich kids who were bussed into the Ninth Ward and bussed safely away again at the end of the day, there was a spot where you could climb over the levee and find yourself in a grove of pecan, scrub pine, and the tall broad-leafed trees called misbelieves by Ninth Warders and Japanese plums by the rest of the city. The area was so quiet that it felt like you'd stepped out of New Orleans and into some sleepy country village. It wasn't private enough for all their purposes, but they often came here to talk.

"You don't have to," Gary said. "You *want* to." He knew it was a petty, immature thing to say, but he couldn't help it. He had honestly thought they would work at the Jolly Corner together or not at all.

"Course I *want* to. I want to be a *cook*. You know that, G. I want to be a real cook. But I thought it was at least a couple years away. At this job, I'd already *be* one."

"I know you want to be a cook. I thought you wanted a lot of other stuff, too."

"What are you talking about?"

"I thought you wanted us to be together."

"We are together. Nothing's gonna change that."

"Bullshit." Gary pushed his shades up on his nose, trying to hide the shimmer of tears that had been threatening for several minutes now. "You'd have to go in right after school and work till the middle of the night. We'd never see each other."

"I won't be working every day. And Marlon thinks I'm too young to work the graveyard shift. He wants me to come in at four and work till midnight. You could come downtown and meet me."

"Yeah, sure. My parents won't even let me work in the Quarter. You think they're gonna let me go down there and party with you in the middle of the night?"

"You could on weekends."

"Whatever," said Gary. He couldn't look at Rickey, so he stared out at the river. A huge gray tanker loomed up near the French Quarter. Beyond it he could see the silver webwork of the bridge.

"I can't believe you're taking it this way. You act like I'm fixing to sleep with another person or something. It's just a *job*."

"Fuck off, Rickey. Do what you gotta do, but don't start lying to me. It's not *just a job* to you. It's the goddamn key to your future, the way you see it."

"I guess," said Rickey. "No, I know it. You're right. That's why I gotta do it. And maybe that's why you don't want me to, cause you think I'm gonna leave you behind. Well, I'm not."

"As far as cooking goes, you already have."

"So quit the Feed-U and come to work with me. Just come in from, like, four to seven whenever you can, and help me make the dinner special. I don't think Marlon will mind, and you'll learn a lot. I can even pay you out of what I make."

"You can't do that."

"Sure I can. I give most of my money to my mom, and I spend the rest of it on cookbooks. I just won't buy as many cookbooks."

Gary thought about it. He knew he was being selfish, and he could see that Rickey was making a tremendous effort not to be. But this in itself disturbed him because it was like a reversal of their usual roles. He just knew everything was going to change if Rickey took that job.

"You do what you gotta do," he said. "But I'm not quitting the Feed-U."

"Why not?"

"Cause Sal needs me, and I'm good at my job. I don't want to leave it so I can be your assistant for a couple hours a day."

"Sous chef."

"What?"

"In the kitchen, you don't call it an *assistant*. You call it a sous chef."

"Pretty fancy language for a place like the Jolly Corner."

Rickey looked wounded, and Gary felt a small, savage pleasure of which he was not at all proud. "Sorry," he said. "It's a good job, and you're gonna kick ass there. I just wish things had worked out different."

"You'll be eighteen in less than a year," said Rickey. "Then they won't be able to tell you where to work."

"A lot of things are gonna be different when we're eighteen," Gary said. But for the first time, he felt scared of what those things would be.

Rickey understood why Gary didn't want to quit his job. At the Feed-U, they knew every inch of the line and could work faster and better than any of the other cooks. They were rollers, and being a roller was a fine feeling. But Rickey believed that part of a good cook's job was knowing when to take risks. He wondered if Gary wasn't a little afraid of risks.

Part of it was that damn Catholic upbringing, that mindset that seemed to equate questioning authority with worshiping Satan. (Gary never had told Rickey about his last confession, and Rickey would have been very surprised to learn of it.) Part of it was just his placid character, and Rickey couldn't really fault that, since it was part of what he'd always loved about Gary. But he still found his friend's cautiousness exasperating at times. Rickey was so excited about his new job that nothing could truly spoil it, but he would have been even happier if Gary had been coming to work with him.

Once he'd given Sal his notice, those last two weeks at the Feed-U were like heaven and hell rolled into one. It wasn't Sal's fault; he'd never expected a couple of teenage kids to work for him forever, and he was pleased to be keeping one of them. It wasn't Gary's fault either; after his initial reaction, he'd shown every sign of being happy for Rickey. So Rickey guessed it was his own fault. He was so eager to be cooking real food that it felt as if the two weeks would never end. At the same time, he wasn't sure he *wanted* them to end, because he knew how badly he was going to miss working with Gary. They seemed to sync up perfectly over the course of those fourteen days, shadowing each other's moves, watching each other's back, getting through the rushes without a hitch.

But finally the two weeks were over. On his first day of work at the Jolly Corner, Rickey couldn't concentrate on any of his classes. As soon as the last bell rang, he hurried to his locker to grab the houndstooth check pants he'd stashed there. Brenda had bought him three pairs of the pants, had even hemmed them for him. Rickey wondered if part of the reason she'd been so supportive about the job was that it meant he would be spending less time with Gary, but he was still willing to accept the fringe benefits of her support.

As he opened his locker, a small envelope fell out, slightly crumpled from being shoved through one of the vents in the metal door. The envelope held a card with a picture of Snoopy wearing sunglasses. Inside the card was the printed legend **YOU'RE THE**

COOLEST! and a message in Gary's neat handwriting: "Dear Chef, GOOD LUCK today. Try not to poison anybody, but if you do, just blame it on the day crew. I'm proud of you. LOVE, G."

Another piece of paper was tucked into the envelope. Rickey pulled it out and blinked at it, stunned: a fifty-dollar gift certificate from G.A. Lotz, the biggest restaurant supply house in New Orleans. Now he could get a really good knife instead of using the crappy house blades. Fifty dollars was a lot of hours at the Feed-U; Gary must have been saving up for weeks. Rickey felt tears prickling at the backs of his eyes and blinked them back hard. This was no time to start feeling guilty. He was grateful for the gift and would put it to good use, but right now he had a job to do.

He caught a bus to the Quarter, got off at Rampart Street, and walked over to Burgundy. "You're early," said Marlon in a peevish tone when Rickey came in.

"Yeah, I thought I'd show up a few minutes early since it's my first day and all. It's not a problem, is it?"

"Well, I didn't want the day cook to meet you just yet."

That didn't sound too good. "I thought he'd be training me," Rickey said.

"No, I'm going to train you."

Rickey almost said *I didn't know you were a cook*, but he stopped himself. "I can go walk around for a few minutes if you want," he said instead.

"No," sighed Marlon. "I suppose we may as well get it over with."

He led Rickey into the kitchen, which was deserted, and handed him a white jacket. Rickey slipped it on over his T-shirt, wishing Marlon wasn't standing there so he could bask in the moment a little. He'd tried on a chef jacket once at Lemoyne's, the restaurant where Brenda worked, but he'd never had one of his own before.

As he was buttoning it up, the cook came through the back door carrying a box of tomatoes. Rickey thought he'd seen the guy at the Hand of Glory, but it was hard to be sure: he was a Quarter type, with his aging face, teenager's hairstyle, and little diamond stud sparkling in his left earlobe. He looked Rickey up and down, then said to Marlon, "I see you got yourself another pretty one."

"He knows how to cook, Cedric. He's been a fry cook at a busy diner."

"I'm sure you hired him for his hard-fried eggs."

"Oh, give it a rest."

"Or was it his crispy bacon?"

"Cedric."

It was as if the two men had forgotten Rickey was still here. He stepped forward and stuck out his hand. "I'm John Rickey," he said. "Everybody calls me Rickey. Nice to meet you."

Cedric looked at Rickey's hand for a second, then clasped it and shook. The guy did have a cook's palm, rough and knife-callused; that was something. "At least it has manners," he said. "Welcome to the Jolly Corner, Rickey. We have a few rules in this kitchen. No smoking over the food. Don't touch my knives. And don't bring your girlfriend in here."

"I wouldn't have hired him if I thought he had a girlfriend," Marlon said peevishly.

"Wishful thinking, Mary. You're always falling for these straight boys."

"I'm not a *straight boy*," said Rickey, stung.

"Excuse me?" said Cedric.

"I have a boyfriend."

"Do you, now?" Cedric lowered his eyelids to a haughty half-mast. "How nice for you." He turned away and started transferring the tomatoes into a colander. Feeling a little lightheaded, Rickey put a hand on the steel countertop to steady himself. He hadn't meant to say anything, and now all of a sudden this bitchy stranger was the first person he'd ever come out to.

"Cedric, you can go on now," said Marlon.

"I was just going to concassé these tomatoes."

"Rickey can do it later."

Cedric shrugged. "Fine with me."

The cook left, and Marlon started showing Rickey around the

kitchen. Rickey thought the line was horribly set up—although the kitchen was tiny, nothing seemed to be within reach of anything else—but of course he didn't say anything. Then an order came in and Marlon stopped to make it. "So you are a cook?" Rickey asked.

"I never trained as one, but when you own a restaurant, you learn how to do everything. More or less."

As he watched Marlon make the order, a cheeseburger and a roast beef dinner special, Rickey decided it was rather less than more. Marlon took out a delicate pink flower-edged plate and slapped down the roast beef slices without removing a large hunk of fat from one. Then he plopped a ladleful of grainy-looking mashed potatoes onto the plate, allowing them to dribble slightly onto the meat. He finished the whole thing with a glossy brown gravy that had the appearance of a sauce designed to hide a multitude of sins. The cheeseburger looked all right, but it went onto an ugly blue and brown plate. He saw Rickey looking at it and said, "We don't match up the tableware here. It's part of our eclectic look."

"But that one looks kinda dirty," Rickey could not restrain himself from saying.

"The glaze is just a little cracked. A lot of this stuff came from thrift stores. I'm not made of money, you know."

Marlon stared at Rickey as if daring him to say anything else. Rickey handed Marlon the mustard bottle and kept his mouth shut.

7

After a couple of weeks, Rickey's new job seemed to be working out. He made his first dinner special, a beef stew adapted from a recipe by Elizabeth David. It sold well and the customers liked it. Unfortunately, Rickey had no experience converting cookbook recipes to restaurant dimensions, and no one at the Jolly Corner was capable of teaching him. And though he loved Elizabeth David, he realized afterward that she might not have been the best choice since she didn't even give measurements in her recipes. Afraid there wouldn't be enough, he had made so much that they had to donate a lot of it to a homeless shelter on Rampart Street. But he didn't make any other big mistakes, or at least none worse than Cedric and the other older cook made. His next special, a braised pork shank with cherries from Cooper Stark's trendy new cookbook, turned out perfect with hardly any left over. After two months, Marlon gave him a fifty-cent raise.

Gary was making good money at the Feed-U, better than Rickey got at the Jolly Corner, and they started savings accounts with the idea of getting an apartment when they were both eighteen. They didn't have as much time together as before, but it was more than Gary had expected. All in all, things were looking pretty good.

It was a cold gray day a couple of weeks after their Christmas break. Marlon had given Rickey three days off, telling him to rest up before they started getting ready for Mardi Gras; every restaurant in the French Quarter was insanely busy for two or three weeks at Carnival time. Gary had the afternoon off too. Getting off the school bus at Rickey's house, they saw two cars parked there, Brenda's Plymouth and an unfamiliar BMW with rental plates.

"What's your mom doing home?" said Gary.

"I don't know."

"Looks like y'all got company. Maybe I should go on."

"No, come in. It's probably somebody visiting next door."

"A BMW at the Mathews'?"

"Makes about as much sense as a BMW at our place."

A little nervously, Rickey unlocked the front door, and both boys stepped into the living room. Brenda was sitting on the sofa with her hands folded in her lap. Either her color was high or she was wearing more rouge than usual. In the wing chair across from the sofa sat a tall, broad-chested man in an expensive-looking suit. He stood up when he saw the boys, and Gary noticed little gold Gucci logos on the tops of his penny loafers.

Gary hadn't seen this man in half a decade, and then they'd only met once. It took him several seconds to realize that the big handsome rich guy was Rickey's father, and longer to remember the man's name. He'd told Gary to call him by his first name, like that would make him seem younger or something, but what was it? Something weird, Gary recalled, but what?

"John," said the man, extending his hand in a formal manner.

Rickey glanced once at Gary, as if looking for help, then went forward and shook his father's hand. "Hey, Dad," he said. "I didn't know you were gonna be in town."

"Johnnie, your father and I need to talk to you," said Brenda.

His name was Oskar, Gary suddenly remembered. Oskar with a K. Rickey's paternal grandmother had been German.

"We need to talk to you *privately*," said Oskar, looking past his son at Gary but obviously not recognizing him. *Why should he?* Gary thought. *We were eleven or twelve last time he saw us. He's lucky he recognizes his own kid.*

"Gary, you better go on home, babe," said Brenda.

Rickey turned and fixed Gary with a wide-eyed, trapped-looking stare. *Don't go,* his eyes seemed to plead, but Gary couldn't see what choice he had. "I was just going," he said. "Call me later."

Rickey nodded slightly but didn't speak. With a terrible knot of dread in the pit of his stomach, Gary left the house. He felt as if he'd just abandoned his best friend, and why not? That was exactly what he had done.

Rickey watched him go, then looked back at Brenda and Oskar. They put him in mind of a half-remembered story from some long-ago English class. A ship at sea had to pass between two giant rocks. Most of the time the rocks were still, but occasionally and without warning they would clap together, smashing whatever happened to be between them. That was all he could remember about the story.

"So, uh," he said, "what's up?" He tried to catch his mother's eye, but she looked over at Oskar. It was weird to see the two of them sitting there together. When Oskar had visited before, he'd stayed in a hotel and hadn't come to the house at all.

"John," said Oskar, "your mother asked me here so we could talk about your future. You're going to be eighteen in less than a year."

Eight months and fifteen days, actually, Rickey thought, but he just said, "Right."

"It's time for you to start thinking about what you want to do with your life."

It was funny; though Oskar had lived here for his first thirty-four years, and in California only for the past ten or so, he had no trace of a New Orleans accent. Rickey wondered how he'd gotten rid of it. "I have thought about it," he said. "I want to be a cook, like I'm doing now. But at a better restaurant."

"A cook?" Oskar frowned. He was a doctor, Rickey remembered—a chiropractor. Probably he wouldn't approve of his son working in a restaurant. But he only said, "Why just a cook? Don't you want to be the chef?"

"Well," said Rickey. "I mean, sure. Maybe. But I don't know if I'm good enough. I haven't been doing this very long."

"That's the wrong attitude. You have to make sure you *get* good enough. And in order to do that, you have to stop limiting your horizons."

"You shouldn't keep all your eggs in one basket," Brenda chimed in. Oskar turned his frown upon her. Though the memory seemed impossibly distant—they had split up when he was six—Rickey recalled him giving her that look at the dinner table, and how she had seemed to shrink beneath it. She did not shrink now, but gazed levelly at Rickey and said, "We think you ought to get out of New Orleans for a while."

He hadn't expected this. "Huh?" he said stupidly.

"You need to experience other things," his father said.

"Wait a sec. Is *that* what this is about?" Rickey turned to Brenda. "Is this something you cooked up with Mary Rose and Elmer? Is that why you helped me out when I got this job, too? So me and Gary wouldn't be spending so much time together, and maybe we'd kinda forget about each other, and when you tried to ship me off to California, I'd just say, 'Sure, Momma, where's my ticket?'" He saw tears welling behind her cat's-eye glasses, but he was too angry to care. "Well, screw that. I know what I want to do, and I'm not going to California."

"We're not asking you to go to California," Oskar said.

Rickey blinked. This conversation seemed to keep getting away from him. "You're not?"

"Absolutely not. I can't imagine what made you think so."

Though he had no interest in living with his father, the distaste in Oskar's voice pierced Rickey's heart a little. "So where was I supposed to go?" he said. "Not that I'm going *anywhere*, but what the hell did you think I was gonna do?"

"I'd like to pay your way through cooking school," said Oskar. "Have you ever heard of the Culinary Institute of America?"

"The CIA? Sure. But that's in New York."

"Yes, upstate New York. It's very beautiful there. Very different from New Orleans. And I've been reading up on this CIA. It's the best cooking school in the country. They call it the Harvard of cooking schools."

"Bertie graduated from there," said Brenda. "You remember him." Rickey remembered him well. Bertie had been the head chef at Lemoyne's when Brenda started working there, and Rickey at age seven had thought Bertie was a close relation to God. He'd soon moved on to become chef at a better restaurant. Rickey didn't know what had become of him after that, but he'd never forgotten the big guy in the white coat who picked him up, put a ladle in his hand, and let him stir a huge pot of gumbo. Hell, that was the first time he had ever been on the line.

He suddenly had the disconcerting realization that his parents were a great deal older and wiser than he was. Though he might have grudgingly acknowledged this in theory—and then again, he might not have—he'd never had it so abruptly brought home to him before.

He knew they were manipulating him and he knew why. Once he turned eighteen, they wouldn't be able to legally control him. He could move out of Brenda's house and get an apartment with Gary if he pleased. He knew he should tell them that was exactly what he planned to do. But he'd read about the CIA, how hardcore it was and how you were just about guaranteed a great cooking job if you graduated from there. He had wondered if he might be good enough to get through their two-year program, but it was very expensive. There were only two breaks—two weeks each, summer and winter—so as well as tuition, you had to board in a dormitory forty-eight weeks of the year. They offered a few scholarships, but Rickey's grade point average was nowhere near high enough to qualify. He'd never even thought of the CIA as a real-life possibility for himself.

"Are you serious?" he said to his father.

"I wouldn't make an offer like that if I wasn't serious."

"Can I take some time to think about it?"

"I'll be in town until tomorrow night," said Oskar. "You're not going to school tomorrow. I've made us lunch reservations at Commander's Palace."

Rickey looked at Brenda. "All of us?"

"Just you two," Brenda told him. "Y'all got plenty catching up to do."

"Two *years*?" said Gary.

Rickey had called an hour ago and said to meet him behind the levee. They were sitting across from each other, not touching. It was pretty dark, but between the light from the Andry Street Wharf downriver and that reflected off the water's shining surface, they could see each other quite well. In fact, Rickey could see the expression on Gary's face a bit more clearly than he wanted to.

"I'd come home for every break," he said. "Two weeks at a time. And you could come up and visit."

Gary didn't say anything, so Rickey kept talking. "There's no classes on weekend. If you came to see me, I could spend the whole weekend with you."

Gary took off his glasses and stared at Rickey, but remained silent.

"Dude, will you *say* something?"

"What—" Gary's voice was hoarse, as if something were caught in his throat. "What do you want me to say?"

"Well, I mean … do you think I should do it?"

"It doesn't matter what I think."

"Course it does. It matters to me."

"Yeah, it matters to you now." Gary closed his eyes, then buried his face in his hands, so that his voice came out muffled. "But if I said I didn't want you to go, and you didn't go, you'd hold it against me. You'd always wonder if you could've done it."

"I—" Rickey was going to deny this, but realized it was probably true.

"You'd end up leaving me without ever leaving New Orleans. That'd be a lot worse than having you leave me for New York."

"I wouldn't be *leaving* you."

Gary looked up for a second, then dropped his head into his hands again.

"I mean, I don't want to break up. I want to do this thing and come back to you. It'd make things a lot better for us, G. I could get a good job right away. I could start making good money. We wouldn't have to scratch out a living the way we will if we both get kitchen jobs right out of high school. But I don't … I don't want to stop being your boyfriend. I'm not gonna tell you to be faithful to me for two years, but I will if you will."

"Rickey …"

"What?"

"We're kids. C'mon. I love you, I know you love me, but we've hardly *lived* yet. You're gonna meet all kinds of people up there. I'm gonna be lonely as hell down here. We don't *know* if we'll be faithful to each other. We *can't* know."

"Well, can we try?"

Gary lifted his head. "So you're really gonna do it?"

Rickey could not quite speak, but he made himself nod. He'd pretty much known he was going to do it as soon as he realized his father was serious about the offer.

"Will you just tell me one thing? The truth?"

"Sure."

"That night … the night after we made dinner … when I asked you not to leave me? I said, 'Whatever happens, just don't go,' and you said you weren't going anywhere?"

"Yeah?"

"Did you at least mean it then?"

"Oh, G …" Rickey had promised himself he wasn't going to cry, but that was when he started losing it. He moved over to sit beside Gary. They wrapped their arms around each other and sat there shivering, though even with the breeze off the river it was an unusually balmy night. Rickey forgot his promise to himself and let his tears soak the shoulder of Gary's jacket.

Gary stared out at the river. He had learned very little geography in school, but he'd heard somewhere that all the rivers in the country flowed into the Mississippi sooner or later. He supposed that if you followed the river far enough it might lead to the Hudson Valley, and when Rickey was up there, he'd be looking at the same water Gary would eventually see in New Orleans. Though this was no comfort at all, Gary's eyes stayed dry.

Mary Rose Stubbs sat in her darkened living room. It was long past midnight, but sleep eluded her. She knew her son had gone out to meet Rickey, and she knew what Rickey was probably going to tell him.

This was the best plan the parents had been able to come up with. They hoped the boys were just going through some kind of phase, that their friendship had become too intense and was preventing them from seeing all the other possibilities life might hold for them. But the parents didn't want to separate the boys by force, and they knew that soon they wouldn't be able to. Gary would turn eighteen in six months, Rickey soon after that, and then they could do whatever they wanted. If things continued as they'd been going, the parents were afraid of losing them entirely.

Mary Rose was surprised when Brenda came up with the best idea anybody had had so far. Mary Rose liked Brenda, but she'd always considered her a flighty woman not overly blessed with brains. Yet it had been Brenda who first pointed out that it might be better to separate the boys by giving one of them something he really wanted. The Stubbses had no money to send Gary to cooking school, and Mary Rose wasn't sure he would have gone anyway; he wasn't as serious about cooking as Rickey seemed to be. But Brenda thought there was a pretty good chance her ex-husband might pay to send Rickey to school if she presented it to him right. Mary Rose was afraid that ten years in California might have perverted the man's mind, but apparently he didn't want a gay son any more than the rest of them did; he had agreed to the plan after only a little arm-twisting on Brenda's part.

Now it just remained to be seen whether Rickey would accept the offer. Brenda believed he would, but she wasn't certain. "Sometimes I feel like I don't know him no more," she'd said.

"I know just what you mean," Mary Rose had told her. "They so caught up in each other, seems like they don't even care for us."

"Did either of you ever think maybe we been driving them away?" said Elmer, but he didn't press the issue, and Mary Rose didn't give the point any credence. If the boys couldn't appreciate the fact that their families wanted what was best for them, maybe they would understand later. If not, separating them was still the best thing to do. She didn't know how far things had gone, but she believed there was something unnatural between them. Once she had loved Rickey almost like a child of her own. Now she wished Gary had never met him. He'd always been the ringleader, and she was quite certain that

Gary would never have gotten in all this trouble without his help. She had wanted to ban him from the house, but Elmer put his foot down: "He's just a kid, and whatever else is going on, he's still our son's best friend."

She thought about Gary's behavior over the past year. He had seemed increasingly distant from the family, it was true, but Mary Rose hadn't raised five other children without learning that that was the normal course of action for teenagers. Moreover, something else had seemed different about him. Gary was smart enough; his teachers said so. But he'd always seemed … what? … a bit vague, maybe. A bit melancholy. She attributed it to his having so many brothers and sisters with whom to share the attention, and she thanked God that he wasn't a spoiled brat like some people's youngest kids. Over the past year, though, Gary had changed. He was more focused somehow, as if he'd seen a future he wanted and had decided to work for it. She could barely bring herself to admit it, but he seemed happier than he'd ever been before. The vagueness and the touch of melancholy were gone.

It crossed her mind that maybe she and the other parents were doing a bad thing. They didn't mean to; they only wanted to help the boys, but what if they were wrong?

Mary Rose reached into the pocket of her dress, found her rosary, and began telling the beads. Slowly her doubt receded. Of course she was doing the right thing. Gary and Rickey had very likely committed a mortal sin, or would soon. They thought they were being very discreet, and the parents had no proof, but you could see it in the way they looked at each other. They were endangering their immortal souls. They had to be stopped, and if they could be stopped in a way that didn't really hurt either of them, then that was not a bad thing.

She heard a key in the front door and stuffed the rosary back into her pocket. Gary came into the foyer. She had been afraid he would have Rickey with him, but he was alone. Even in the darkness of the living room, she could see the stricken, lost look on his face. He looked as if somebody had managed to beat him half to death without leaving a mark on him.

His eyes adjusted to the darkness and he saw Mary Rose sitting there on the sofa. She thought he might ignore her or even yell at her, but he just stood there looking at her. His expression was too much to bear, and after a minute she held out her arms.

Except for an occasional pat on the shoulder or swat on the butt when he said something fresh, Mary Rose had not touched her youngest son in several months. Though she was not proud of her feelings, she was disgusted at the thought of what he might be doing with Rickey, and she hadn't wanted to get close to him. But now he came to her, crawled onto the sofa, curled up in her lap, and sobbed there like he hadn't done since he was a little boy. He was nearly a foot taller than Mary Rose now, but she held him as best she could, stroking his hair and not minding when his sharp bones poked into her flesh. He was still her baby and it was her duty to comfort him, just as it was her duty to help him out of this mess he'd gotten himself into.

8

There is a little green space at the river end of Audubon Park whose proper name is Avenger Park, but which for some reason is popularly known as "The Butterfly." This park is closed at night, but Rickey and Gary knew several ways in, and they thought they had the place to themselves. They climbed down the sea wall and sat in a grove of scrubby trees on the river batture, the muddy strip of land beyond the levee. It was here that the night of heroic drunkenness began.

They'd borrowed Elmer's car, so they didn't intend to drink too much. But somehow they ended up at The Butterfly with a quart of orange juice and a fifth of cheap tequila, swigging alternately from one, then the other. Soon they reached that stage of drunkenness where getting even drunker seems like the finest idea in the world. Rickey sprawled on the ground, propped his head against Gary's leg, and sucked at the neck of the bottle. "You know what?" he slurred. "I might not even get into the stupid school."

"What? The CIA?"

"Yeah ... I mean, they don't let in everybody who applies. I got the application. It looks pretty hard."

"You'll get in. Your grades are OK, and you said they require, what? Six months of restaurant experience? You already got a lot more than that."

"I gotta have two letters of recommendation from people in the industry too."

"So you ask Sal and Marlon to write you one. Big deal."

"I gotta do some kinda math test."

"What you mean, math test?"

"Like ..." Rickey tipped more tequila into his mouth, not noticing that a good deal of it was running down his chin and soaking the collar of his shirt. "Like word problems and shit ... like, 'A side of beef weighs 225 pounds and costs eighty-five cents a pound. How much does the whole side of beef cost?'"

"That's a big fucking piece of meat."

"Yeah, but I can't *say* that. I gotta work the *math*."

Gary thought about it for a minute. "$191.25," he said.

"See, I can't even do that on paper."

"Sure you can. It's just mulpli ... multifi ... shit."

"How can you do it in your head when you're too drunk to even say the *word*?"

"I don't know," Gary admitted. "Math's just easy."

"Not for me it isn't."

"Look. You just *take* the number of pounds and *times* it by the price—"

"Oh God," Rickey groaned, "don't tell me now. I'm not gonna remember."

"Well, I'll give you some pointers another time."

"Don't know why you even wanna help me," Rickey said rather sulkily.

"Cause I want you to do it if it's what you want to do."

"That's fucked up."

"Why? You want me to, like, threaten you or something? Tell you I'll never talk to you again if you go?"

"Kinda."

"Would that make you change your mind about going?"

Rickey thrust the bottle away, rolled over onto his stomach, and buried his face in Gary's lap. "No," he admitted in a very muffled voice.

"Well, see, I can't win."

"Least you got one thing to be happy for."

"What's that?"

"The rule."

"Oh yeah, the rule." Gary reached for the bottle and took a long drink. The tequila burned his throat and nearly made him gag. "Ugggh ..."

"Don't puke! Don't you dare puke! Say the rule!"

"There is ... agh."

"*Say* it."

Gary coughed, took a deep breath, and wiped his eyes. "There is always alcohol," he said.

"There is always alcohol," Rickey repeated. "Just remember that and you'll be fine."

"Sure," said Gary.

"Aw, don't get all bummed out. We're gonna be OK."

"I'm not getting bummed out."

"Yes you are. I can tell. C'mon, dude …" Rickey sat up and gave Gary a very sloppy kiss on the cheek.

"Jeez. It's like being kissed by Mescalito."

"C'mon…"

Gary relaxed a little and turned his head so that Rickey could reach his mouth. Soon they forgot their conversation entirely. They didn't usually make out in public places, even deserted ones. But the tequila made them incautious, and they didn't notice that they had company until a voice said, "Hey, lookit the little faggots!"

They pulled away from each other and looked around to see three young men in white baseball caps advancing on them from the downtown side of the batture. Though there was no way to be sure, Rickey immediately pegged them as Tulane frat boys. He got to his feet and gripped the neck of the tequila bottle. If he could find something to smash it on, the broken end would make a pretty good weapon. These Greeks wouldn't be counting on that kind of Ninth Ward defense. "Fuck off," he said.

"*Fuck off*," mocked the biggest whitecap in a high-pitched voice. "What are you gonna do, fag? Make me?"

"Yeah, sure." Rickey hefted the bottle. "You wanna try something?"

"We'll try something, all right." The guy's accent was harsh, nasal, unnaturally full of R's and L's. Midwestern, maybe. "We'll kick your faggot asses for you."

"Three against two, huh? Tough guys. C'mon, then. You look like a bunch of pussies to me."

As he spoke these last words, Rickey felt the tequila bottle snatched out of his hand. He'd been focusing on the big whitecap, and he thought one of the others had circled around behind him until he saw Gary rushing at the three guys, his arm cocked back, the upraised bottle glittering in the moonlight. "Jesus fucking Christ!" said one of the whitecaps, then turned and ran as Gary plowed into the other two.

"FUCK YOU FUCK YOU FUCK YOU!" Gary yelled. At the bottom of its arc, the tequila bottle connected with the big whitecap's head. It did not break, but the guy went to his knees anyway. He managed to get one arm in front of his face, which was probably the only reason Gary didn't brain him with the next swing of the bottle. Instead, it glanced off his forehead, but apparently that was enough. The guy flopped to the ground. His head lolled and his cap fell off.

All this had taken about five seconds, and Rickey watched it dumbly, his mouth hanging open. They'd been in a few street fights and school fights over the years, but he had never seen Gary do anything like this before. The remaining whitecap looked equally stunned for a moment—he hadn't expected any resistance at all from a couple of little fags, Rickey supposed. But when Gary advanced on him, he didn't run like his friend had done. Instead he half-crouched in a kind of fighting stance, kicked out at Gary's arm, and managed to knock the bottle out of his hand. It was probably just a lucky kick, but it looked like some kind of karate. Rickey launched himself at the guy, hit him in the back, and drove him forward onto the ground. The guy got his arms under him and flipped himself over somehow. In another second he might have wrestled Rickey down and pinned him, but Gary darted around behind them and gave the guy a good hard kick in the balls. The guy's body just sort of jackknifed. Rickey scrambled up, grabbed Gary's arm, and said, "Run!"

"I'm not in the fucking mood for this!" Gary panted as they half-ran, half-staggered across the batture.

"Me neither—let's get outta here—"

"Let's go after the one that ran!"

"No, dude—c'mon—" Rickey had thought he was in pretty good shape from several months of full-time kitchen work, but his wind was failing him as they scrambled up the wire-covered rocks that comprised the sea wall. He dragged Gary across the parking lot, through a small playground, past a set of railroad tracks and into a thick grove of trees. Among the drooping branches it was pitch-black. He stumbled against a section of wire mesh fence, felt his way along it, and came to a sagging spot. Where the wire met the ground, he thought there was enough leeway to pull it up and shimmy beneath. "Here," he whispered, finding a handful of Gary's jacket and yanking on it.

"What?"

"There's a fence. I'm pulling it up. See if you can slide under."

Rickey felt Gary hesitate—maybe he wanted to go back and beat on the whitecaps some more. "Get your ass under there," he hissed, and Gary did. Rickey followed him. They came out on some kind of dirt track. A ways along it, there was a little more light. Rickey could make out more fences, a gazebo, and a very weirdly shaped tree silhouetted against the sky. As he watched, the tree moved, tore a leafy branch off another tree, and ate it. "Dude!" said Rickey. "We're in the zoo! Look, there's the giraffe."

"COOL!" Gary howled, hoisting the bottle as if proposing a toast. A few inches of tequila still sloshed in the bottom.

"Oh my God!" Rickey started laughing. "You saved the liquor!"

"Course I saved the liquor." Gary scowled. "You think I was gonna waste it on those fucking Greeks?"

"Nuh-uh, you kicked their asses without it. C'mon."

"I just wasn't in the mood for that kinda shit," Gary mumbled as he followed Rickey toward a clearing up ahead. On the other side of the clearing rose the Audubon Zoo's most famous landmark, Monkey Hill. Thirty feet high, it had been built by WPA workers in the 1930s so that children growing up below sea level could have the experience of playing on a hill. Virtually every kid in New Orleans had climbed it and rolled down again, but Rickey was willing to bet most kids hadn't sat on the summit doing tequila shots. He pulled Gary to the top, pried the bottle from his resisting hand, and swigged the burning taste of victory.

When the police cruiser came rolling slowly through the park an hour later—when two cops who seemed to be hiding a certain amount of amusement rousted them off the hill and poured them into the back of the car—when they threw up more or less in tandem on the cruiser's floor—even when their parents arrived to retrieve them from Central Lockup in the cold and merciless hours just before dawn, Rickey couldn't bring himself to regret a thing about the evening. The memory of Gary dropping two frat boys and making a third run like a scared little bitch through Avenger Park was worth every bit of it.

9

They suffered remarkably little disgrace over their arrest in the Audubon Zoo. It was as if their parents were relieved that they'd gotten in trouble for something normal, like public underage drunkenness. The next day, Brenda had even said, "Aw, just about everybody gets took in sometime in their lives."

"You been to jail, Momma?" Rickey had asked, interested.

"Well, not jail exactly. But when I was a girl, me and my little friend Antoinette tried to steal candy out the store, and the grocer kept us there till our folks come to get us."

"I guess you weren't cut out for a life of crime."

"And you ain't either, mister."

One week after Mardi Gras, before the kitchen-ache had even left his back and feet, Rickey came home from school and found a letter from the CIA. He tossed the other mail—a water bill, a K&B advertising circular, and a card from Brenda's sister—on the kitchen table and sat down to open his letter. He stuck his finger under the flap of the envelope, then paused. As long as he didn't know what was in the letter, life could go on as before. He was pretty happy, he realized. The Jolly Corner had its problems—he'd wanted to make something with ginger a couple of days ago, and Marlon had told him they didn't use "exotic spices"—but he knew it was a far better job than most seventeen-year-old cooks could hope for. And being with Gary, well, that was great. That was probably the best thing that was ever going to happen to him, and he knew he might destroy it by going to New York.

Still, he really, really wanted that CIA education.

The day after offering to send him to cooking school, Rickey's father had taken him to lunch at Commander's Palace, one of the oldest and best Creole restaurants in New Orleans. Rickey had been very impressed with the elegant main dining room and the impeccable service, but most of all he'd been taken with the food. He had expected it to be old-school stodgy, swimming in pools of butter like most of the stuff they served at Lemoyne's. Instead it was prepared with bright flavors and a deft touch. Though there were plenty of traditional elements—turtle soup, meunière sauce, and the like—it wasn't the kind of stuff you could get at ten or twelve other high-end restaurants around the city. It was, in fact, the first food Rickey had ever tasted that seemed to speak with the chef's own voice.

He didn't know if the chef talked to everyone or if Oskar had maybe slipped somebody a twenty, but as they were finishing lunch, the chef stopped by their table, shook their hands, and said to Rickey, "I hear you're going to the CIA." It turned out the chef had graduated from there and considered it one of the most valuable experiences of his life. If a CIA education could not only get you a job like that guy had, but could also help you give your food a coherent voice, then Rickey didn't think he could afford to turn it down.

He hesitated a second longer, then ripped open the envelope and pulled out the letter.

> Dear John Rickey:
>
> We are pleased to inform you that your application to the Culinary Institute of America has been accepted ...

"Congratulations," said Gary. Rickey could tell he was really trying to look happy, though the truth had been visible in his eyes when he took off his shades for a moment.

Gary was at work at the Feed-U, and Rickey had come to show him the letter. Now Sal Keller walked over to look at it. "Huh," he said, somehow managing to pack decades of skepticism into a single syllable. "Flipping burgers just wasn't good enough for you?"

"'Fraid not."

"So you gonna come back from that place and open your own restaurant?"

Rickey doubted it—where would he ever get the money?—but he just shrugged. "Maybe."

"Gonna be my competition, huh?"

"No. I'm gonna go after the diners who *don't* want to take a chance on ptomaine poisoning with every meal."

Sal pulled a filthy side towel from his apron and snapped it at Rickey, who ducked out of the way. "That's the thanks I get for writing you that damn letter," Sal said.

"No, seriously, Sal, thanks again for that. I appreciated the hell out of it." He had, too. Sal had obviously labored over the document—"This young man is hard working, inteligent, and fermiliar with all asspects of the fry cook's job"—and Rickey had let Sal send it even after learning that he only needed one recommendation from a food-service professional. Marlon's endorsement had been more literate and probably more useful, but not nearly as heartfelt.

Sal grunted something that might have been "Welcome" and disappeared into the back. Gary scanned the letter once more, then handed it back to Rickey. "I really am happy for you," he said, but he seemed to be swaying on his feet just a little.

"Dude, are you OK?"

"Yeah. I'm fine."

"You sure?"

"Course I'm sure. I been ready for this, Rickey. I didn't think they were gonna turn you down. I didn't *want* them to turn you down—I can see how bad you want to go."

"I'm kinda scared, though," Rickey admitted.

"Be pretty crazy if you weren't. You never even been out of Louisiana. Who knows what it's like up there?"

"I been to Mississippi."

"Just the Gulf Coast. I don't think that counts."

Rickey was about to say something else, but just then an old man came in and ordered the all-day breakfast special. Gary turned away to crack eggs onto the grill. Rickey got himself a cup of coffee and sat at the counter watching Gary work. The strings of Gary's apron had caused the back of his shirt to ride up, exposing a small triangle of skin just above the waistband of his jeans. Rickey tried to look away, to think about something else, but his eyes kept returning to that little patch of bare skin. He knew just how it would taste if he put his lips there, salty with perspiration and, beneath that, faintly sweet. He wondered how much longer that taste would belong to him, and whether someone else would be tasting it this time next year. A small, sharp blade twisted deep in his gut. He put down his cup of coffee.

"Want a warm-up?" said Gary, there with the pot.

"Nah … it's old. I better go. I got a book report to write." Rickey checked his pocket for the CIA letter and stood up. "Hey."

"What?"

"What time you get off tonight?"

"I don't know. About eight." Gary shrugged. "I could probably leave earlier if it's slow. Why?"

"My mom's going to a movie with Mr. Claude. I know she won't be back before eleven. Come over, OK?"

"Sure, I guess—"

"Don't *guess*. It's important." Rickey put his hand on the counter, not quite touching Gary's. "Look, I'll pick you up. I got the car anyway. I'll come get you at seven."

"Why? What's so important?"

"What do you *think*?" Rickey said, wondering if he was beginning to lose Gary already. He sought out Gary's eyes with his own, felt his pupils dilating. "Come *on*, dude. I'll pick you up. OK?"

"Oh," said Gary, finally getting it. "Yeah, OK. I'll see you at seven."

Rickey left the diner. As he crossed the parking lot, one of the neighborhood winos asked him for fifty cents. Rickey gave him a quarter. "Godblessya," croaked the wino, but Rickey hardly heard him. His mind was racing. There had been a time, not long ago, when Gary would have known what he meant as soon as he'd said they would have the house to themselves. But of course that was before Rickey had decided to leave. Could he blame Gary for shutting off his heart just a little?

He couldn't, he knew. But he wasn't sure he could stand it, either.

"Ow!" said Gary. "Damn, Rickey!"

"*What?* You want me to *stop?*"

"No, just be careful."

"I'm *being* careful," Rickey said impatiently and started fucking him again, way too hard, circling Gary's wrists with rough fingers and pinning him to the bed. Gary tried to relax into it, but his head was buried in the pillow and he couldn't see Rickey's face. He didn't like being fucked from behind, didn't like it at all. Rickey knew that, but had flipped him over anyway.

"Let me turn over?" he said without much hope.

"*No*, dude, c'mon, this feels really good ..." Rickey's sharp chin dug into Gary's shoulder, causing a small flare of pain. "You like that, huh?"

Usually when Rickey said that, he really wanted to know the answer. Now it was just meaningless dirty talk. Gary nearly sobbed, managed to suppress it but for a small sound in his throat.

"Yeah," said Rickey, almost splitting him in two. "You like that."

Gary pushed his face deeper into the pillow and wondered why Rickey was mad at him even though Rickey was the one going away. Afterward, he lay beside Rickey in the narrow bed. All was silent. Gary wanted to say something, but for the first time he could think of nothing to say. On the nightstand, the digital clock's red numerals flicked inexorably toward eleven.

"You OK?" Rickey said at last.

"Seems like you been asking me that question all day."

"Well, are you?"

"What the hell you want me to say, Rickey? I keep saying yes because that's what you want to hear."

"Fuck you!" said Rickey. "Since when do you just tell me what I want to hear? Since when do I ask you a question if I don't want to know the answer?"

"Since about last October, I'd say."

"You mean when I got the job at the Jolly Corner? Dude, that's not fair."

"Life's not fair."

"Now you sound like your mom." Indeed, *Life ain't fair* was one of Mary Rose's pet expressions, and Gary had only said it because he knew it would annoy Rickey. Now he kept his mouth shut, knowing

Rickey couldn't do the same for long. Sure enough, after just a few seconds Rickey threw the covers back and said, "I don't feel like laying around in here. I'm gonna go get something to drink."

"Don't go on my account," said Gary, getting up from the other side of the bed. "I'm leaving anyway."

"What you mean, you're leaving?"

"I gotta get home. I came here straight from the diner, remember? I still got homework to do."

"Oh, sorry," said Rickey. "Excuse the hell out of me. I thought maybe we had some important stuff to talk about, but I wouldn't want to keep you from your *homework*."

Gary stepped into his pants, pulled them up, and buckled them before he turned back to Rickey. "Now you want to talk?" he said. "Now that you're through fucking me like I was some cheap piece of meat, you want to talk to me?"

Rickey had been staring at Gary; now his eyes dropped. "Seemed like you liked it OK," he said.

"Yeah? How'd you figure that?"

"Well," said Rickey uncertainly. "I mean, you came, didn't you?"

"Rickey, I'm so goddamn crazy for you, I don't think there's any way you could fuck me that I *wouldn't* come. But I didn't feel close to you. I felt like you were just using me to get off. And you hurt me."

"I didn't hurt you."

Gary extended his arms so that Rickey could see the small finger-shaped bruises forming on his wrists. "You want to look at my ass?" he said. "I think you bruised it too."

"No, I …" Rickey stopped, swallowed hard, looked away. "I didn't mean to," he said. "I didn't mean to do *any* of that stuff to you. I don't know why I did it."

"I don't either," said Gary. He was still pretty upset, though his anger was ebbing as quickly as it always did.

"I'm so scared to leave you," Rickey said. "I'm scared we won't be able to handle it. I'm scared we won't be together any more."

"I don't know what to tell you." Gary sat down on the edge of the bed. Rickey moved over to wrap his arms around Gary's shoulders and press his face into Gary's back. This was one of Rickey's usual patterns, Gary reflected: bitter remorse after doing something terrible. He reached up and enfolded Rickey's hands in his own. "I mean, I'm scared of all those things too," he said. "But we got no choice. We just gotta try."

And so they tried.

First they tried to get through the few months remaining to them, and to enjoy each other as much as they had before. It wasn't as difficult as they feared it might be; they had never been able to hold any kind of grudge against each other, and the spark between them was, if anything, stronger than ever. Sometimes they were able to forget that anything had changed. But the calendar always reminded them. The CIA admitted new students several times a year, but Brenda and Oskar had decided that Rickey should work through the summer and save up some money to pay his incidental expenses. He would start school in September.

They also tried to make things more bearable by working together again. Gary turned eighteen, put in his notice at the Feed-U, and told his parents—gently but firmly—that he would now be working at the Jolly Corner regardless of how they felt about the place. Elmer and Mary Rose accepted this with no argument, both because they knew Rickey would be leaving soon and because they didn't want Gary to move out of the house now that he was of legal age to do so. Rickey badgered Marlon into hiring Gary even though the restaurant was entering its slow season. Marlon bitched about the extra hours, moaned about the extra money, and completely neglected to tell his two young cooks that customers were saying the food had never been better. Rickey and Gary knew it anyway; they were having the time of their lives. They'd grown accustomed to working apart, so being back in the kitchen together was like sex after a long dry spell—not that they'd had a sexual dry spell yet, but that was how they imagined it to be. Every shift was a blast, every dinner special a culinary masterpiece, at least in their minds. No New Orleans summer had ever seemed to pass so quickly. No two New Orleanians had ever wished so hard that the sodden, joyless month of August would go on forever.

But September came too soon. Rickey had a copy of the CIA textbook, *The New Professional Chef*, that he'd pre-ordered from the campus bookstore. He had a slightly ratty assortment of the collared shirts and dress pants students were expected to wear to their lecture courses. He had a roommate assignment, some guy from Boston named Philip Muller. He had a brand-new suitcase—he'd never owned one before, since he'd never been anywhere—and a one-way plane ticket to New York. About the only thing he didn't have was the ability to believe he was really going. It still seemed like a fantasy, and sometimes late at night, alone in his room, he would take out the plane ticket and pore over it in wonder and dread.

All through his last week at home, Rickey walked around with a strange feeling in his stomach that was part excitement and part nausea. He worked his final shift at the Jolly Corner. He slept over at Gary's house for two nights, then had Gary sleep at his house for two more. They didn't ask for permission or even care if their parents knew where they were. Though he had wanted to go to the CIA, and still wanted to, Rickey couldn't help feeling tricked now that the moment of departure was nearly here. He would wake up during the night in a kind of panic and realize Gary was awake too; they would cling to each other like a pair of octopuses, not letting go until they were exhausted, sore, and three-quarters asleep again. By the end of the week their eyes were ringed with dark circles. It was Sunday, and Rickey had to leave on Monday.

Elmer had slipped Gary some cash and told him to buy Rickey dinner. Gary had some cash of his own and had already been planning to take Rickey out, but with Elmer's money they were able to go to a nice Uptown restaurant. They sat in a softly lit dining room sipping Bloody Marys, pacing themselves because they didn't want to get too drunk tonight; they were a little afraid of what might happen if they did. Rickey did not find his shrimp appetizer to be entirely successful—"It's like it can't decide if it wants to be Creole or Chinese"—but he pronounced his entrée the best duck he'd ever had.

"See," said Gary, who was eating a decent but unspectacular pork roulade. "That's why you gotta go to the CIA."

"Why?"

"Because even tonight you can't stop analyzing the food. You're obsessed. I'm an OK cook—I'm pretty fast and all—but you got a real talent. You need to be somewhere they'll recognize it."

"What if they don't, though? What if everybody else in the class already knows how to make French sauces and shit?"

"They won't."

"What if they do?"

Gary shrugged. "Then I guess you learn fast and you get better than them."

Their eyes met across the table and exchanged a series of subtle, silent messages: *you OK?—I think so; you?—pretty much—maybe we can do this—yeah, maybe.*

They were like that the whole rest of the evening, careful, polite, not wanting to speak one unhappy word or shed a single tear in case it opened the floodgates. It was probably the most courteous night they had ever spent together, and that in itself felt strange and wrong. The later it got, the more Rickey worried about how it was going to end. They were home now, in his room, and he didn't want to have to deal with both Gary and Brenda in the morning. He wished he and Gary had just spent tonight at one of the hotels near the airport. He could have left straight from there, and Gary could have seen him off with no parents around. They should have spent their money on that instead of the nice dinner, but it was too late now.

He was still worrying when Gary sat up and said, "It's almost morning. I better go and let you get some sleep."

"I don't think I can sleep," said Rickey.

"You might be surprised. Anyway, I'm gonna go."

His voice was light, unconcerned. Rickey watched him dress, pulled on his own T-shirt and boxers, followed Gary to the front door and out onto the porch. "Are you even gonna say goodbye to me?" he asked.

Gary's calm expression faltered for a second, and he looked away. When he looked back, he seemed to be maintaining the expression by some tremendous effort. "Do me a favor?" he said.

"What?"

"Just say 'See you tomorrow.'"

"But—"

"Please, Rickey. It's the only way I can do this."

Rickey understood. He put his arms around Gary's neck, but tried not to hold him much tighter than he would have on any other night. He kissed Gary once, trying not to linger any more than he normally would have. "See you tomorrow," he said, and just managed to keep his voice from cracking.

"Sure," said Gary. "See you tomorrow."

Rickey watched him walk down the porch steps and unlock the door of Elmer's car. There suddenly seemed to be any number of things—Gary's loose-limbed gait, the soft curls of hair at the back of his neck, the way his jeans hung low on his hips—that he had never noticed fully enough and now did not have time to absorb. "I love you," he called.

Gary looked quickly up at him. His glasses caught the streetlight and Rickey could not see even a hint of his eyes. He smiled a little, raised one hand in a kind of sketchy salute, and got into the car.

Rickey sank onto the steps as Gary drove away. He wrapped his arms around his knees and watched the taillights dwindle. He knew he should go back in the house—at least try to get some sleep, and it wasn't the greatest idea to sit out here at four-thirty in the morning—but he couldn't quite make himself move yet. He squinted into the darkness, searching for a last hint of Gary's taillights. They were gone. He rested his forehead on his knees, squeezed his eyes shut tight, and hoped to hell that the CIA was going to be worth all this.

Gary drove all the way home, undressed, and got into bed before any trace of emotion caught up with him. He wasn't sure how he had suppressed it, but he was glad he had been able to. Rickey was already scared half to death; he hadn't needed a big farewell scene. And Gary knew that if he had let himself get started, he would have cried all the tears in the world. He simply wouldn't have been able to stop. See you tomorrow; that had been good.

Now, alone in bed, he thought he would cry. But he didn't. He just hugged his pillow—he thought he could still catch the scent of Rickey's skin on it, very faint—and stared into the darkness. He knew quite matter-of-factly that he would never see Rickey again. Of course, that was ridiculous. Rickey would be home for Christmas in three months. But three months was an eternity to them, who had never been apart for more than a couple of days since they'd met. And two years, the full length of Rickey's CIA curriculum? That was incomprehensible. He'd always assumed that heartbreak was just an expression, but now there was an actual pain in his heart, a dull, steady ache that seemed to be settling in for a while. He felt as if someone had died; he felt like a small child being asked to fathom the concept of Forever.

For the first time in years—maybe the first time ever—Gary thought he could understand his mother's religious faith. If you believed in that stuff, really believed it without question, then you always knew your loved ones would return to you. No matter how long they stayed away, even if they died, you would see them again eventually. That must be so comforting—if you could believe. He just couldn't any more. Where he had once had a little faith, there was now nothing but a big, black X like the one in an algebra problem. But he'd run into very few algebra problems he couldn't solve. He had no idea what the value of this X might be, or whether it had any value at all.

10

Rickey found his first airplane ride disappointingly uneventful. He had thought it would be glamorous, scary, or both. Instead it was so boring that he fell asleep an hour out of New Orleans. He woke up when he heard the meal cart coming down the aisle, but upon catching a whiff of the food, he decided not to eat any.

Brenda had called the CIA admissions office and obtained explicit instructions on how he should get to the campus. Nevertheless, the logistics were harrowing. First he had to catch a bus from Newark Airport to Grand Central Station. He experienced a weird sense of dissonance as the Manhattan skyline came into view through the bus window. Buildings he'd seen in a hundred movies and TV shows were suddenly spread out in front of him, seeming somehow less real than they had onscreen. As the bus entered the city, Rickey pressed his face to the window, marveling at the density of restaurants, stores, signs, and people. In New Orleans there were mostly just black people and white people, the majority of them rather fat and scruffily dressed. Now he saw people of every color and shape imaginable, people in turbans, people in traditional African and Asian dress, mysterious-looking men in long black coats and wide-brimmed hats with strange curls of hair hanging down on either side of their faces. He couldn't take his eyes off the people until the bus came to a stop and the driver announced, "Grand Central Station."

He was hungry from skipping lunch on the plane, so at the oyster bar in the basement of the terminal he ordered a dozen assorted raw oysters. They were very expensive, but he figured this could be the beginning of his New York education. He was used to fat gray Gulf oysters, and most of these seemed very small by comparison, but their flavors more than made up for it. Some were coppery, like the taste of blood in a rare steak. Some were sweet. One had an odd creamy texture. Rickey found himself thinking of a Christmas candy sampler; there was that same element of risk and adventure, not knowing what you'd get next. When he finished them, he wanted another dozen, but he couldn't afford it. Instead he picked up his suitcase and went looking for the train to Poughkeepsie.

On his way to the track he passed a newsstand, bought a postcard of the Empire State Building and addressed it to Gary. *There's all kinds of oysters in the world,* he wrote. *Wish you were here to share them.* He didn't sign it *Love* because he knew Gary's parents might read it. Instead he wrote, *Be Good and Keep The Faith—Rickey.* Gary would know what that meant. Rickey fished a stamp out of his luggage, affixed it to the postcard, and dropped his missive into an old-fashioned, copper-colored mailbox in the terminal. This would be the first installment in a voluminous correspondence.

> Dear Gary,
> Being up here is like being on another planet. The school is really out in the country. The campus is surrounded by trees which are already starting to change color for Fall. The leaves are red, yellow, and orange. They don't just turn brown and dry up like in New Orleans. There's mountains off in the distance. They are called the Catskills and I heard there used to be a lot of fancy resort hotels up there. Somebody said they were full of comedians.
>
> Classes started on Monday. For the next 6 weeks I have Culinary Math, Introduction to Gastronomy, Product Knowledge, and Food Safety. The math sucks, of course. The only good thing about it is that sometimes we get to bring our knives, but just to portion carrots and shit. Intro to Gastronomy is great. At first I thought it was going to suck too, because we started with etiquette. Who cares? I'm going to be in a kitchen all my life. I don't need to know how to use fingerbowls. But then the teacher started talking about the history of the chef in French cuisine and that

was really interesting. Did you ever hear of Antonin Carême? He was the father of haute cuisine. He invented the "pièce montée," which is a dessert shaped like a famous statue or building. Napoleon loved to have them at his royal banquets. We also learned about Plato, who was a philosopher in olden times. He said there is a perfect version of every dish and the cook's job is to find it.

My roommate, Phil Muller, is OK. He's in my Intro class too. He's 19 and worked in his uncle's deli in Boston before he came here. You should hear him talk. Yesterday he asked me if I had a "shoppinna" (that's what it sounded like) and it took me forever to figure out he was talking about a steel (sharpener). The really funny thing is he thinks I have an accent!

Well, I have a bunch of stupid-ass decimal homework to do, so I better go. I miss you. Be Good and Keep The Faith.

Love,
Rickey

Dear Rickey,
Sounds like you are having an exciting time. Sorry the math sucks so hard. Remember, decimals are just tens.

Everything is about the same here. I made chicken cacciatore for the dinner special tonight. Marlon thought it was great, but big deal, I could make it in my sleep. I think I'm going to put in my notice at the Jolly Corner. I just don't like that whole scene. I'd rather work with cooks who won't be grabbing my ass all the time. I mean, since you're not one of them.

I'm being good and it's easy to keep the faith since there is nobody I want to break it with.

Love,
G.

Dear Gary,
Who grabbed your ass? I knew those bitches would start some shit like that as soon as I left New Orleans. Tell them to quit or they'll have me to answer to at Xmas.

I went drinking with a bunch of people from Intro. The drinking age is 21 up here and they actually card people, if you can believe that. I always thought getting carded was just a myth. But one of the older guys bought pitchers for the table. While we were drinking, they started asking me about New Orleans cuisine. They think it's really spicy and everything is blackened. (Fuck Paul Prudhomme!) They even think locals actually eat alligator. I tried to introduce them to reality. I think they were interested, but then Muller, my roommate, said "All you need to know about New Orleans is that they feed on the bottom feeders."

I said "Yeah, because they taste good."

He said "It's all right for a regional cuisine, but I'm appalled by its current trendiness." He really talks like that. I wonder if everybody in Boston does.

I said the trendiness doesn't have anything to do with what we really eat in N.O. Then I asked him if he grew up eating baked beans and cod every day. I think he was surprised that I had heard of Boston baked beans. Up here, if you're from anywhere south of Washington D.C, everybody just assumes you are a retard.

It's cool, though. Everybody gives each other shit all the time. I guess that is good training for working in a restaurant.

Miss you. Do you have another job lined up yet? Make those Jolly Corner BITCHES, especially Cedric, keep their hands to themselves.

Love,
Rickey

Dear Gary,
I know you are very busy coming up with brilliant dinner specials and fighting off all the cooks and waiters who want to grab your ass, but if I can go to these fucked-up classes all day and do homework all night and still find time to write you, I think you could drop me a line. My Product Knowledge class is pretty cool because we're learning about purchasing and seeing some ingredients I never saw before. Remember the first time we made dinner together? I showed you the Julia Child cookbook and said I'd never seen a parsnip? Well, now I've seen one. Of course, that's probably not what you remember most about that night. It better not be!

WRITE ME YOU FUCKER. Just because I went out and had a little fun doesn't mean I don't hate being away from you.

Love,
Rickey

Dear Rickey,
Sorry I didn't write sooner. I put in my 2-week notice and Marlon has been working me to death. He has me making Italian specials every night. My theory is that he's feeding Cedric the dishes so C. can try and figure out how to make them when I leave. Well, fat chance. It took me 10+ years of cooking next to my mom and sisters to learn that stuff.

I wasn't mad that you went out drinking. I've been doing quite a bit of that myself. Also smoking a lot of weed, which is the one good thing about the Jolly Corner (connections). But your roommate sounds like kind of a dick. What's wrong with bottom feeders?

Soon as I finish my 2 weeks at the Corner, I'll start at Terrio's, a po-boy place right off Canal. There's no challenge to it but they pay better than Marlon and can give me more hours. I'll mainly be working lunch, but might be able to pick up some night shifts too. If not, I'll spend my evenings with my friends Jack, Jim, Jose, and Dixie.

Love,
G.

Dear Gary,
Watch out for those so-called "friends" of yours, especially Jose. You know what happened last time we drank tequila.

Dude, what are you working in a po-boy place for? I know you want to save up some money, but it's important to keep learning too. You're not going to learn anything frying seafood and slicing roast beef. I will be making good money when I get back to New Orleans. Please don't think you have to build up a big savings account at the expense of your career.

I finished my first four classes and am now in Meat Identification. We're learning the anatomy of pigs, cows, etc. It's kind of gross, but interesting. Next week we do Meat Fabrication, where we actually get to cut things up. FINALLY!!! I think I forgot how to hold a knife. (Not really.)

Well, gotta go. Tonight I have to write a 2-page paper on subprimal cuts.

Love,
Rickey

Dear Rickey,
I know you think you're automatically going to get some bad-ass line job as soon as you graduate from the CIA, but I'd just like to have a financial cushion in case it's not as great as you think it's going to be. If

I have to deal with living at home for 2 more years, I need to be making money. I want to give some to my folks so they won't have an excuse to treat me like a kid, and I want to put some in savings. Plus, I won't lie to you, I have a weekly liquor budget that I'm not about to give up. Don't tell me to be careful. You're not here. I'm going to try like hell to get through these 2 years and keep the faith and all that good shit. But I'm not going to do it sober. I'm not sober right now and I probably shouldn't mail this. I guess I'm going to, though. Sorry.

When you get back here and get your bad-ass job in a good kitchen, then maybe you can convince them to hire me and I'll learn whatever you want me to learn. Until then, to be honest, I don't really give a shit. I'm just marking time.

Love,
G.

Rickey didn't have much money for incidental expenses like long-distance bills, but he called Gary as soon as he got that letter. Elmer answered the phone. Though it was nine P.M. in New Orleans and Gary's shift ended at six, he wasn't home yet.

"Is he OK?" Rickey asked.

"I don't know," Elmer admitted. "Seems like he might be a little down. I guess he really misses you. To tell you the truth, we don't see a lot of him."

"Is he just out drinking all the time?"

"He don't tell us nothing, Rickey. He might be drinking, he might be going to the movies. If me and his momma try to ask him anything, he just says, 'I'm eighteen. Don't worry about me.'"

"That doesn't sound like Gary."

"I don't know what to tell you," said Elmer, sounding older and sadder than Rickey remembered.

"Well, tell him to call me when he gets in. Or leave him a note if you go to bed. I don't care how late it is. I want to talk to him."

But Gary didn't call that night or the next. The following day, Rickey had a few minutes between classes. He ran back to his room, called New Orleans Information, and got the number for Terrio's Po-Boys. The girl who answered the phone seemed to have no idea who Gary was. After Rickey had told her twice that he worked in the kitchen, she put the phone down on the counter with a bang. Faintly, Rickey could hear her shouting, "To—NY! We got anybody named Gary working here?" Her juicy Yat accent and the general air of confused incompetence made a wave of homesickness wash over him.

After what seemed like ages, Gary picked up the phone. "Who's this?" he said.

"It's me."

"Rickey? What are you doing calling me at work?"

"Dude, what is it? Three in the afternoon there? It's not like I'm pulling you off the lunch line."

"Well, I'm not supposed to get calls here."

It's a fucking sandwich shop! Rickey felt like saying. *If they fire you over a phone call—and from the sound of it, they don't give a shit—you just get another crappy job!* But he managed to suppress the urge. Instead he said, "I was kinda worried when I read your letter, and then you didn't return my phone call. I just wanted to make sure you were OK."

"Oh … I was gonna call you soon. I haven't been feeling too good, is all."

"That's just when you *should* call me."

"I figured you were busy," Gary said so wanly that Rickey felt like crying.

"Well, are you OK? Will you call me tonight?"

"Yeah. What time are you gonna be there?"

"I'll be in my room all night after eight—seven your time. Make sure and call me, OK? Please?"

"I will," said Gary. He hesitated, and Rickey thought he was going to hang up. Then he said, "Thanks for calling."

Gary did call Rickey at the dorm that night, and they had a good conversation, though Rickey was still worried at the end of it. Rickey's roommate, Phil Muller, was out of the room for most of the conversation, but a couple of minutes before Rickey hung up, Muller came in and sat down at his desk. At the other end of the line, Gary was talking about one of the cooks at Terrio's, an old guy who tried to give all the other kitchen people religious pamphlets. If you took a pass on the Jesus literature, he'd say, "Well, then, how's about some nice maryjane?"

Rickey laughed. Gary did too, and for a moment things were completely comfortable. Then Gary said, "I guess I better go. If I don't run up the phone bill too much, maybe I can call you again next week."

"I wish you would. It's really good to hear your voice."

"Yeah, same here. I miss you like hell, you know."

"I know," said Rickey. "I miss you too."

"I love you."

Rickey glanced over at Muller, who seemed to be absorbed in his textbook. "I love you too," he said.

He had been lying on his bed throughout the conversation. As he stood to put the phone back on its cradle, Muller looked up. "Your girlfriend?" he said.

Rickey knew he should say yes. Why complicate things? But he just couldn't quite make himself do it. He mentally flipped through a selection of possible responses and settled on, "Not exactly."

"I know how *that* goes," said Muller. He gave Rickey a conspiratory smirk before returning to his book.

No you don't, Rickey thought, but this time he kept quiet.

11

Gary thought this Thanksgiving might be the most depressing day of his life. Since Brenda was such a terrible cook, she and Rickey had been eating Thanksgiving dinner at the Stubbs house for ten years now. This year Brenda had gotten her gentleman friend to take her to Commander's Palace, because she'd been jealous ever since Rickey ate there with his father. Gary hadn't wanted her to come over anyway. He had not seen Brenda since Rickey left, and he didn't particularly want to. He knew it had been her idea to send Rickey to New York; his own parents didn't know anything about the CIA and would never have come up with such an effective plan.

The house was full of brothers, sisters, aunts, uncles, and assorted children. Gary felt lost in the middle of it all. He nibbled at a plate of food and let his brother-in-law keep refilling his wine glass. After dinner, when everybody else was either cleaning up the kitchen or half-asleep in front of the football game, he slipped out and caught a bus to the French Quarter.

He'd been doing most of his drinking at a bar on Iberville Street near Rampart, well off the tourist track, but the place was empty tonight. It was mostly frequented by cooks, dishwashers, and other restaurant people, and they were probably all working the Thanksgiving dinner shift or home with their families. Gary drank a beer and walked over toward Bourbon Street. He didn't have any particular destination in mind; he just wanted to be around people. But even Bourbon was pretty dead. The trash in the gutter had the look of ancient artifacts. The touts outside the strip clubs had all but abandoned their spiels. He kept walking, past the bright display windows and garish plastic signs, down into the darker and more local part. He paused outside the Hand of Glory, but decided not to go in. He didn't feel like being anywhere he'd been with Rickey. Instead he went into one of the big gay dance clubs that had taken over most of the corner buildings in this area. He had never set foot in one of these places before, and he wouldn't have gone in now except that it looked crowded.

The darkness of the place was pierced by several sharp beams of multicolored light from some kind of machine mounted on the ceiling. Ribbons of cigarette and pot smoke twisted through these beams, making the air seem to writhe in tandem with the bodies on the dance floor. Gary went to get a drink, but stopped in amazement at the sight of a muscular black man gyrating on the bartop. The man wore only thick-soled Doc Marten boots, a leather gun belt, and a neon-green rubber ring around the base of his penis, which was uncircumcised and huge. The pouch of the gun belt was full of crumpled bills. He had been dancing with his eyes closed, but now he opened them, saw Gary, and beckoned him forward.

Gary glanced over his shoulder, certain the dancer must be motioning to somebody else. When he looked back around, the dancer nodded emphatically, pointed at him, smiled. Gary shook his head and dove back into the crowd. By the time he worked his way around to the far side of the bar, he hoped the dancer would have found a new target.

He managed to get a drink, downed it quickly, and got another. It was too loud in the club to really talk to anybody, which was fine by him. After the second drink he started feeling a little better. He was standing at the bar waiting to order a third when he felt somebody move in close beside him. He turned and saw the dancer from the bartop, now dressed in a tight white T-shirt and a pair of leather shorts that didn't leave much more to imagination than the rubber ring had. The guy leaned in even closer and spoke into Gary's ear. "You thought I was trying to get you to tip me, didn't you?"

Gary knew he should say something, but he was distracted by the guy's smell, a tangy mixture of sweat, soap, and leather. He caught himself wondering how that would translate on his tongue, and when he realized what he was thinking, he bit the inside of his cheek hard enough to make his eyes water. The dancer was still watching him expectantly. Gary finally managed to make himself shrug.

"I wasn't looking for a tip," the guy said. "I just wanted to tell you I thought you were cute."

And then he smiled a wide, white, gorgeous smile that (Gary realized later, at least as far as he could remember) probably changed the whole course of the evening. Gary had always been a sucker for a beautiful smile with a touch of the devil in it. That was one of the first things he had noticed about Rickey, when he started noticing Rickey in that way. In fact, this guy's smile reminded him a little of Rickey's.

"Thanks," said Gary, trying to sound like somebody who had been in this kind of place before. "So, uh, since I didn't tip you, can I at least buy you a drink?"

"Sure," said the dancer. "My name's ——"

Gary was sure he must have learned the guy's name at some point. Probably he had told the guy his name too. For all he knew, he might have told the guy his entire life story. But somehow, from that point onward, the night deliquesced into a sick swirl of more drinks, a cocaine-laced joint smoked in a bathroom stall, another bar, yet more drinks, a vertiginous cab ride, and an iron staircase that seemed impossible to navigate. He must have navigated it eventually, though, because he remembered that it led to a wooden gallery with a splintered railing. Beyond the gallery his memory went completely blank, as if a heavy velvet curtain had been pulled over whatever went on after that. Usually, no matter how drunk he had been, there were a few disjointed flashes. They might not make any sense, they might be embarrassing, but they were there.

This time, try as he might, he could recall nothing. There was the staircase; there was the gallery; then he was waking up to watery early-morning light, just enough to make out the shape of a pale brown water stain on a ceiling he'd never seen before. He experienced two terrible realizations simultaneously. The first was that he was not only hung over, but also still drunk. The second was that someone, definitely not Rickey, was asleep beside him.

He sat up fast and immediately wished he hadn't. When the room had more or less stopped spinning, he turned his head and looked at the guy next to him on the bed. It was the dancer from the club, his beautiful naked body stretched out long and lean like that of a sleeping panther. His big uncut cock lolled on his muscular stomach, partially erect as if he were dreaming of using it—maybe dreaming of whatever they'd done last night?

Gary looked down at himself. He was shirtless and shoeless, but still had his pants on, though they were unzipped. There were no telltale tissues, lotion bottles, or such things nearby. His ass wasn't sore, as it surely would have been if the guy had fucked him. He racked his brain, but it was no good: he just couldn't remember.

There was a clock on the wall across the room, but Gary couldn't make out the time. He had no idea where his glasses were. He clutched his head, massaged his temples briefly, then began the long and painful process of getting out of bed, finding his things, and leaving this place without waking the guy up. Whatever they had done, Gary didn't want to talk about it.

He let himself out of the apartment while its occupant slept on. Probably that was a shitty thing to do, but he'd already done the shittiest thing imaginable; what did one more small sin matter?

Outside, the sunlight hit him in the face like a shock of cold water. He navigated the vaguely familiar-looking gallery and staircase, went through a small cluttered courtyard, and found himself on a deserted sidewalk somewhere in the Marigny. He was miles away from home and feeling sicker by the minute. Nevertheless, he started walking. He knew he deserved all this and far worse.

12

"You going to the demo tonight?" Rickey's friend Dave Fiorello asked him.

"Just a sec," said Rickey. They were in Skill Development I, the first real kitchen class in the CIA curriculum. The big tiled kitchen was full of students in tall paper toques, check pants, kerchiefs, and double-breasted white jackets with their names embroidered on the left breasts. Rickey was finishing up his daily knife cuts. Each day the Skills I students had to mince and slice various combinations of onions, shallots, parsley, tomatoes, and carrots to demonstrate their knife proficiency to the teacher. Most of the cuts were sensible stuff you'd need in any kitchen. Right now, though, Rickey was trying to do a tourner, a cut he hated with a passion and couldn't imagine ever using in the real world. Why would you need carrots or potatoes whittled into the shape of a seven-sided football? It was a waste of time, but he wasn't about to tell that to his Skills chef, an iron-jawed guy who looked like he might have learned how to cook in the Marines.

He finished the tourner, dropped it into his hotel pan, and looked up at Fiorello, a big amiable kid from the Jersey shore. "What demo?" he said.

"Cooper Stark's doing a cooking demo in the Anheuser-Busch Theatre tonight. Chef said we should try to go."

"I didn't hear him."

Fiorello shrugged. "I guess that was when you were in the walk-in."

"Hell yeah, I'll go. I got his cookbook. He does some cool stuff."

"I don't know," said Phil Muller, who was also in the Skills class. He was pretty slow with his knife and was laboring to finish his cuts. "I don't think he's all that."

"So don't go," said Fiorello.

"Yeah, but I figure Chef'll ride our asses if we blow it off."

"So go then!" said Fiorello, shaking his head. "I swear to God, Muller, you can always find the downside of anything."

"Ahh, fuck you, Fiorello ... I don't care, I just heard Stark was kinda ... *funny*."

"What do you mean?" said Fiorello.

"You know." Muller seesawed one hand in the air. "*Funny*."

"You mean gay?" Fiorello asked. Muller scowled, then nodded. "Big deal, so he's gay," said Fiorello. "Everybody knows that. Who gives a fuck?"

"Hey, whatever turns you on," said Muller. He completed his cuts, scooped them into his hotel pan, and walked off toward the chef's desk.

"Cooper Stark is gay?" said Rickey.

"That's the buzz," said Fiorello. "Supposedly he's pretty open about it. I don't know why anybody cares. You're good in the kitchen, what difference does it make what you do in the bedroom?"

"But I thought ..." Rickey wasn't sure what he was trying to say. He paused, and Fiorello gave him an inquiring look. "I don't know. Can you get away with that in most kitchens? Don't you think he gets his ass ranked to hell and back?"

"Probably he used to. I doubt anybody ranks his ass now that he owns two restaurants in New York City." Fiorello picked up his hotel pan. "But you know, Rickey, he didn't get where he is now by worrying about what people thought of him. Sometimes it's worth taking a little ranking to be true to yourself, you know?"

Rickey looked up, alarmed, but Fiorello had already headed off toward the chef's desk. "Fuck," Rickey whispered, wondering just how much he'd said. He knew one thing, though: he wanted to see that demo more than ever.

As an A.M. student, he was out of class by one-thirty. He ate lunch in the dining room, which still had high vaulted ceiling and stained glass windows from when the school had been a Jesuit seminary. Then he walked across the quad to his dormitory, did his homework (a two-page paper on veal stock), and wrote a letter to Gary.

Dear Gary,

What up, dawg? Seems like I haven't heard from you in a while. I tried to call the day after Thanksgiving but you weren't home. T-Day here was OK. The Intro to Hot Foods class made turkey legs and dressing for everybody. The dressing wasn't as good as your mom's—no oysters. I missed you. Remember last year when everybody was watching football and we snuck out back to my house? You know what I mean. I can't wait to see you at Xmas. Well, I'd write more but I am going to a cooking demo tonight (Cooper Stark!) and I want to catch a nap first. Please write or call me soon. Be Good and Keep the Faith.

Love,
Rickey

At 8:45 he woke up to the sound of his alarm beeping. The demo was at 9:15. Rickey went to the communal bathroom to brush his teeth and splash water on his face, then pulled on some halfway-clean clothes and hurried back across the quad toward Roth Hall, which housed the demo theatre and all the classrooms. It was very cold up here now, and his wardrobe was wholly unsuited to a Hudson Valley winter—watching him pull a thin sweater over his chef jacket one morning, Muller had commented, "What's that supposed to be, a negligee?" But he couldn't afford any warmer clothes and wasn't about to write his father for more money. He lived in Hudson, the dorm closest to Roth, so it wasn't as if he had to be outside much anyway.

In the foyer of Roth Hall it was toasty-warm. Down the corridor, students were streaming into the theatre. Rickey scanned the tiers of stadium seating and found an empty spot near the front. From here he could see the pans of mise-en-place on the counter of the little demo kitchen and the nervous expressions on the faces of the two white-jacketed students who had been selected to assist Chef Stark. Rickey could understand their nervousness: all these demos were taped and archived in the school's video library, so any mistakes would be preserved for future generations.

9:15 came and went. The student assistants conferred in whispers; then one of them disappeared through the door at the back of the demo kitchen. By 9:30 a sullen muttering had begun to spread through the audience. "Wonder if he's this late at his own fucking restaurants," a kid behind Rickey said, and somebody else said "Probably." At 9:40 the student assistant came back and held up five fingers to the audience. A few people booed. "Some of us got up at three AM," a girl—probably a pastry student—called out, and the other pastry students gave her a little round of applause.

At five minutes until ten, Cooper Stark finally came through the demo kitchen door holding up his hands in a gesture of mock surrender. The audience clapped for him, but not as much as they would have done at 9:15 or even 9:30. Rickey sat up straighter trying to get a good look at the man. He was tall, broad through the shoulders, younger than Rickey had expected—maybe thirty-five. He wore a very high paper toque and a snowy chef jacket with red piping at the cuffs and collar. His name and the logo of his first restaurant, Star K—a red letter K in a stylized gold star—were embroidered on the jacket's left breast. His complexion was very pale, and against all the white, his cropped hair and deep-set eyes looked almost black.

"Sorry to keep everybody waiting," he said in a deep unaccented voice that was picked up by the small microphone clipped to his jacket. "Had a hard time getting out of Gaffney's, if you want to know the truth."

Reluctant laughter rippled through the audience. Gaffney's was the Irish pub in Hyde Park where CIA students did much of their drinking, and everybody in the theatre had probably had trouble getting out of there at one time or another.

"Anyway, I'm Cooper Stark, I got my associate degree here in 1975, and I've never regretted it. Well, maybe a little when my student loans came due, but I managed to pay those off a few years ago. Now I'm just trying to pay off the restaurant loans ..."

His whole presentation went like that: slightly self-deprecating, mildly irreverent, charismatic. Within ten minutes he had won over all the people pissed off by his tardiness. Within the hour he had made duck breasts with sun-dried cherries and balsamic vinegar, green peppercorn polenta, and a mascarpone tart topped with kiwifruit. His face, enormous on the display screen at the front of the theatre, remained serenely handsome all the while; he never even appeared to break a sweat. While he was cooking he told funny anecdotes from the Star K and his other restaurant, Capers. Rickey had never thought of himself as being impressed by star power, but just now he couldn't help feeling that Cooper Stark might be the epitome of cool.

He expected Stark to duck out of the theatre immediately after the demo, but the chef stayed to shake hands, sign cookbooks, and answer questions posed by students who stuck around to talk to him. Rickey made his way to the front. A fat girl in a reindeer-patterned sweater was saying, "What did you mean, you don't have to chill pie dough? Everybody knows you have to chill pie dough!"

"Well, of course I'm not a pastry chef," Stark said. "What do I know, really? I'm just going by what worked for me." He looked past the girl, saw Rickey standing there, and gave him a big smile. "Hi there!" he said.

"Hi—uh, I just wanted to thank you for your braised pork shank recipe in *Stark Raving Flavors*. I made that as one of the first dinner specials in my first real cooking job, and it worked out real well."

"The one with the cherries? I love cherries, man. They're so sexy. Even when they're dried, you just plump them in some nice liquid and it's like they're ready for another go-round."

"Yeah," said Rickey, a little nonplussed.

"Excuse my metaphor. I'm sublimating—must've been working too hard and not playing enough." There were other students coming up behind Rickey now, but Stark didn't even glance at them. "So, your first real cooking job, huh? Where was that?"

"Just a little place in New Orleans."

"The Big Easy." Rickey hated that nickname, but he nodded. "I love New Orleans. Stayed down there for a month once and gained ten pounds. You gotta love a place that doesn't fear butter."

"That's us, awright."

"You're from there? I can tell by your accent. I like that."

"Well," said Rickey, enjoying the attention Stark was paying him but not wanting to monopolize the man's time. "Thanks a lot, Chef Stark."

"Coop. My friends call me Coop. You're not leaving already?"

"I, uh … I don't guess I have to."

"Stick around for a few minutes. I'll be getting out of here soon. What say we grab a cup of coffee and you can catch me up on New Orleans?"

"Sure." Rickey had no idea why Cooper Stark would want to have coffee with him, but he wasn't about to refuse.

"Why don't you just wait for me over there—what's your name?"

"Rickey."

"Well, then…" Stark reached out and grasped Rickey's unresisting hand. "I'm extremely glad to meet you, Rickey. Just chill out and wait for me. I won't be long at all, I promise."

He talked and signed books for another twenty minutes while Rickey sat in the front row of seats wondering what was up. Should he stay? Had Stark meant the invitation sincerely, or would it be politer to just slip away and not be a nuisance? He wasn't sure, but he really wanted to talk to the chef a little more, so he stayed put. Eventually a custodian came into the theatre and flipped the lights off and on. The last students began to trickle out and Stark came over to Rickey. He was grinning widely, not a bit tired as far as Rickey could see. "You still want to get that coffee?" he said, pulling off his toque and unbuttoning his jacket. "I'm not going to ruin you for your early classes, am I?"

"It's Friday. I don't have class tomorrow."

"Excellent!" said Stark, putting a hand on Rickey's shoulder as they walked up the stairs together.

The café in Roth Hall was closed, so they drove to a diner in Hyde Park. Stark had some kind of little Italian roadster that seemed to cover the miles in a matter of seconds, but maybe it was just that

Rickey was no longer used to being up so late: a sense of unreality had begun to pervade the evening. A cup of strong, milky coffee cleared his head a little. Stark asked a bunch of questions about New Orleans restaurants, most of which Rickey had never been to. When he hit upon a place Rickey did know, he would ask all about what Rickey had eaten there and what he'd thought of it. He nodded attentively at Rickey's answers and commented on some of them as if they were deeply wise and fascinating. "I never had a conversation like this before," Rickey said after a while.

"Don't you have anybody to talk to about this stuff? It's a shame if you don't. You're a natural—I can tell, because I always was too. People like us need outlets for our obsessions." Stark laughed a little, as if to offset the breathtaking egotism of what he'd just said. It was a habit Rickey recognized from his demo, and it was quite effective.

"Well, I do, but—"

"See, Rickey, it's so hard to find people who really care about this shit. Even most of the students at your school, it's just a way for them to get a better paycheck. And there's nothing wrong with that. But I can tell it goes deeper for you." Stark leaned forward a little and pinned Rickey with those intense dark eyes. "You're so young. Have you ever even *met* anybody who cares as much about food as you do?"

"I'm not sure," Rickey admitted. Stark's gaze made him feel reckless, and he decided to reveal himself as he'd been wanting to do all evening. "My boyfriend's a cook," he said. "I talk about food with him."

"Sure," said Stark, smiling as if he'd won some kind of bet. "I thought you were probably gay."

"You did?"

"Oh, don't sound so dismayed. It's not that obvious. I can just tell because I'm an old faggot myself." That little laugh again, and Rickey wondered what it meant.

"So haven't you taken a lot of shit for it? Isn't it really tough in the kitchen?"

"Oooh yeah," said Stark. "But so am I. Nobody ever fucks with me more than a couple of times. And so are you, too, Rickey. I can tell. You're tough enough to deal with it, and you're just going to get tougher."

"I guess."

"If you stay in the business, you will. Trust me. You know what Elizabeth David told me when I met her? This was years ago, when I was just starting out and she had her shop in London. Her employees were terrified of her. She said, 'Young man, this business will make you into a monster one way or another. Just be a monster with exquisite taste.'"

"You met Elizabeth David?" Rickey tried not to sound as ridiculously impressed as he felt.

"Sure. I saw her again a couple of years ago. Beautiful old lady, but mean?" Stark shook his head. "She still seemed to like me, though. Gave me a Le Creuset Dutch oven she said she'd had for twenty years. That baby made my suitcase pretty fucking heavy, let me tell you."

"Wow," said Rickey, giving up on trying to sound nonchalant.

"She'd love you," Stark said. "She seems to appreciate handsome young men. Likes having them around, to a point."

"To what kinda point?"

"To the point that they start getting on her nerves, I guess. Which I can understand all too well." Stark sighed. "I'm kind of a train-wreck personality right now, Rickey. You'll have to excuse me if I say anything weird. I just split up with my partner of ten years. He moved out a couple of months ago." From the way he said *partner*, Rickey could tell he meant his boyfriend.

"Damn … that's gotta suck." It was a stupid thing to say, but Stark's eyes softened as if he were grateful for any expression of sympathy, and Rickey felt the first inkling of a real kinship with him. They were both alone in the world, weren't they? Of course he'd be going back to Gary, would see him in just a few weeks, but who knew what would happen after that? Despite all the people he'd met up here, he had been lonely for two solid months now. Coop could understand that kind of loneliness, was living it just like Rickey was.

"Yeah," said Coop. "I'm pretty much a mess. I've been drinking, getting high all the time, doing a lot of coke … Say, do you like coke?"

The sadness left his eyes and they seemed to glitter, as if by just mentioning the drug he had perked up a little.

"Well," said Rickey. "Yeah. I mean, I had it a few times." He'd had it once, at a party thrown by one of the waiters at the Jolly Corner.

"You want to do some?"

"Sure."

Coop dropped a ten-dollar bill on the table to pay for their two coffees. On the way out to the car he put his arm around Rickey's shoulders and said, "I'm so glad I met you. I haven't talked to anybody like this in months."

He's not actually flirting *with me, is he?* Rickey wondered, then dismissed the thought. A guy like Cooper Stark wouldn't be interested in somebody so young and inexperienced. He didn't have to worry—Coop had probably just invited him for coffee as a kindness, and they'd happened to hit it off. Maybe they would forge a longtime friendship. Coop could introduce him around in the restaurant world, watch his back a little, advise him.

In the car, with a small light shining from the open glove compartment, Coop took a gold credit card and a tiny glassine bag from his wallet. "Look at us," he said as he tapped the powder onto the back of the card. "What a couple of waste-case stereotypes, right?"

"You got a hundred-dollar bill we can snort it with?"

"You know, I think I do." Coop pulled one out and rolled it into a crisp tube, which he offered to Rickey. "After you," he said, holding up the cocaine-heaped credit card so that Rickey had to lean in close to him to reach it. Rickey took a blast and felt his heart speed up as soon as the stuff hit the back of his sinuses. This was obviously a lot better than what the Jolly Corner crowd had had. His eyes watered and he nearly sneezed. He felt like a prize dork, but Coop just grinned at him and said, "You look so young—you make me feel like I'm corrupting a minor," then snorted the rest of the cocaine off the back of the card. "You want some more?"

"I guess I could stand another line," Rickey said.

"I've got more at my office. Let's drive down there, what do you say?" Without waiting for an answer, Coop started the car and pulled out onto Route 9. About twenty miles later, when they exited Route 9 for the interstate, Rickey said, "Where's your office?"

"New York."

"The city?"

"Yeah. I meant my office at Star K. You're up for it, right?"

"Sure," said Rickey. It suddenly seemed like the most glamorous of ideas, blasting down the highway toward the big city with this famous chef, on their way to an all-night private party. He didn't think he had ever felt so cool in his entire life. He wished Gary could see him now. It crossed his mind that Gary might not really like what he saw, but that was silly: if Gary were here, he'd be having just as much fun as Rickey was.

The cocaine had energized them, and they laughed and talked trash all the way to New York. It should have been about a ninety-minute drive, but at Coop's pace it took just over an hour. They crossed a bridge and exited onto Riverside Drive. Rickey could see dark, deserted-looking high-rise tenements on the left. A paranoid fantasy flashed through his mind: Coop was some kind of sadist freak who had brought him all the way to New York just to dump him off in a bad neighborhood with no warm coat, no money, and no hope. He shook his head. Where had that come from? The coke, probably. Coop wasn't going to dump him off, and anyway he was from the Ninth Ward; he'd take his chances in just about any neighborhood if he had to.

Soon they had left Riverside Drive and were winding along the avenues and cross streets of midtown Manhattan. "There's Le Cirque," Coop pointed out, but Rickey was looking back at the gorgeous deco spire of the Chrysler Building. By the time he turned around, they had passed whatever Coop wanted him to see. "Where?" he said.

"Le Cirque. Famous French restaurant. I ate there once with Julia Child. Don't know how impressed she was—the quality goes up and down like a yoyo, but when it's good, it's really fucking good."

"You must know everybody."

"Well, you meet a lot of people in this business. Julia's great—she's like some kind of culinary grandma to me. She calls me up and says, 'Are you being good, Cooper?' and I usually have to say, 'No, Julia.' You ought to come up to Cambridge with me sometime—I'll introduce you to her. She'd like you."

Overwhelmed by the possibility of meeting the author of the first cookbook he had ever used, Rickey could think of nothing to say. Fortunately, they had now reached Star K and were pulling up in the loading zone outside the restaurant. Coop bounded out of the car, came around to Rickey's side, and opened the passenger door. "Welcome to my empire," he said with his weird little laugh.

It was well after midnight now and the restaurant was closed, but Coop unlocked the front door and ushered Rickey in. The foyer was full of enormous stylized star sculptures in copper and brushed steel. They dangled from the ceiling, hung on the walls, and jutted from the floor like invitations to put out an eye. In the bar just beyond, a woman sat at a table with a ledger and a stack of receipts in front of her. She looked up when she heard them come in, then rose from the table and came to greet them. She appeared young from a distance, but as she got closer Rickey saw that she was in her mid-forties, with little delicate-framed glasses and a red rinse in her hair.

"Hi, Ella," said Coop. "What the hell are you still doing here?"

"Trying to make sense of your books, that's what." She looked Rickey up and down, then shook her head. "Oh, Coop, have you no shame? This one's just a *baby*."

"Ella . . ."

"How old are you, young man?"

"Ignore this harpy," said Coop, putting a hand on Rickey's shoulder and steering him through the bar. Rickey glanced back at the woman, but she had returned to the ledger, still shaking her head. Except for her voice, she had reminded him a great deal of his mother. At the thought of Brenda he felt a pang even sharper than the one he'd had when thinking of Gary. He wasn't sure what Gary would make of his adventures this evening, but he knew Brenda would take a dim view of them. For a moment he wished he were back home on Tricou Street, safe in his own bed, never having so much as seen the CIA or Cooper Stark.

But the moment passed. Brenda had sent him away, and Gary apparently couldn't be bothered to keep in touch with him. He might as well have a good time while he could. He followed Coop through the dining room and into the kitchen. The night porter was leaning on a counter near the grill smoking a joint, which he dropped and stepped on when he saw them. "*Hola*, Chef!" he said.

"*Hola*, Juanito. You dropped your *mota* there."

"I'm sorry, Chef, I was just—"

"Christ, I don't care," said Coop, cutting the man off with a weary wave of his hand. "I hate to see good drugs go to waste, that's all. Of course, those probably weren't good drugs," he added *sotto voce* as he led Rickey past the hot line. "Who knows what kind of fucking dirtweed these dishwashers get?"

At the rear of the kitchen was a narrow ill-lit staircase, and at the top of it, Coop's office: a small room whose desk, shelves, and floor were chaotically piled with papers, boxes, bottles, shopping bags, food and wine publications, and hundreds of cookbooks. Coop cleared a stack of *Bon Appetit*s off one end of the leather sofa so Rickey could sit down. From the wall he removed a framed copy of his three-star *New York Times* review. "Hold that," he said, handing the frame to Rickey. Rickey propped it up in his lap and read the first lines: "Too often in Manhattan, a beautiful restaurant is like a rose with a hidden canker, an eye-pleasing front for mediocre or downright bad food. Happily, this is not the case with Cooper Stark's new venture ..."

"Here we go," said Coop, taking back the frame and dumping several big rocks of cocaine from a Baggie onto the glass. He pushed a box of his own cookbooks out of the way, sat next to Rickey, and started breaking up the rocks with his credit card. "This isn't too much for us, is it?" he asked.

"Oh, no," said Rickey. "I got no limit as far as coke is concerned." He thought it might be true: at the waiter's party he had done an awful lot, not even really liking it all that much but for some reason wanting to do more anyway.

"That's so cool," said Coop. "You're just extremely cool, Rickey. You've got it going on. Most of the people I meet, I don't feel anything in common with them. I'm really glad I met you. We're going to be good friends."

Rickey couldn't help but feel flattered. He did wonder a little why Coop wanted to be good friends with an eighteen-year-old kid, but maybe he was a particularly cool eighteen-year-old and just hadn't realized it. Gary thought so, didn't he? Or he had at one time. Maybe Coop was able to see past his youth and ignorance to all the things they had in common. He congratulated himself on his heretofore unsuspected coolness as Coop handed him the picture frame and a cut-down soda straw.

They sucked up quite a number of lines—Rickey lost count after the third set—and Coop started telling stories about evil bosses he'd had, maniacal cooks he'd worked with, waiters who had sex with customers between courses, and other restaurant yarns. Many of these stories concluded with, "And that was the end of *him*!" Rickey was never sure if this meant the person had died, gotten fired, left the business in disgrace, or what. As he talked, Coop laid his arm along the back of the sofa so that his fingers dangled down and brushed Rickey's shoulder. It made Rickey a little uncomfortable, but he figured it was just a casual gesture, something Coop would do with any good friend. He was still telling himself that when Coop leaned over, cupped his face with the other hand, and kissed him softly on the mouth.

The kiss felt dangerous, tender, and good. Rickey found himself involuntarily relaxing into it. Instead, after several seconds, he made himself pull back.

"I've been wanting to do that all night," Coop said.

"I . . ." Rickey fought back the pleasant wave of warmth that was trying to spread through his lower belly. "I *can't* do that, Coop. I told you about my boyfriend. I love him."

"Of course you do." Coop held Rickey's gaze. His eyes were very steady and sincere. "I'm no threat to your boyfriend, Rickey. You'll be going home to him when you graduate. I'll be here in New York. Maybe I'll see you if you come up here—I'd like that—but it's a long way from New York to New Orleans." Coop let his hand slide to the back of Rickey's neck, began stroking the side of Rickey's throat with his thumb. It tickled in a maddening, exciting way. "But we sure could have a lot of fun while you're up here."

"I know we could," Rickey said a little unsteadily. "But I can't."

"You're very sweet and very loyal. But you're far too young to plight your troth to one person." Rickey guessed his incomprehension showed in his face, because Coop rephrased it: "To be faithful to one person. It's an admirable goal, but almost impossible at your age. Hell, it's almost impossible at *my* age. You owe yourself a few adventures before you even think about settling down."

Rickey thought about it, or rather he tried to. It was difficult to think with Coop's warm hand on his neck and a hard-on that was urging him to listen to Coop. While he was trying to think, Coop kissed him again. This time Rickey was unable to keep his arms from sliding around Coop's neck and pulling him closer. Maybe Coop was right; maybe unfaithfulness was inevitable between him and Gary. If so, at least Rickey would be with someone who wasn't trying to break them up. And who *really* knew how to kiss, and probably do a lot of other things too. This man would manipulate his body and take charge of him in ways Gary had never even thought of, and suddenly that idea seemed very appealing.

"I just want to make you feel good," Coop whispered as if hearing his thoughts. "I can do things to you that'll blow your mind. I can teach you things ... your boyfriend will actually *benefit* from your being with me."

Some kind of alarm went off in Rickey's head. That was the most patently self-serving line of bullshit he had ever heard. All at once he found himself wondering if the whole evening had been like that, and he'd just been too stupid to realize it until Coop took things a step too far. Coop made as if to resume kissing him, but Rickey turned his head so that Coop's mouth only found his cheek. He sat up straight, disentangled himself from Coop, and got off the couch. "I'm not doing this," he said, crossing the office and standing by the desk with his back to Coop. "Maybe you're right about everything, and I'm sorry if I gave you the wrong idea by coming down here. It's not that

I wouldn't *like* to be with you. I totally would. But I really love Gary and I'm not gonna cheat on him if I can help it."

When he felt that he had control of himself, Rickey turned around to look at Coop, figuring he'd be angry. But Coop was smiling at him, charming as ever. "I understand," Coop said with a little shrug. "But it was worth a try. You're so damn cute, I couldn't help myself."

"I guess I better get back to campus," Rickey said. His voice sounded faint in his own ears.

"Don't be mad."

"I'm not mad," said Rickey. His head had begun to ache in a strange way, as if each separate bone of his skull were hurting in its own distinct manner. "I think I'm just really tired."

"I'll bet you are. How about if I take you to Grand Central? The train'll get you to Poughkeepsie in about an hour, maybe ninety minutes, and you can cab it from there."

Rickey had hoped Coop would drive him back—the trains had been difficult enough to figure out when he was sober—but he didn't want to ask for a ride. Then a terrible fact occurred to him: he only had about five dollars in his pocket. "I, uh, can't really afford to take the train," he said, hating the words as he spoke them.

"Say no more." Coop took out his wallet, removed the cocaine-encrusted hundred-dollar bill, and handed it to Rickey. Though it would pay for the train ride and cab fare with enough left over to buy a warm coat, accepting it still made him feel cheap.

As they drove again through the nearly deserted predawn streets, Coop asked, "When did you first get together with your boyfriend?"

"Couple years ago."

"What were you? Sixteen? Seventeen?"

"Uh, we were sixteen."

"Ah," sighed Coop. "The trouble with being sixteen yourself is that you can't appreciate the sheer carnal pleasure of fucking a sixteen-year-old."

"Say what?"

"The forbidden aspect isn't there. I bet it's still fun, though. So what do you two like doing? Do you fuck him? Does he fuck you? Do you suck dick? Eat ass? What's your favorite thing to do?"

"I'm not gonna tell you that!" said Rickey, appalled. "God! What makes you think—"

"Sorry—sorry—jeez." Coop lifted his hands from the wheel in the same surrendering gesture he'd used when he was forty minutes late for his demo. "Forget it. Just trying to salvage something from the evening. A little grist for the fantasy mill ... anyway, here's Grand Central. You know what to do? Just get the Metro North."

"Thanks," said Rickey quietly.

"Take my card, OK? I'll write my private number on the back ... here. Look, I meant what I said about wanting us to be friends. Can I get your number too?" Rickey wrote it on the back of another business card, which Coop stowed in his wallet.

"I'll call you soon, I promise," Coop said, gripping Rickey's shoulders and planting a kiss on his forehead. "We'll go visit Julia."

Rickey got out of the car. The cold wrapped itself around him at once. His breath made a frosty plume in the air. Coop revved his engine and drove away fast without waiting to make sure Rickey got into the station.

The train hadn't seemed so bad when he first took it to school, but at this time of the morning it was deserted and bleak. The lights in the cars seemed very bright. Rickey wanted to sleep, but the cocaine kept him unpleasantly alert. His mind wouldn't stop yammering at him. *Cooper Stark wanted me*, he thought, *that talented, rich, famous, handsome guy wanted me—I must have been crazy to say no. But I just couldn't do that to Gary. But what if Gary doesn't even care? Maybe I should have done it. No, it wasn't right. But I wanted to. But that was so creepy, what he said in the car—I guess I'm glad I didn't. But damn, I still wanted to ... I wonder if he really will introduce me to Julia Child. Maybe I should have done it just to meet Julia ... God, that's so sleazy ... Oh, hell, I don't know ...*

The sun was up by the time he disembarked in Poughkeepsie, and the light felt like daggers in his eyes. He caught a cab back to the CIA and let himself into his dorm room, hoping he still had some of the Excedrin PM he'd bought when trying to adjust to an early-morning schedule. Hearing Rickey come in, Muller sat up in bed rubbing his eyes. "Your fucking *friend* called about ten times last night," he said.

"What? Gary? When'd he call?"

"*I* don't know. Around midnight, and then, like, twice more. Kept waking me up."

"Did he say to call him back?"

"Fuck, man, I don't know. If you do, tell him some people around here like to sleep through the night, OK?"

Rickey dragged the phone out into the hall before realizing that it was only about six-thirty in New Orleans. He wanted to call anyway, but forced himself to wait. Now he couldn't take the Excedrin PM because he didn't want to go to sleep before he had tried to reach Gary. Instead he grabbed his *Pro Chef* and walked over to Roth Hall before remembering that today was Saturday and no meals would be served in the dining room. He wasn't hungry anyway. He went down to the riverside cliffs and sat shivering in a little gazebo somebody had built there. Very near Hudson Hall and almost always deserted, this was where Rickey came when he wanted to be alone on campus. He got very cold here sometimes, but he felt comfortable near the river; it reminded him of the spot behind the Mississippi levee where he and Gary used to go.

Flipping through his textbook, he managed to kill an hour before returning to his room. Muller was gone. Rickey dialed Gary's number and got Mary Rose. "I been up," she said when Rickey apologized for calling so early. "Gary ain't here."

"Is something wrong? My roommate said he kept trying to call me all night."

"Well, a boy y'all went to school with got shot a couple days ago. Gary might be at the hospital trying to visit him right now."

"Shot? Who? What's his name?"

"I think Gary said it was Terrell. Terrell Washington? That sounds familiar?"

"Sure," said Rickey. "Jeez. What happened? Is he gonna be OK?"

"I don't know nothing else about it. Gary don't tell us nothing."

It was like a nightmarish repeat of the last conversation he'd had with Elmer, so Rickey just said, "Please tell him to call me" and got off the phone. His mind was reeling. He couldn't imagine Terrell Washington, that runty big-mouthed kid, lying in the hospital with a bullet wound. And as if everything else wasn't bad enough, Mary Rose—who had once been like a second mother to Rickey—now sounded like she wouldn't care if she never heard his voice again.

He swallowed four Excedrin PMs and managed to catch a few hours of fitful sleep. When he woke up, he knew he had dreamed about Gary and that it had been bad, though he couldn't remember any details. He picked up the phone and dialed Terrio's Po-Boys in New Orleans. "Is Gary there?" he said when the counter girl answered.

"Gary don't work here no more."

"What?"

"He quit yesterday. Didn't even put in his notice or nothing. If you talk to him, tell him Tony's real mad at him, awright?"

Rickey crawled back into bed and pulled his pillow over his face. He didn't remove it when he heard Muller come in, putter around the room for a few minutes, and leave again. A few minutes later somebody knocked on the door. Rickey didn't answer. The knob turned and the person came in anyway. "Rick?" said Dave Fiorello, who lived down the hall. "You OK?"

"I'm fine," said Rickey in a muffled voice.

"Muller said he thought you were crying."

"Tell Muller thanks a lot."

"Aw, I think he's just worried about you. He's almost human sometimes. Listen, you OK for real? I know it's easy to get burned out here, all the shit we have to do. You want to go into town and shoot a little pool at Gaffney's or something?"

"I'm OK," said Rickey, removing the pillow from his head with a tremendous effort. "I just had a rough night. Did some stuff I probably shouldn't have."

"You went off with Cooper Stark, didn't you? After the demo?"

"Aw, fuck. Does everybody know about that?"

"Well, you know, this is a small school. Shit gets around. It's cool, though. Nothing wrong with getting to know famous chefs. Maybe you can do your externship at one of his restaurants."

"Yeah. Maybe."

"Well," said Fiorello, apparently getting the message that Rickey didn't want to talk, "I guess I better try to finish up that veal stock paper. I'll be around if you change your mind about shooting some pool, OK?"

"... yeahsure ..."

Rickey burrowed back under the pillow, willing the phone to ring. It remained silent. All he wanted in the world was to talk to Gary ... but what would he say? He couldn't very well tell Gary about his night with Cooper Stark, could he? Maybe he should. It wasn't as if anything had happened. But it sounded like Gary was already losing it: drinking too much, quitting his job without notice. "I'm losing it too," Rickey said aloud. "We're both losing it. Oh hell, G, what made us think we could ever do this?" Then he really did start to cry.

That was how most of the weekend went. By Sunday afternoon, several of Rickey's friends had gotten word that something was wrong. Led by Dave Fiorello, they came to his room, all but dragged him out of bed, and took him to Gaffney's. He didn't really want to go, but he felt a little better once he was there. Since he wasn't much of a pool player, he stayed at the table and guarded a succession of pitchers while the others played. By the time they all headed back to campus, he had a pretty good buzz going.

They parked in the big student lot and began the long, cold hike back to the dorms. The campus commons had recently been decorated for the holidays, trees and buildings sparkling with tiny white lights. It wasn't the kind of Christmas decoration Rickey was used to—in New Orleans, people's tastes ran more to tinsel garlands, life-sized plastic Santas, and flashing lights in every color of the rainbow—but it looked pretty. In front of Roth Hall the group split up to go to their respective dorms. Rickey was left with Dave Fiorello and Phil Muller. As they headed toward Hudson Hall, Fiorello snapped his fingers.

"Shit. I forgot to look up something for that Skills paper. I guess I'll go see if the library's still open."

"What are you so worried about, Fiorello?" said Muller. "It's just a stupid two-page paper on veal stock."

"I think I remember reading an article where President Metz talked about roasting the bones versus leaving them raw. I figure Chef might be impressed if I quoted it."

"You fucking kiss-ass."

"I know, but I could really use the grade. My last paper sucked. See you guys later, OK?"

"Bye," said Rickey. "Thanks."

"So what's up with you anyway?" said Muller after they had walked on in silence for a few moments. "Somebody at home die or something?"

"No," said Rickey, caught off guard. Despite their being roommates, Muller hardly ever showed any personal interest in him. "It's just … you remember my friend Gary, who kept calling the other night?"

"I wish I didn't. You ever get hold of him?"

"No, but I talked to his mom. A guy we went to school with got shot."

"Shot!"

"Yeah, but that's not it really. I mean, I feel awful for Terrell, but I'm from New Orleans. You know? People get shot pretty often."

"I never heard about that. I thought it was all Hurricanes and plantation houses."

Rickey laughed. "Try malt liquor and crack houses. In my neighborhood, anyway. But, I mean, I hated to hear about Terrell, but it didn't surprise me much. We had friends get shot before. What worries me is, Gary still hasn't called me back."

"Maybe he figures you already heard the news from his mom, you don't need to hear it again from him."

"It's not exactly like that," Rickey said carefully. "See, Gary's my best friend. We been best friends since we were in the fourth grade. It's like, we're each other's main person in life, you know?"

"Uh huh," said Muller. They were passing through a small grove of trees and Rickey could not see his face.

"We always tried to work in the same kitchens. We spent all our free time together, too. We did ... pretty much everything together, I guess."

"So what's the problem?" said Muller. They were out of the shadows now, and Rickey glanced over at him. Muller's hands were jammed deep in the pockets of his coat. His profile was unreadable.

"I don't know," said Rickey. "One of the reasons my parents sent me up here was because they thought I should, like, expand my horizons. I guess they thought me and Gary were spending too much time together. But there isn't really anybody else I *want* to spend that much time with. And I don't think Gary's doing so good since I been gone."

"But that's his problem, right?"

"If it's Gary's problem, it's my problem too," said Rickey. He started to get the feeling he was talking too much, but beer and loneliness had loosened his tongue and he couldn't seem to stop himself. "That's just how we are. I gotta make sure he gets through the two years I'm up here. Then I'm going back to New Orleans and we're gonna get an apartment together. We'll be OK if we can last that long."

"Uh huh."

"I just miss him really bad."

"Well," said Muller, running his key card through the lock that let them into the dorm, "I guess it'll all work out. I'm kinda hungry. Think I'll go up to the lounge and see if anybody left some chips lying around or something."

"Sure," said Rickey. He went on down the hall to his room, let himself in, and lay down on his bed. In a few minutes he felt as if he had never left.

13

Gary stood at a bus stop on Tulane Avenue holding a bag that contained the latest issues of *Sports Illustrated* and *NBA Roundup*. He'd meant to bring them to Terrell, but the receptionist at Charity Hospital had told him the Washingtons weren't accepting any visitors. As he was leaving, he passed a woman on the steps who looked just like Terrell. When Gary asked, she said she was Terrell's big sister. He tried to give her the magazines, but she said, "He ain't gonna be able to use those, baby" and hurried away in tears.

As far as Gary had heard, Terrell had been shot accidentally in some kind of drive-by thing near his house. Of course there might be more to it, but that was the basic story. The guy who'd told him about it—another Frederick Douglass alumnus who sometimes caught the same morning bus as Gary—said Terrell still had a bullet in his chest, but didn't know how serious it was.

Growing up in the Ninth Ward, Gary and Rickey had had acquaintances get shot before, but never anyone they knew as well as Terrell. Gary had gotten off the bus and gone to work, but he couldn't seem to concentrate on any of the mundane tasks at hand. He burned a basket of shrimp, put mayonnaise on no-mayo orders, absentmindedly dropped a handful of shredded lettuce in the fryer oil. There had been a time when he would have laughed these things off, but he didn't find himself laughing much at anything these days. And why laugh, really? What had happened to Terrell was no anomaly; sometimes in New Orleans it seemed that young black men who lived to adulthood were more unusual than young black men who died of gunshots. And Rickey was gone—who knew if he'd ever come back? And even if he did come back, how could Gary look him in the eye after the terrible things he might have done with that go-go dancer?

So when the manager came in just before lunch rush and started bitching about the time clock, Gary wasn't in the mood to listen to him. It seemed that people were forgetting to clock out at the end of their shifts, clocking each other in, and shoving pennies in the clock in an attempt to make it jump ahead. Gary hadn't tried the latter thing, but he'd done the other two. Had his time card been accurate, he would probably be out of a job by now, as he was almost always late. But he still didn't appreciate hearing the manager bray at the lunch crew, calling them a bunch of lazy, thieving slobs as they slammed together ten po-boys at a time. He decided he was never going to listen to that voice again. He didn't quit on the spot—he wasn't looking to fuck over the rest of the crew—but at the end of his shift he found the manager adding up receipts in the front of the house and said, "Hey, Tony, I quit."

"What?" said Tony. "You're putting in notice? This is a hell of a time to tell me—"

"No, I'm not putting in notice. I just quit."

The manager gawked as if Gary were a mouse that had just turned around and bitten his toe off. Probably he was trying to think of something to say, but Gary didn't wait to hear it. He went back into the kitchen and told the rest of the crew what he had done. They high-fived him halfheartedly, glad to see somebody getting out of the place but sorry it wasn't one of them. "What you gonna do now?" the dishwasher asked him.

"I don't know," said Gary. "Get drunk."

"Listen to that spoiled white boy," said the head cook, who went by the name of Cootie. "'*I'm gonna get drunk. I don't need no job.*'"

"Aw, I need a job. I just stood this one as long as I can."

"Well, I heard that."

"They got a opening for head dishwasher over by the Pirate Lafitte Grill," said the dishwasher. "Pays good. I ain't got the experience, but you might."

"Shut up, Dwayne," said Cootie. "The boy's a cook. He don't want no damn dishwashing job."

"I might check it out," said Gary. "I don't care about cooking as much as some people do."

But instead of going to look for a new job, he stopped by his favorite bar on Iberville Street. Somehow the afternoon and most of the evening slipped away. The more he drank, the easier it was to justify the next drink by telling himself he deserved it for standing up to that asshole Tony. An annoying small voice in his head told him he hadn't stood up to anybody, he'd just walked out, but he ignored it. Around midnight he plugged a handful of change into the pay phone and tried to call Rickey. Rickey's roommate said he was out. Suddenly the bar, which had seemed warm and convivial, now felt like a lonely place. Gary paid his tab and left.

Once home, he called Rickey's room again. Rickey was still out and Gary could tell the roommate was pissed at being woken up. Even so, he couldn't help saying, "Do you know where he went?"

"Last I saw, he was talking to the chef who gave the demo tonight," said the roommate. "After that, how the hell should I know? I'm not his mom."

"Thanks," said Gary. As he hung up, all the alcohol he'd drunk seemed to desert him. He was stone cold sober and paranoid. He knew in his gut that Rickey was with somebody. The visiting chef? Probably they weren't supposed to fraternize with the students. Another kid, then? Hell, it didn't matter who the person was. It could be the Holy Lord Jesus incarnate and Gary would still hate him.

He thought he had prepared himself for the possibility—the likelihood—that Rickey would meet other guys up there. Now he wondered whether it was even possible to prepare for such a thing. He didn't think it was, not if you really loved the other person. How could anybody stand feeling this way—not even knowing the truth, just wondering, worrying, getting horrible pictures in his head?

In the next hour or so he went through a number of possibilities. He would catch the next Greyhound bus to New York and get there in … what? Two, three days. The train, then? It wasn't much faster. All he knew about buying a plane ticket was that you had to do it far in advance. What if he rented a car … or borrowed Elmer's … no. None of it was any good. Rickey was going to do whatever he was going to do. Gary knew he couldn't change it. By telling himself this over and over, he managed to keep his hands off the telephone until nearly three in the morning. Then he started thinking maybe he'd let his imagination get away from him. Maybe Rickey had just gone into Hyde Park with some friends—he'd talked about doing that before. And maybe he'd gotten back to campus by now, but his roommate was asleep, or just hadn't bothered to tell him Gary had called.

He watched his fingers dial the number as if from a distance, as if he had no control over them. He willed Rickey to be there, willed it so hard that a sharp sliver of pain lanced through his head. When the roommate answered, sounding sleepier and more pissed off than ever, he actually hated Rickey for an instant. In that instant he could have cheerfully cursed Rickey's name. But all he said was, "Uh, I guess he's not back yet ..."

"God, what are you, retarded? I already told you Rickey's out and I'm trying to get some sleep here. You call back one more time, I'll report your pal to the R.A. for causing a disturbance in the dorm—"

Gary hung up before the guy had finished saying "dorm." He left his room, padded downstairs to the kitchen, and found a half-full fifth of Early Times in one of the cabinets. Back in his room, he huddled in the dark, swigging from the bottle and willing the phone to ring. All he wanted in the world was to talk to Rickey ... but what would he say? How could he accuse Rickey of being with someone else when he had almost certainly done the same thing himself?

The phone remained silent. Gary never really slept, but eventually he drank enough to lull himself into a kind of stupor. The bottle slipped to the floor, spilling what little bourbon remained to be spilled.

He was not hung over the next day, but filled with a cold resolve. Rickey didn't care about him any more. He knew that now, and it was time to start dealing with it. The first step was to stop being so selfish. As Mary Rose had often reminded him when he got upset about something as a child, there were people much worse off than he. He'd go visit Terrell, bring him some magazines to take his mind off the pain he must be in.

After he was turned away at the hospital, he decided the second step was to find a new job. He might never live with Rickey now, but that didn't mean he had to live with his parents forever. He got on the bus and rode back toward the Central Business District. It wasn't a long walk from Charity to the Pirate Lafitte Grill on Poydras Street, but after a couple of years working long kitchen hours, Gary had gotten into the habit of saving his feet whenever he could. Riding the bus through the CBD, he took *NBA Roundup* out of the bag and leafed through it. Even the news that Karl Malone had been named to next year's Olympic basketball team couldn't cheer him up, so he left the magazines on the bus. Maybe somebody else would be able to get some pleasure out of them.

He got off at Poydras and crossed a busy six-lane intersection to reach the restaurant. It was a rundown-looking seafood place, the kind you often saw downtown: undistinguished, anonymous, but attempting to pull in the tourists by using a name connected with New Orleans history to make them think they'd heard of it. A restaurant on Royal Street was called Pere Antoine's after the nearby alley, named in turn for one of the early priests of St. Louis Cathedral. Though its fried seafood was nothing special, the place was always packed with tourists. Rickey had often voiced his theory that these people thought they were eating at *the* Antoine's, which was named after a completely different guy. The Pirate Lafitte Grill looked like that kind of place, but less prosperous because it didn't have the Quarter's walk-in business.

He sat in the dining room breathing several decades' worth of fry vapors as he filled out an application. Before he had finished listing his previous places of employment, a middle-aged, café-au-lait-colored man in cook's whites came out of the kitchen and paused at his table. "You applyin for the dishwasher job?"

"Yeah."

"How many restaurants you worked in?"

"Three."

"How come you left your last position?"

Gary pondered a variety of responses before deciding he didn't care about this job enough to lie. "My boss was an asshole," he said.

"Hazard of the motherfuckin trade," the man said agreeably

enough. "I'm an asshole too. All my cooks say so. Think you could work for me?"

"I don't know. You gonna be an asshole all the time, or just when I deserve it?"

"You ever gonna admit you deserve it?"

They looked at each other for a long moment. Then the man's face broke into a crooked grin. "I ain't had nothin but criminals and crybabies applyin for this job," he said. "I need somebody knows his way around the kitchen. Somebody can get my pots clean when I need 'em, not when he feels like it. Can you do that?"

"Sure."

"Then you're hired."

"Don't you even want to see my application?" said Gary.

"Cracker boy, if you can get me clean pots when I need clean pots, I don't give a shit about your application. I don't even need to know your motherfuckin *name*." The man stuck out a callused, burn-scarred hand. "But just in case you need to know mine, I'm Chef Irvin. Any chance you can start tonight?"

14

By the next week, Rickey was doing better. The last traces of the cocaine hangover had left him, and his Skills class was keeping him so busy that he had little time or energy to worry about the fact that he still hadn't heard from Gary. When he did think about it, there was a stubbornness in his heart that was not relieved in the slightest by the letter he got one day:

> Dear Rickey,
> Sorry I didn't write sooner. I couldn't really think of anything to say. I got a new job. It's at The Pirate Lafitte Grill, a seafood place in the CBD. I started out as head dishwasher but the chef found out I knew how to cook and put me on the line. He's pretty cool. My mom said she told you about Terrell Washington getting shot. He didn't make it. I heard he would have been paralyzed if he lived, so who knows what is best. I couldn't go to the funeral because I had to work. Speaking of work, I guess I better get going. Hope you still like school.
>
> G.

Rickey crumpled up several abortive responses, most of which started with lines like What the fuck do you care if I still like school, or Why write me at all if you don't have anything to say, or If you don't love me anymore, why don't you have the balls to TELL me so instead of just leaving it out of your letter, but then again when did you ever have the balls to tell anybody anything they didn't want to hear, but I thought maybe I deserved better than that, but I guess I'm just stupid ... It was this last attempt that made him abandon the idea of writing back altogether. This wasn't the kind of thing they could work out on paper or over the phone. They'd deal with it when he went home for Christmas, when they could see and touch each other. Surely that would make things a little easier. It was only a couple of weeks away. He decided to call Brenda and see if she had made his flight reservations yet.

"I been meaning to call you, babe," she said when he got hold of her.

"Did you book my flights? When am I coming home?"

"Well, that's what I wanted to talk to you about."

Rickey felt a flicker of disquiet, but he brushed it off as paranoia. "Is there a problem?"

"No, not exactly. It's just, well, Claude wants to take me on a Carnival Cruise and we thought it might be better if you didn't come back to New Orleans until your next break."

"My next break's not until summer," he said as a cold invisible hand wrapped itself around his heart. "And I gotta do my externship then. I want to come home now."

"We just think it'd be better if you didn't."

"Momma ..." Rickey tried to keep a tremor out of his voice, then decided he didn't care if she heard it. "What is this shit? I never been away from home for Christmas before. I don't want to stay here. I don't think the campus is even open."

"Your father's gonna send you some extra money. You can get a nice hotel room or something."

"I can't believe this. You really want to go to the Virgin Islands that bad?"

"Cozumel."

"What?"

"That's where the cruise goes. It's in Mexico."

"Whatever. Go to Mexico, then. Stay there and get a job in a tequila factory, I don't care. I'm still coming home in two weeks. I'll book my own goddamn flight. I'll stay at the house by myself."

"You can't do that, babe."

"Why not?"

"It just ain't a good idea."

"I don't care. It's still my home, right?"

"I got the locks changed," said Brenda, at least having the decency to sound ashamed. "Your keys don't work no more."

Rickey closed his eyes and gripped the receiver as hard as he could, hoping the pain in his fingers would ward off the dizziness that had begun to wash over him. "This isn't about you going on a cruise at all, is it?" he said. "That's just an excuse. You're not letting me come home because you want to keep me and Gary apart. You and Elmer and Mary Rose. You don't think you've driven the wedge quite deep enough yet, and you're afraid we might still be able to fix things if we see each other at Christmas."

"Johnnie—"

"Well, fuck that. I don't need you or your house. *Your* house, right? Not mine any more. I don't even have a key. Fuck it. I'll stay with Gary, and if his folks won't let me, I'll get a room somewhere. If I gotta stay in a cheap hotel for Christmas, I might as well do it in New Orleans, *where I can see my boyfriend*."

He slammed the phone down. His heart was beating against the wall of his chest like a trapped bird. His vision began to gray at the edges, and he realized he was close to hyperventilating. He rested his head on his knees and made himself breathe deeply for several minutes, until he felt close to being in control again. Then he called Gary's house. For once, Gary answered, and instead of saying anything about the letter, Rickey filled him in on the Christmas situation. "I was hoping maybe I could stay with y'all," he finished.

"I'd like you to," said Gary. "But I don't think my folks would let you. Sounds like they all got together and planned this."

"Doesn't that piss you off?"

"Course it does."

"You don't sound all that pissed off."

"Well, you didn't sound all that pissed off when they worked it out for you to go to the CIA."

"What's that supposed to mean?"

"You figure it out."

"I told my mom I'd get a hotel room in New Orleans if I couldn't stay with you," Rickey said. "But you sound like you don't even care if I'm there."

"I do care. I just don't know what you expect me to do about it."

"Maybe I shouldn't come home."

"Maybe you shouldn't."

"Well, maybe I just won't. Maybe I'll find something better to do up here."

"If that's what you want."

"What do *you* want? Do you care? Do you want to see me?"

"I don't know, Rickey. I don't know what to say."

"Gary …"

"Nobody calls me that any more," Gary said rather snottily. "I got a nickname at work. Chef Irvin started calling me G-man and now that's what everybody calls me."

"Who cares, dude? I'll call you whatever you like. I'm just not sure if you really want me to call you at all any more."

"I don't know what to tell you."

"Tell me if I should come home or not."

"I can't decide that for you."

"Well, I guess that's my answer then." He heard Gary start to say something else, but he sent the phone crashing onto the receiver. What a day. He'd never hung up on anybody before, and now within twenty minutes he'd hung up on the two people he loved most in the world. But they obviously didn't love him back any more, so fuck them. Not only would he refuse to feel guilty for hanging up on them, Rickey decided; he would refuse to talk to them if they called back.

They didn't call back.

Gary put down the phone and walked upstairs to his room. He didn't blame Rickey for hanging up on him. He knew he'd been an asshole, but he hadn't been able to help it. He missed Rickey so badly and felt so sure things were over between them that he didn't know what to say when they talked, and it all came out wrong.

Probably Rickey didn't really want to come home for Christmas anyway. Probably he'd rather stay up there with whomever he'd met, and he was just upset because he felt like Brenda had put one over on him. Rickey always hated it when he thought somebody had put one over on him. He didn't even seem to realize that the parents had done just that by sending him to New York. It was like he thought the whole CIA thing had been his own idea.

Gary realized he was wearing a T-shirt Rickey had sent him, heather-gray with the CIA logo in blue. He felt vaguely bogus wearing such a thing when he'd never attended the school, but he'd liked it because Rickey had slept in it for a week, then mailed it to him without washing it. When he first took it out of the envelope, Rickey's familiar scent had hit him like a long-lost memory, and he'd worn it constantly until it just smelled like his own boring skin. Now he pulled it over his head, balled it up, and stuffed it under the bed.

As he rummaged through his drawer for a clean shirt, Gary decided to go in to work. He wasn't on the schedule today, but Chef Irvin could usually find him some prep to do. Before the Pirate Lafitte Grill, work had been something he tolerated. He'd gotten into restaurant work because Rickey was interested in it, and he'd never minded it much, but he'd never really loved it. Now the restaurant was the only place where he felt competent and in control. The busier he was, the less he had to think about the rest of his life, and that was a comfort. The food was nothing special, but Chef Irvin seemed to think Gary was good at his job, which made Gary want to please him more than any other boss he'd ever had. He thought maybe he was actually starting to understand why some people spent their whole lives in restaurant kitchens.

I could just climb down to the tracks and wait for the train to come, Rickey thought. *Probably wouldn't hurt too much, and it would make a HUGE mess for them to deal with.*

The Amtrak express came barreling along the river several times a day. An item in the campus newspaper, *La Papillote*, had recently warned students to stay away from the tracks. Sitting in the gazebo by the cliffs, Rickey watched two trains pass and imagined them mangling him. But he didn't really want to die; he just wanted everybody to be sorry for the way they had treated him, and his state of mind was such that he could imagine nothing short of his death triggering such remorse.

With a gloveless, cold-purpled forefinger he traced carvings on the silvery wood of the picnic table: **TORY ♥'s JENNIFER, A.M. CREW KIX ASS, J.P.S. '84**. A wind was kicking up, seeming to chase away the last of the daylight. Rickey pulled his new heavy coat more tightly around him. He'd found it at a secondhand store in Hyde Park, paid for it with $40 of the $100 Cooper Stark had given him, and spent the rest on sweaters and a wool-lined hat with earflaps. He'd never owned a hat in his life, thought this one was a godawful stupid-looking thing, and had not been able to make himself wear it more than a handful of times. The rest of the purchases were invaluable. He had not enjoyed spending the money, but he was a lot warmer now.

All at once he knew what he would do. He'd call Coop, mention that he was going to be alone and adrift for the holidays, and see what happened. Of course Coop had promised to call him and hadn't yet, but a guy with two restaurants had to be busy. Maybe if Rickey called, Coop would invite him down to the city for Christmas, and then who knew what might happen? It could be the beginning of a whole different life. Maybe Rickey would never return to New Orleans at all. Something deep within him set up a dismal wailing at this thought, but he ignored it. As he walked back to the dorm, he saw something strange in the air, thousands of tiny brilliant specks swirling against the slate-colored sky. Snow, he realized as a few flakes landed on the arm of his coat. He'd seen it a couple of times in New Orleans, but seldom more than flurries. This was the real thing, and it struck him now as some kind of good omen.

He found Coop's business card in his desk drawer and dialed the number Coop had written on the back. After four rings, an answering machine picked up. "I'm not here," said Coop's voice, "but you know what to do."

"Hey, uh, this is Rickey. I had a great time with you last week and, well, I thought we should keep in touch. I found out I'm gonna be here over Christmas, I'm not going home, so … call me if you feel like getting together, I guess. I'll be at the dorm until, uh, December twenty-second. Hope to hear from you." Rickey recited the number in case Coop had mislaid it and hung up, feeling apprehensive and a little horny just from hearing Coop's voice. He knelt by the window above his bed and stared out at the snow, which had begun to accumulate on the brick ledge outside. It looked a lot like the fake stuff they used to decorate Santa's Village at Lakeside Mall in Metairie, but Rickey thought it was magical anyway, a harbinger of adventure. He spent the rest of the evening gazing at it as it fell. If he was also waiting for the phone to ring, he barely admitted it to himself.

He awoke folded awkwardly on his bed, half-sitting, his cheekbone sore against the windowsill. The sky was cottony-pale, the campus blanketed in white. Muller's bed was empty. The clock read 7:46. Somehow Rickey had slept all night at the window. The phone had not rung, and now he was late for class.

"Mr. Rickey! Thanks for gracing us with your presence," the chef barked as Rickey rushed into the kitchen still tying his kerchief. "Smell those burnt pots in the sink? They're all yours."

"Thanks for waking me up, asshole," he hissed as he passed Muller's table on his way to the sink. He heard Muller mutter something in return, and the other students at the table laughed, but Rickey was already running hot water and could not make out what Muller had said.

By that night he began to suspect that Coop wasn't going to call him back. By midweek he was sure of it. He told himself he would not call Coop again; he'd only sound desperate and pathetic. The next day, feeling numb, he heard himself speaking into Coop's answering machine: "I just wanted to make sure you got my message ... uh, it's Rickey ... call me if you get a chance."

He could think of nothing but Coop and Gary and Brenda. He hated them all, but would have dropped everything at a kind word from any of them. He couldn't sleep even when he took four Excedrin PMs. In Skills class he failed to hold up his end of a heavy pan of veal bones as they came out of the oven, and only his oven partner's quick reflexes kept the sloshing molten fat from hurting anybody. The snow crunched pleasantly underfoot as he walked back to his room, but Rickey was past being able to enjoy it. He lay in bed and thought about how stupid he was for believing Coop really wanted to be his friend. Somebody like that wouldn't want him for a friend. He was just a cheap little piece of shit, maybe good enough to fuck, certainly not good enough to be friends with if he wouldn't put out. Remembering some of the things he had said to Coop that night, the coke-fueled *bon mots* and flights of fancy, he writhed in embarrassment and wished he could take back the last two weeks. No, the last three months; if he had it to do over again, he'd realize that what he had with Gary was worth any amount of culinary education. He would just stay home, where he'd once belonged and now was not even welcome.

After a few hours alone with the mute telephone and his own self-loathing, Rickey got up, went to the campus bookstore, and bought a Poughkeepsie newspaper. If he was going to rent a room for Christmas, he figured he'd better start looking.

15

"What the fuck you think this is, your jack-off break? This is LUNCH RUSH, you motherfuckin pussies, so how 'bout RUSHIN a little?"

Chef Irvin's hands seemed to blur as he spoke, but his voice was calm and affable. The chef almost always seemed less agitated than anyone else in the kitchen, and he put out twice as many plates as any of them. The rest of the lunch crew was unspectacular—a couple of them seemed even greener than Gary, though they'd been here longer—but with Chef Irvin egging them on, they could do a hundred covers in forty minutes without much trouble. Gary hadn't expected it to be so busy on Christmas Eve. He guessed maybe people were doing their last-minute shopping on Canal Street, but he didn't really care one way or the other. He wished he could just forget Christmas this year.

After lunch, he started prepping up lemons for the night crew. Chef Irvin wanted them cut in something he called a Van Dyke, which just meant halving them in a zigzag fashion to garnish plates. Gary went to the back of the kitchen to get a crate of lemons, doglegging around the hole in the floor near the walk-in. You could see not just the floor joists but the foundation of the building through the hole. This was actually a pretty nasty kitchen, Gary thought. Some of the equipment was so old as to be dangerous, and everything was covered with a sticky glaze of half-rancid cooking oil. It was a hardcore place, though. The chef made it so.

He entered the little hallway leading to the fire door where some of the less perishable produce was kept. Chef Irvin was sitting on an upturned pickle bucket smoking a cigarette, pinching it between two hard brown fingers and and sucking at it as deeply as if it were a joint. "Awright, G-man," he said. "Good service today."

"Thanks, Chef."

"You ever work in a place this busy before?"

"Not even close. I mean, we were pretty busy over at Terrio's, but it was a lot easier."

"Ain't much to makin sandwiches," Chef Irvin conceded. "I known plenty cooks who could even fuck that up, though, get in the weeds and start whinin, 'Oh, woe, I ain't got enough bread. Oh, boo-hoo, I can't fit all this shit in my motherfuckin fry basket.' You musta learned somethin over there, cause you a lot faster than I thought you'd be."

"I got pretty fast at the very first place I worked. Diner in the Ninth Ward, over by where I grew up. The Feed-U?"

"What, Sal Keller's place? Well, fuck my ass. See what happens when I don't bother lookin at people's applications. I knew you worked for that bastard Sal, I'd a put you on the line right away."

"Did you work at the Feed-U?"

"Hell, no. I worked with Sal about thirty-five years ago at Escargot's in the Hotel Bienvenu. Shitty place. *Shitty* goddamn place, worst I ever worked. Sally was a good cook, though. We was just kids then."

Gary had been too busy to think about Rickey all through lunch service, but talk of the Feed-U and the thought of the two young cooks working together reminded him. A shadow must have crossed his face, because Chef Irvin said, "I notice somethin got you down lately."

"Lately?" said Gary, and shrugged. "I been miserable since before you hired me, I guess. I actually feel better since I got this job—it keeps my mind off shit."

"Work'll do that," Chef Irvin agreed, shaking another cigarette from a battered pack of Tareytons, then offering the pack to Gary, who took one. He didn't really want it, but he liked standing back here talking to the chef. The first drag tasted like a dried dog turd, and he let it burn without inhaling a second time.

"I had a cook workin for me once always seemed worried about somethin," said Chef Irvin. "Never said a fuckin word, but I could just tell. Turned out his wife was a drunk, home with the baby. Started a grease fire one night tryin to cook some Tater Tots, burned herself up, burned up the motherfuckin baby too, how you like that shit? I'd a give him some time off if he'd a told me what was goin on."

"It's nothing like that. It's just . . . I don't know. Personal."

"Shut my big fuckin mouth, then. Put it out your mind."

"What would you do if you had a friend you came up with?" said Gary, not hearing him. "They were a cook too, and they were your best friend, and you always worked together, and you thought it meant something, and all of a sudden they ditched you and went off to cooking school? Like, 'Well, this is good enough for *you*, but I gotta learn to be a *real* cook'?" Gary warmed to his subject, forgetting that he hadn't even cared that much about cooking until he began working at the Pirate Lafitte Grill. "What if they were like, 'Oh, I'll come back when I graduate,' but you started thinking they were never gonna come back? And what if your whole life just seemed to suck without them?"

"Well," said the chef dryly, "first of all I guess I'd settle on a pronoun."

Gary looked up, so surprised to hear Chef Irvin use the word *pronoun* that he did not immediately catch the chef's meaning.

"Barrin that, I'd ask myself how come they had to go away to learn to cook. They got a cookin program at Delgado, and plenty cooks come up in New Orleans restaurants without goin to school at all. Could be your friend didn't expect to learn much workin with you. You a pretty good cook, so how come you hired on here as a fuckin *dishwasher*? Don't tell me, it ain't none of my business." The chef held up a scarred palm as Gary started to answer. "And don't get me wrong. I don't give a fuck about ambition, career plannin, all that crap. I did, I wouldn't be workin here. But maybe your friend got more ambition than me and you."

"That's for sure," said Gary.

"Well, you doin one fuck of a lot better than you were a few weeks ago, least as far as cookin's concerned. I tell you one thing, though. If that friend of yours makes you happy, hang onto 'em any way you can. Ain't too often in this life you meet another person makes you really happy. Listen to this shit," Chef Irvin said, stubbing out his cigarette on the sole of his shoe. "Motherfuckin Hallmark Cards oughta hire me. Make me head of the motherfuckin inspirational division."

"It'd be a loss to the restaurant world, Chef."

"It'd be a loss to my left ass cheek." The chef reached over and plucked the half-burned cigarette out of Gary's hand. "Gimme that if you ain't gonna smoke it. I never seen no white boy smoke a Tareyton anyway."

"It's not that. I just never smoked a cigarette when I was sober before. I don't think I got a taste for it."

"Just as well. It's bound to kill me one day, but I tell you what— if my feet feel like they do today, I'm gonna be ready to go." Chef Irvin heaved himself up from the pickle bucket, sighing hugely. "Say, G-man, ain't you got some lemons to cut?"

Gary hauled the crate of lemons into the kitchen, set them by the small cutting board (another cook was using the big cutting board to quarter potatoes for salad), and got to work. As he drew his paring knife in a zigzag pattern through lemon after lemon, he kept hearing Chef Irvin's papery voice saying *If that friend of yours makes you happy, hang onto 'em any way you can.* It was good advice. Trouble was, he didn't know if there was still any way he could hang on.

There had been no room advertised for rent that Rickey could afford. Everybody wanted a month's deposit or more. Even staying in the Super 8 Motel on Route 9 would have cost him nearly $400. Finally, in desperation, he had asked the bartender at Gaffney's whether there were any really bad sections of Poughkeepsie. "Well," she'd said doubtfully, "most of it's not *too* bad … but you might not want to be on West Main after dark."

Within two hours he had borrowed Dave Fiorello's car, driven to West Main, and found a cheap room in what he guessed was popularly known as a flophouse. It was an old red brick building with a faded sign on the front, *Apartments Now Available* with a cartoon of a smiling 1950s-style doorman. If there had ever been a real doorman, he had disappeared sometime between the fifties and 1991. The apartments were single threadbare rooms, each containing a card table, a chair, a sink, a radiator, and a very hard bed. The bathrooms were down the hall on alternate floors. The landlady had offered Rickey a room on a bathroom floor for an extra $20, and Rickey had taken it. That was his Christmas splurge.

He lay half-asleep in the hard bed wondering why he could hear faraway bells. Sometimes, if a Sunday morning was very clear, it was possible to hear the bells of St. Louis Cathedral all the way over in the Lower Ninth Ward. But why was it so cold? Then he came all the way awake with the terrible knowledge that he was in a rented room in Poughkeepsie and it was Christmas morning.

He didn't want to get up, but he was so cold he was almost shivering, and he couldn't afford to get sick. He rolled out of bed, crossed the room, and fiddled with the radiator for a few minutes. He'd never seen one before and hadn't yet gotten the hang of adjusting it. Hoping it would warm up eventually, he put his coat on and sat on the edge of the bed. That soon got too depressing, so he opened the window and leaned out to see what was going on. The street was even emptier than usual. The ghettos of New Orleans could be menacing, but they were noisy, flashy, undeniably alive. The bad part of Poughkeepsie—if that was what this was—seemed not so much dangerous as desolate.

He glanced at the building across the street and saw a big-breasted, blonde-haired black woman leaning out one of its windows, scanning the street just as he was doing. She noticed him, waved, and called, "Merry Christmas, baby."

"Merry Christmas," Rickey called back.

"You wanna come help me celebrate?"

"No thanks."

"Aw, c'mon. I ain't gonna charge you nothin. You cute and it's Christmas."

"Thanks anyway," Rickey said, and shut the window. As long as he had his coat on, he decided he might as well go see if he could find a cup of coffee. He walked down three flights of stairs, let himself out into the empty morning, and went to the Caribbean market on the corner. Their coffee was horrible, bitter and oily-tasting, but he'd been drinking it for a few days now and figured he would just about get used to it by the time school started again. On impulse, he asked the counterman to give him his change in quarters. It came to more than three dollars, enough for a call to New Orleans.

He set his coffee on the ledge of the pay phone outside the store, plugged the quarters into the slot, and began to dial Gary's number. As he pressed the buttons, he pictured the scene in the Stubbs house. They'd all be sitting around in their bathrobes drinking Community Coffee spiked with eggnog from the Brown's Velvet dairy. The little kids would be half out of their minds on candy, the adults debating how soon they needed to start dinner. Their crappy artificial tree would be teetering in the corner, looking like the fire hazard it was. Rickey wondered if any of the cardboard ornaments he'd made as a kid were hanging on that tree, or if Mary Rose had thought it best to leave them in the box this year.

He paused with his finger on the last digit, then abruptly racked the receiver. All his quarters came jingling down into the coin-return slot like a cruel parody of sleighbells. He scooped them out and shoved them into his pocket. What had he been thinking? Just because it was Christmas morning didn't mean Gary wanted to talk to him. He wasn't a part of that family any more. He wasn't a part of any family. Hot coffee slopped over the edge of the cup and onto his fingers as he walked back to his room, and he relished the small pain.

"Merry Christmas, babe," said Mary Rose, handing Gary a small envelope.

"Merry Christmas," Elmer echoed.

Gary opened the envelope and tried to smile. It was a $50 gift certificate from G.A. Lotz, and while he could certainly use it, he felt as if he'd come full circle from the day Rickey had started work at the Jolly Corner and Gary had given him the exact same present. That had been the beginning of his losing Rickey, he guessed, so this must be the final step.

"Thanks, Momma," he said. "Thanks, Daddy. I'll pick up a good chef's knife with this. The ones at the restaurant are crap."

"I just hope you know we so proud of you," said Mary Rose. "You been doing so much better since you got this new job."

Better than what? he wondered. Did they think he was somehow cured now that Rickey was gone? Was he learning to hold his liquor better, so that they could no longer tell how much he'd been drinking? Or was working at a job where he felt useful really making him easier to live with? He had no idea, but he guessed it was OK if they believed he was doing better. He was trying to be a hard-assed line cook now, but he couldn't help having been born with a peaceful soul, and he still had no desire to cause anyone trouble or pain.

"Ga—RY!" his sister Rosalie hollered from the kitchen. "You gonna help me with these artichokes or what?" Gary winced. He knew his family wasn't going to change what they called him—if he asked them to, they'd probably laugh themselves silly—but he almost always thought of himself as G-man now. It was what everybody at work called him and how he introduced himself to people he met elsewhere. Gary was his old self, immature, romantic, and trusting. Gary was the kid who had believed Rickey when he said he wouldn't go away. G-man was alone in the world and fine with it; he didn't really need anybody.

"Go on and help your sister," said Elmer. As Gary got up from the sofa, Elmer gave him an awkward little hug and said, "Your momma's right—we real proud of you."

Gary suddenly felt like throwing his arms around Elmer and dissolving into tears. *Hardass*, he thought. *Nobody cries on the hot line.* The urge receded a little as he went into the kitchen and started trimming the artichokes. He had them nearly ready to go in the big stockpot when Rosalie said, "You talked to Rickey today?"

"I don't really keep in touch with Rickey any more."

"Oh, Gary." Rosalie favored him with the tragic eyes she'd inherited from Mary Rose. "You probably think you sound tough or something, don't you? Well, you don't. You sound like you got a broken heart. You sound like that all the time, and I'm sick and tired of it."

"What do you know about it?" said Gary, irritated.

"Well, I know Rickey's your boyfriend. I hope y'all didn't think you ever kept that from me. And I know Momma had something to do with Brenda sending him away to school."

"Momma and Daddy both, you mean."

"Oh, come on. You know Daddy just goes along with whatever Momma wants. He would've never tried to send Rickey away if it was up to him."

"If you know all that, how come you never said anything before?"

"I didn't think it was my business."

"Yeah, well, maybe you also thought they were right about me and Rickey."

"Gary." Rosalie reached over and grabbed him by the wrist, immobilizing his knife hand. "What do I do for a living?"

"You work at Krauss," Gary said grudgingly. He'd enjoyed going to see her at the downtown department store when he was small, riding in the old-fashioned wooden elevators operated by ladies in white gloves.

"Where at?"

"In the shoe department."

"So you think I never met a gay man before? Hell, half my damn customers are drag queens."

Gary was surprised by this knowledge, but tried not to show it. "So?" he said.

"*So*?" she mocked in a gruff voice. "Listen to my tough baby brother. *So* it's not gonna cross my eyes if you admit you love Rickey and try to get him back here where he belongs."

"I thought you were supposed to be a good Catholic."

"We don't all interpret it the way Momma does."

"But the priest said it was wrong. He told me that years ago, right before I … before I knew for sure."

"What priest?"

"I don't know. Some priest out in Chalmette."

"Well, what the hell you went to *Chalmette* for? Why didn't you talk to Father Mike at our church? God, Gary, you grew up with Father Mike."

"That's exactly why I didn't talk to him."

"I see what you mean … I wish you would've, though. I did."

"What? About *me*?"

"Well, yeah. When I first started thinking you were gay, I talked to him about it. I knew how I felt, but I wanted to understand the Church's position. Momma talked to him too."

Gary was speechless for a long moment. "So what did he tell you?" he managed to say at last.

"He told us not to judge," Rosalie said quietly. "He told us it wasn't our place to decide what God thought of you. I wish Momma would've listened to him."

"Well, goddamn."

"Gary!"

"Sorry. I didn't mean it that way. It's just … I don't know. Maybe things could've been different, that's all."

"They still could be."

"I don't think so."

"Yes they can," Rosalie insisted. "You haven't been happy since Rickey left. I bet he's not happy either. Y'all belong together. You need to get him back here, and if he won't come, then I guess you'll just have to go up there."

"Are you crazy? I'm not going to New York."

"Why not?"

"I got a good job."

"They got jobs up there."

"I like it here."

"You don't seem like you like anything any more. The other day Tommy asked me how come you were sad all the time. Then he said, 'I bet it's cause Rickey went away. Let's get Rickey to come back so Gary won't be sad no more.'"

"He's just a little kid. He can't understand it."

"I think he understands it perfectly," said Rosalie. "I think you oughta listen to him."

Gary busied himself mincing garlic for the artichoke stuffing. He didn't want to look at Rosalie, because he knew she would have that annoying I'm-your-big-sister-and-you know-I'm-right expression on her face. He had been seeing it all his life and didn't feel like looking at it now.

By ten o'clock that night, everyone else had gorged themselves and gone home or upstairs to bed. Gary was wide awake and restless. He'd thought Rickey might call today from wherever he was, but now it was probably too late to hope so. He decided to go downtown for a while. Remembering what had happened on Thanksgiving night—or, rather, not remembering it—he didn't intend to go to Bourbon Street, just to the little bar he frequented on Iberville.

Driving Elmer's car up St. Claude, he saw houses decorated with Christmas lights and couldn't help thinking about how he and Rickey used to ride out to Metairie to look at the lights there. They'd never admit that they planned it, but every year since they'd learned to drive, they always seemed to end up on one particular street in Metairie sometime during the Christmas season. The people on this block went crazy for Christmas, decorating their houses and yards with thousands of lights, mechanical Santas and snowmen and Nativity scenes that actually moved, giant candy canes, piped-in music, entire North Pole villages. Last year Rickey had wondered aloud if prospective homeowners got grilled when they tried to buy a house there—"How much are you prepared to spend on lights? What's your position on Disney characters—pro or con? If you believe in keeping Christ in Christmas, are you opposed to putting Frosty next to Him?" It was always like that—they made fun of the spectacle, but it went without saying that they kind of loved it too. Gary thought he would probably want to kill himself if he went within a mile of that block this year.

The Quarter was more crowded than he'd expected it to be, and he had to park way down on Dauphine. As he crossed St. Ann on his way to the bar, somebody called his name. He turned and saw a big, handsome black man coming toward him, but he couldn't place the guy immediately. Somebody from the Jolly Corner? He didn't think so, and he was not enlightened when the guy said, "I'm Ken."

"Sorry," Gary said. "You look kinda familiar, but I'm drawing a blank."

"Don't worry about it. You were so fucked up that night, I'd have been surprised if you remembered your *own* name."

"Oh my God." Gary suddenly pictured the guy in tight leather shorts instead of the sweater and jeans he wore now. "Oh shit ..."

"Did you get home OK the next morning?"

"Yeah," said Gary, remembering how he had stumbled down the iron staircase in the blinding early-morning light. "Uh, I'm sorry if it was rude of me to leave like that. I just didn't know what else to do."

"Not at all. I was worried about you. You were so upset when we got back to my place, I thought I better just put you to bed."

"You mean we didn't ... ?"

"What? Have sex? Baby, that would have been date rape on my part, because you just didn't seem to know what you were doing. Oh, we made out a little, but you kept saying some guy's name, and you said you were sorry, and then you started to cry, and that was when I took your shoes off and called it a night."

"Jeez," said Gary. He knew he should be embarrassed, but instead he felt a cautious, creeping elation. "Well, thanks for taking care of me."

"No problem, honey. You want to get a drink now?"

"I better not."

"OK. You know where I am if things change."

In the bar on Iberville, Gary drank a screwdriver and mused on the encounter. He hadn't realized how much cheating on Rickey had affected him until he found out he hadn't done it. The knowledge was like a weight off his soul, and he now thought that night had been the beginning of his letting things get so fucked up with Rickey. He wondered if they were too fucked up to fix, or if Rosalie had been right after all.

The bartender noticed that Gary had finished his drink. "Hey, G-man, you ready for another one?"

"No thanks, T.J.," he said. The words felt foreign in his mouth, but he found that he didn't care. "I think I'm just gonna go on home. I don't really feel like drinking tonight."

16

Rickey swigged from a two-dollar bottle of eggnog that came with the liquor already mixed in. It was terrible stuff, but it had gone on sale at the Caribbean market the day after Christmas. He'd been drinking it ever since. There was nothing else to do here but read, and the only books he had with him were *The New Professional Chef* and George Orwell's *Down and Out in Paris and London.* The *Pro Chef* made him hungry and was too heavy to read in bed. He'd thought the Orwell would be a distraction, but his hands ached with cold if he held the book for very long, and the story was just depressing him further. He didn't have to pawn his coat like Orwell had, but otherwise the life of a Parisian *plongeur* didn't sound all that much worse than his situation right now. At least George Orwell was in France. It was embarrassing to be down and out in Poughkeepsie.

He heard the faint staccato pop of faraway explosions. *Gunshots?* he wondered blearily. He hadn't heard gunshots here, and the sound made him feel almost homesick. It wasn't *nice* to hear gunfire out on the streets, but it was normal where he came from, and when you were safe in your own bed there was almost an element of comfort to it. The bed here did not feel safe, so there was no comfort.

When the sound came again, Rickey realized it was not gunshots but fireworks. He rolled out of bed and went to the window. At the very edge of the dirty glass he could just make out shimmering flowers of light, purple and gold in the midnight sky. It was a new year, and Rickey wasn't sure whether to be appalled or glad that 1991 was over.

Dear Rickey,

Happy New Year, sweetheart. I love you.

I'm still totally gone on you, see? I thought I better get that out of the way right up front. If you're not interested, you can quit reading now.

I hope you didn't quit reading. I thought about you a lot over Christmas. I really missed you and I'm sorry I didn't tell you to come home. I thought maybe you didn't want to. But I should've just said "Yes, Rickey, of course you should come home because the whole holiday is just going to suck without you," which it pretty much did. Just because I was scared to speak up, I let you stay there when I wanted you here. I was scared, OK? I admit it. You once told me I should never be scared to say anything to you, and I never was before you left, but now I am. I'm going to send you this anyway, though, because I'm more scared of losing you than saying something you don't want to hear.

So anyway, I'm sorry if you had a shitty holiday, but at the same time I kind of wished it on you, because you weren't with me where you belong. Me, I just worked my ass off at the Pirate Lafitte. Cooked, went home, slept, got up, cooked some more. Joy to the world, huh?

I feel like I can do this now. I was willing to try before, but I didn't really believe I could do it. I've regained my faith in us, if that makes any sense. Do you still have yours? If you do, then let's try to get back to where we were before, or else find some other place to be. But wherever we are, let's please be together. I have been lost without you.

Love,
G.

Rickey sat at his desk holding the letter, tears streaming down his face. He hoped Muller wouldn't suddenly walk in and see him, because he didn't think there was any way he could pretend not to be simultaneously heartbroken, relieved, and elated. The letter had been waiting for him when he got back to school, and his two-week flophouse vacation was already beginning to take on the hazy quality of a bad dream.

He called Gary's house and got Rosalie, who said Gary was at work. "Just tell him I got his letter and I said 'absolutely,'" Rickey told her.

"I hope that means what it sounds like."

"I guess it does."

After reading the letter once more, he stuck it between the pages of his *Pro Chef* where he would see it often. Then he went off to the library to find an article on *à la minute* sauces that his Skills teacher had recommended before the holidays. Now that things were looking up, maybe he'd actually be able to enjoy school again.

"I'm telling you, man." Phil Muller stabbed his fork into a small pile of steamed Brussels sprouts, spearing one. "It was a *love letter* from a *guy*. Rickey's a fag."

"Whoa, back up a sec," said Dave Fiorello. They were in Alumni Hall, the Jesuit-chapel-turned-dining-room. "Why were you looking at Rickey's *Pro Chef* anyway?"

Muller scowled. "I forgot mine at home over Christmas," he said. "My mom's mailing it to me."

"How the fuck do you forget your main textbook when you're packing to come back to school, Muller?"

"It doesn't matter," said Muller, shoveling gaufrette potatoes into his mouth. "What I'm worried about is this letter."

"So what'd you read it for?"

"It was staring me in the face when I opened the book."

"And you just couldn't tear yourself away."

"I knew I shouldn't read it, but Rickey said some stuff to me before, and I thought I ought to find out about him for sure."

"Why?"

"Well, because I have to live with the guy, for one."

"Muller, I don't know who Rickey wants to sleep with, but I can guarantee it isn't you." Fiorello bent over his veal blanquette so he wouldn't have to look at Muller's face. Muller was really starting to piss him off.

"Don't even talk like that." Muller gave a theatrical little shudder of disgust. "I wasn't thinking about that. But I still have to get dressed in front of him, shower with him ..."

"Oh, so you're worried it might be catching?"

"What the fuck, Fiorello? What am I supposed to do? I got a faggot for a roommate! Whose side are you on?"

"I'm on Rickey's side, you asshole!" Fiorello felt like throwing his plate at Muller, but he was still hungry, so he resisted. "I mean, he's a nice kid, and you've been on his case since Day One. He's poor, he's from a hick city, he's a faggot. Now you're reading his mail and shit. What makes you think this letter was from a guy, anyway? You said it was signed with an initial."

"I could tell." Muller was sullen now. "It just sounded like a guy."

"Uh-huh."

"It said something about being on the line at a restaurant. That doesn't sound like a girl wrote it."

"Muller. Look around you. See those people at that table over there? And there? And that one just walked by? Those are girls. See what they're wearing? Chef's whites. I hate to break it to you, but the world is changing."

"Ahh, most of them are in Baking and Pastry Arts. The chick track."

"Muller, did anybody ever tell you you're an asshole?"

"He did WHAT?" said Rickey.

"I wasn't sure I should tell you," Fiorello said nervously. "But I thought you had a right to know."

"I'm gonna kill him."

"Rickey—"

"That snot-nosed pencil-dick motherfucker. Seriously, Dave, I'm gonna kill him. He might think he's met some faggots before, but I bet he never met one from the Ninth Ward."

"Rickey, I know you want to kick Muller's ass. Hell, *I* want to kick his ass. But don't do anything stupid. It's not worth getting thrown out of school over."

"You think they'd throw me out?"

"For fighting? Sure. You know we're supposed to—what is it the dean said at orientation?—'conduct ourselves like professional chefs at all times.'"

"I know professional chefs who'd kick his ass over something like this."

"Well, but you know they'd throw you out of here if you did. Is that what you want?"

"I guess not," said Rickey reflectively. "Maybe. I like it here, but maybe it's not the right place for me."

"What do you mean? I think you're one of the best cooks in our Skills class. Chef does too—I can tell."

"You think?"

"He never rolls his eyes when you bring your plate up to his desk. Me, I get an eye-roll once in a while. Some people get it almost every day."

"Huh," said Rickey, who hadn't noticed. Until he returned from Christmas break and got Gary's letter, he had been too unhappy to know if he was doing a good job or not. "Well, what should I do, Fiorello? I really want to kill Muller."

"Don't kill him. Go to the R.A. and ask for a room transfer. Tell him your roommate's been going through your stuff and spreading, like, homophobic slurs about you. I bet you'll get transferred right away."

"I'm not gonna say anything about homophobic slurs."

"Why not?"

"Because I don't want to talk about it."

"Rickey, the R.A.'s not going to care if you're gay. It's none of anybody's business."

"You wanna bet? Muller's already spreading this shit. I confirm it to the R.A., and next thing you know, nobody's gonna want to room with me."

"Well, I'd room with you. Maybe my roommate would trade with you." Fiorello said this without much hope; he knew his roommate thought Muller was an asshole. That was going to be the problem, he thought—not that no one would agree to room with Rickey, but that no one would agree to room with Muller. "Or maybe they'll give you a single. Or you could even move into a three-person room that only has two—somebody must've dropped out over the break. Hell, wouldn't anything be better than staying with Muller?"

"I guess."

But Rickey didn't want to talk to the R.A. He didn't think he should have to retreat because of something Muller had done. He'd talk to Gary about it first, he decided. Gary had apparently regained the good sense and dependability Rickey had always expected of him, so he would abide by whatever Gary thought he should do. They hadn't spoken since Rickey received the letter, though he was sure that Rosalie had given Gary his message and that Gary had known what it meant. Today was Thursday, the day Gary usually worked a double shift at the Pirate Lafitte Grill, so he couldn't call tonight. First thing after class tomorrow he would call.

By the time he finally got a chance to talk to Gary, though, switching roommates was no longer an issue at all.

"These were supposed to show up already butchered," said the Skills chef, looking at several large hotel pans full of whole chickens. He picked one up by the tip of a drumstick, let it fall back into the pan, and shrugged. "Well, this'll be a chance for you to practice what you learned in Fabrication. Break them down to suprême cuts and put the rest aside for the beginning Skills classes to use in stock."

"What's a suprême cut?" Rickey asked Dave Fiorello as the students started grabbing chickens and opening knife kits. He'd heard the term, but couldn't remember what it meant.

"Boned-out breast with the wing joint still attached."

"Oh, an *airline* cut," said Rickey. He heard Phil Muller give a derisive little snort behind him, but he was determined to ignore

Muller until after he'd spoken to Gary tonight. It wouldn't be easy, since Muller was in his group, but he intended to try.

"I'll break it down," said Muller, slapping a chicken onto their cutting board. "We do this all the time at my uncle's deli." Fiorello and the other member of their group, a girl named Brittany, walked off to collect the vegetables for the day's assignment. Muller positioned his knife at the center of the chicken's breastbone and brought the blade down. Maybe the cutting board was slippery, or maybe Muller's knife wasn't sharp; at any rate, instead of parting neatly into two halves, the chicken slid out from under the knife blade and went skidding onto the floor.

"Fuck!" said Muller, glaring at his knife as if it had betrayed him.

"Don't worry about it," said Rickey. "We can just rinse it off." He bent to pick up the chicken. Just as he did so, Muller took a step forward, and the back of Rickey's hand accidentally brushed his thigh. Muller recoiled, gave Rickey a little shove, and snarled, "Save it for your boyfriend, faggot."

Later, Rickey could not swear to the exact sequence of events that happened next. He remembered feeling not angry, but incredulous that Muller had shoved him. The fucker had actually *shoved* him, a girly little push on the shoulder. You didn't just shove somebody and expect him to stand there and take it, did you? Maybe in Boston you did; Rickey couldn't say. In the Lower Ninth Ward you sure as hell didn't.

A number of images raced through his mind: Fiorello telling him they were expected to conduct themselves like professional chefs; Gary writing that brave letter, sealing it, and dropping it in the mailbox; Muller reading it shamelessly as if it were some piece of trash lying around for public consumption. These were the pictures in his head as he set the chicken back on the cutting board, half-turned, and swung at Muller, catching him just under the left cheekbone, then in the gut. Muller doubled over and Rickey slammed his knee under Muller's chin, then grabbed him by the neck, propelled him backward across the kitchen, and shoved him up against one of the big reach-in refrigerators. With his back against the cold steel, Muller tried to make some kind of recovery and managed to clobber Rickey once on the side of the head, but then Chef was there, screaming at them, pulling them apart as easily as he might have separated a pair of tussling kittens, then knocking their heads together. "I'LL TEACH YOU LITTLE SHITS TO FIGHT IN MY KITCHEN," Rickey heard as stars exploded across his field of vision. When they cleared, he saw all the Skills students clustered around him, Muller, and the chef. Dave Fiorello was at the front of the pack, looking as if he didn't know whether to feel disappointed or pleased.

Standing there, and later in the dean's office, Rickey could not shake a creeping sense of beatitude. His knuckles and the knot on the side of his head where Muller had hit him throbbed in tandem, but he could not make himself care. He had fucked up very badly; he knew that. But the more he thought about it, the more ridiculously happy he felt. It was like some kind of drug that just kept getting stronger and stronger.

Sitting in a hard wooden chair before the dean's desk, he looked over at Phil Muller's glowering face and saw a crust of blood on Muller's swollen upper lip, and he was happy. Listening to the dean's lecture on conduct grossly inappropriate for CIA students, he was happy. The dean asked whether they had any explanation for their actions, and Rickey tried not to smile as Muller stammered, "He just, like, *attacked* me. He's always had a problem with me."

"Mr. Rickey? Do you have a problem with Mr. Muller? ... Is something funny, Mr. Rickey?"

"No, I was just wondering what kinda problem he thought I had with him that made him go through my mail."

He felt even happier as he watched Muller twitch. *Didn't think I knew about that, huh?* He almost laughed aloud and managed to suppress it.

"I didn't *go through his mail*," Muller told the dean. "I borrowed one of his textbooks and there was a letter in it. I didn't even read the whole thing."

Let's ask Dave Fiorello about that, Rickey thought, but said nothing. He didn't want to drag Fiorello into this. It would all come out the same in the end anyway. He leaned back in his chair, crossed his arms over his chest, and tried to tamp down the flame of happiness that seemed to be centered just below his ribcage.

"It doesn't really matter who did what," said the dean. "If you'd come to me with these problems sooner, maybe I could have helped. As it is, you've flagrantly disregarded our code of conduct, and I have no choice but to expel you both."

"You can't do that!" Phil Muller cried. Rickey closed his eyes. An observer might have thought he was wincing, but in truth he was only trying to blink back tears of joy.

Gary was due at work in an hour, and it took very nearly that long to ride the bus from his house to Poydras Street, so he almost didn't answer the phone. He grabbed it on the fourth ring because he thought it might be somebody for Rosalie; she'd recently applied for some jobs. Instead, as soon as he said hello, Rickey's voice said, "I'm coming home."

"What—"

"Do you still want me to?"

"Course I do," Gary answered without having to think about it. "But what happened?"

Work was momentarily forgotten as he leaned against the wall by the telephone table and listened to Rickey tell the tale. Though he knew it was absurd, he felt flattered and just a little turned on. He knew Rickey hadn't beaten up the guy just because of his letter, but he had been the catalyst. "I couldn't stand the thought of him reading it," Rickey said. "Not because I was embarrassed about any of the stuff you said, but because it was *ours*, you know? Just ours."

"Oh my God," said Gary. "I missed you so much, I didn't think I could stand it."

"You did?"

"Yeah. I didn't want to tell you how bad it was, cause I knew there was nothing you could do about it, but … How soon can you get home?"

"I'm gonna try to fly out tomorrow. If not, then definitely the day after. I'll call you back as soon as I get my reservation."

"Do you need any money?"

"No. My dad sent me a check for Christmas. It was in the same batch of mail as your letter." Rickey laughed a little ruefully. "I won't need it for this semester now, so I'll fly out as soon as possible even if it costs a lot. Just, uh ..."

"What?"

"Well, get us a hotel room, why don't you? Those places out by the airport aren't real expensive. And pick up a paper. Start looking at some apartments."

"You got it."

They hung up and Gary sprinted for his bus. The driver, who had never spoken to him before and usually looked about as cheerful as an iguana, gave him a big smile. "You look so *happy* today!" she said.

"I should," he told her. "I just got the best news of my life."

"Oh, man," said Dave Fiorello. "I'm sorry you have to leave, but *damn*, it was good to see you take that fucker down."

"I took him down?" Rickey was cramming clothes into his suitcase. They were going to be terribly wrinkled by the time he unpacked them again, but he didn't care. "I didn't think I actually took him down."

"He wasn't on the floor, but he was *down*," said Fiorello. Some of the other guys who had crowded into the room nodded their assent. "If Chef hadn't broken it up, Muller would've been crying for his mommy."

"I bet his mommy isn't too happy with him now," said a kid who wasn't even in their Skills class. Rickey thought his name was Scott.

"What about your folks?" Fiorello asked Rickey. "You gonna be in a lot of trouble or what?"

"Well, my mom's not too thrilled." Rickey had called Brenda right after he spoke to Gary. She had been upset that he was leaving school, but even more upset that he didn't plan to move back in with her. *You still my baby!* she'd sobbed, and Rickey had said, *Momma, I'm always gonna be your son. But I stopped being your baby when you wouldn't let me come home for Christmas.*

"What about your dad?" said Fiorello.

Rickey turned away from his suitcase to look at the other students in the room. "My dad sent me here because he thought it would cure me of being queer," he said. "It didn't, and I don't really give a fuck what he thinks any more." The students gazed back at him, and he studied their faces, searching for derision. He didn't find any; their expressions ranged from neutral to (in the case of Scott) almost worshipful.

"Who the hell sends his kid to *cooking school* to cure him of being *queer*?" a Skills student named Jason said at last, and everyone laughed.

"If you were cured, you wouldn't have put the chicken back on the cutting board before you hit him," Fiorello added.

"What's so queer about that?" said Rickey. "That's just good kitchen habits."

The tension was broken. Rickey started packing again.

"Well, you did us all a big favor anyway," said Fiorello. "If Muller hadn't gotten thrown out too, I swear I would've had to kick his ass just on general principle."

"Yeah," "Damn right," and "Me too," muttered several of the others. Rickey knew most of them would have done no such thing, but he was pretty sure Fiorello would have, and the knowledge made him feel good. If he got much happier, he thought, he wouldn't even need a plane ticket to get back to New Orleans.

"There's a Newark-New Orleans flight tomorrow that's nearly empty," the travel agent had said. "I might be able to get you a last-minute deal … what's the code for New Orleans? MSY? That doesn't make sense …"

Just the thought of the code not making sense had given Rickey a little homesick thrill. On the train to New York, on the bus to the airport, and then on the plane, all he could think was *I'm going home, I'm going home, I'm going home.* The thought sang in his head as the plane took off into the afternoon sky. He glimpsed spidery black treetops through the tiny window and hoped they were the last true winter sight he would ever see. Home was New Orleans, and in some ways home was still the little house on Tricou Street, but mainly home was wherever Gary was and he knew he must never forget that again.

He didn't kid himself that things would be perfect once he got home. He had fucked up not just at school, but in a lot of ways that could not be instantly mended. Rickey couldn't help laughing to himself as he thought of the phone call he'd received late last night: "Rickey? It's Cooper Stark … I wonder if you feel like coming into town for a drink this weekend." But even that problem was easily solved now with the talismanic words: "I'm going home."

Once he was home, though? Who knew? He and Gary were awfully young, and Rickey wasn't going to have a nice well-paying CIA-graduate job, and they might grow up to be old, tired, broken line cooks. But maybe it would be OK. Maybe it would even be fabulous.

He sprawled across the empty row of seats, fell asleep smiling, and did not wake until the plane touched down in the swamp-green city that felt like home enough for a lifetime.

D*U*C*K

A Tale of Men, Birds,
and One's Purpose in Life

This story is dedicated to the memory of Buddy Diliberto,
alive in New Orleans hearts forever;
and to Bobby Hebert,
the only act who could follow him.

I. RICKEY TAKES OUT THE TRASH

Everything you've heard about summer in New Orleans is true. The only tourists who visit during that infernal season are hardy Germans and Australians, who can weather anything, and people from Alabama, Mississippi, and Texas, who are used to it and don't have far to drive. The deepest pits of Hades have nothing on your average August day in the Crescent City. (You can say Crescent City if you like, because the Mississippi River cups the city in a crescent shape. Say "the Big Easy," or, worse, "N'Awlins," and people will know you're a tourist.)

Because of the sun pounding down out of the coppery sky—because of the stickiness that turns the air into a dishcloth from which you feel certain you could wring dirty water if only you could catch hold of it—because of that stink that rises off sidewalks and asphalt parking lots, choking the unwary with ghosts of shrimp shells, dogshit, burning tires and armpits—because the temperature seldom drops below the high eighties even at midnight, the people of the city try to keep their physical exertions to a minimum. In the heat of the day, there might be one old white man in a seersucker suit moving snail-slow along a sidewalk, or a group of black teenagers gesturing languidly at each other on the corner. Certainly there will be an ancient woman carrying a shopping bag and an umbrella; there's no chance of rain, but she's using the thing for a sunshade. These folks, you expect to see. The middle-aged man in the Broad Street neutral ground, standing motionless with a sign in each hand, occasionally putting one of them down to take out a handkerchief and blot the sweat from his smooth ebony dome—he is an unusual sight. His signs are handmade, but neatly printed. One reads THOU SHALT NOT KILL. The other says ENOUGH IS ENOUGH. You don't see him every day, but if you're from New Orleans or know the city well, you understand immediately what he's talking about.

There will be these people, and somewhere nearby there will be a chef hard at work. Kitchen workers don't have the option of keeping their labors to a minimum. Through sweat-soaked Julys and Augusts they preside over stovetop flames and the hot breath of ovens, swampy dish sinks and desert heat-mirages rising off grills.

On this particular August day, a chef named John Rickey was taking out a bag of wet trash, muttering and cursing over it with no idea that a few minutes from now he would be wishing his head were a little harder. He was muttering and cursing not because he thought a chef-owner was too good to take out the trash—he knew better than that—but because he had told one of the low cooks on his kitchen totem pole to do it an hour ago, and the cook hadn't done it. Devonte was a hell of a lot more seasoned than he had been when Rickey hired him, but occasionally he just sort of ... spaced. It might mean he was thinking about the tricked-out car he hoped to buy, or the pussy he hoped to score at his favorite hip-hop club, or nothing at all. This time of year, it might also mean he was thinking about basketball, in which case Rickey's partner and co-chef, G-man, would probably be thinking about it right along with him. But G-man wouldn't space; G-man was the solidest cook in the kitchen.

The whole crew was solid, even Devonte and the new kid, Jacolvy, most of the time. Still, Rickey missed Devonte's predecessor, Shake, with whom he and G-man had been working for years. Shake had snagged a sweet sous chef position at La Pharmacie, a hot new restaurant on Magazine Street. The chef over there had basically poached him from Rickey's restaurant, Liquor, but Rickey didn't hold it against Shake: there wasn't much room for advancement at Liquor and Shake had given them a good three years. He wished he had Shake back just for tonight, though; there were three major conventions in town, Liquor had two-fifty on the books, and they were going to get hammered.

Half-absorbed in these thoughts, still muttering about the trash, Rickey heaved the bag up and over the edge of the Dumpster. The ripe sour-milk smell of garbage wafted toward him, but he barely noticed it; just as the zookeeper ceases to smell elephant shit, this was one of the normal odors of his life. He was turning to go back into the restaurant when his world exploded with a tremendous crack that seemed to come from inside his skull. He felt his knees connect with the concrete apron around the Dumpsters. His field of vision went red, then turned to a field of glittering silver and blue stars that seemed to drip through the air before his eyes like fireworks ... except that his eyes were closed, weren't they? While he was thinking about this, the pain arrived, a huge pair of pincers that grabbed him by the temples and squeezed. Faintly he could hear somebody yelling: "How you like it now, you fucking faggot? You shitfuck! How you like it now, asshole?" Rickey tried to lift his hand to the back of his head where the pain seemed most concentrated—if his fingers encountered wetness and a hole, he would know he'd been shot—but before he could get his arm up, another explosion came. This one bounced his forehead off the concrete, and he passed out.

II. THE LURKER BY THE DUMPSTERS

Rickey's croutons were burning. G-man could smell them from all the way across the kitchen, where he was prepping fresh porcini mushrooms to go with tonight's duck special. "Rickey!" he hollered. "You got shit on fire in here!"

No answer. G-man sighed, crossed the kitchen, and pulled the sheet pan of croutons out of the oven. They were a few shades darker than they probably should have been, but with everything else that needed to be done today, he wasn't going to throw them out. Where was Rickey, though? It wasn't like him to walk off and leave his prep work to die.

"Rickey!" he yelled again.

"I think he took out the trash," said Devonte, coming in from the hall that led to the walk-in cooler, employee restroom, and office.

"Coulda sworn I heard him tell *you* to take out the trash a while ago."

Devonte looked away. "I got to doin somethin else and forgot. Sorry."

"Yeah, well, I just want to know where Rickey is."

G-man laid his knife on the cutting board and headed for the back door, limping a little on the foot that had been bothering him for a couple of months now. It was no big deal, just a bone that felt like it was going to pop out of place every now and then. If he sat down for a minute and flexed his toes the right way, it usually faded to a dull ache. He had just turned thirty-two, Rickey would catch up with him in September, and they had been working in kitchens since they were fifteen: plenty of time to build up a generous assortment of aches, pains, scars, and calluses.

He whacked the pressure bar and stuck his head out the back door, expecting to see Rickey talking to some purveyor who'd just pulled up with an order: that seemed the likeliest thing to delay him. Instead, G-man couldn't immediately process what he was seeing. Because his eyes were weak and light-sensitive, he always wore dark glasses in the kitchen, and for the first couple of seconds after he opened the door, the relentless sunlight blinded him: he just saw dark shapes and bright patches. Then the picture resolved into something horrible. Rickey was lying prone on the ground between the Dumpsters and the restaurant, his face against the hot asphalt. A big guy was standing over him kicking him in the ribs. Lying on the ground beside Rickey's head was a two-by-four with a smear of blood on it.

G-man turned in the half-open doorway as if he was planning to go back into the restaurant. "TERRANCE!" he shouted as loud as he could. "HELP ME!" Then he darted back around the door and into the parking lot. The guy had already taken off running, but G-man caught him easily, rabbit-punched him in the back of the neck, then spun him around and kneed him in the balls. The guy staggered for a second, then fell to the asphalt groaning.

G-man ran back to Rickey. Terrance, their 280-pound grill guy, was already there. "Grab that asshole!" G-man panted. "Don't let him get away!" He dropped to one knee beside Rickey, who was already trying to push himself up onto his forearms. A thin trickle of blood ran from one nostril and his eyes were like twin zeroes in a slot-machine window. "Fucker got the drop on me," he mumbled. "Burned my fucking croutons."

"Yeah, you did. Don't worry about it. Here, lay your head on my leg."

Rickey did, and blood began to soak into the houndstooth fabric of G-man's chef pants. Meanwhile, Terrance had lifted Mr. Two-By-Four as easily as he would a fifty-pound sack of oysters and dragged him back over to the Dumpsters. "You know this asshole?" he said, cuffing the guy on the side of the head to make him turn his face toward G-man.

G-man found it hard to look away from Rickey, but he made himself squint up at the guy's face. Yes, he realized; he *did* know this asshole. Had, in fact, handed him his last paycheck not two weeks ago, after Rickey had fired him.

Rickey wasn't too tyrannical as far as bosses went, but he had a few strict rules, most of which were directed at waiters and other front-of-the-house staff. It wasn't that he failed to discipline his kitchen crew, but that he tended to hire kitchen people he already knew he could trust. The front of the house was trickier. Neither Rickey nor G-man had much experience handling it; as lifelong kitchen guys, they were naturally suspicious of waiters, whom they secretly believed to work half as hard as cooks and make twice as much money. The waiters sensed this ill-concealed animosity, and the turnover rate among Liquor's servers was higher than Rickey and G-man would like it to be.

One of Rickey's most holy rules had to do with chewing gum in the dining room. Some of the servers liked to do it so they wouldn't breathe halitosis fumes on the customers, but Rickey thought it looked tacky and forbade it. He even bought tins of Altoids and left them at the wait station, which mostly got the message across, but apparently this guy—Dave, G-man remembered, his name was Dave Hammond—didn't care for Altoids. The first time Rickey saw him chewing gum on the floor, he gave him a warning. The second time, he lurked in wait behind the kitchen door, and when Dave came through, Rickey smacked him on the back of the head so hard that the wad of gum flew out of his mouth and stuck to the opposite wall. Only Dave's pride had been hurt, but apparently the message still hadn't gotten through, because Rickey caught him folding a stick of gum into his mouth during service a couple of weeks later and gave him his walking papers.

Rickey and G-man had grown up in the Lower Ninth Ward, one of the scrappier parts of a generally scrappy city, and knew how to hold their own in a street fight. G-man was a basically peaceful soul, but even after having most of his rough edges smoothed off by the comparatively genteel world of restaurant ownership, Rickey was maybe a little too inclined to use his fists. No waiter could have put him on the ground in a fair fight, G-man knew that much. Guy must have hidden behind the Dumpsters and waited for Rickey.

"Call the cops," he said to Devonte, who'd just come out the back door. Then he glanced down at Rickey, who was bleeding freely from a gash on the back of his head. "And an ambulance."

"No cops," Rickey gasped. "No ambulance." By gripping G-man's forearm, he managed to lever himself into a kneeling position. Those twin-zero eyes settled on the bloody two-by-four. He groped for it, grabbed one end, and, using it like a cane, pushed himself to his feet. G-man hovered behind him, ready to catch him if he went over backwards. Instead he advanced on Dave and half-raised the board. The waiter struggled in Terrance's massive grip.

"How many times he hit you?" said Terrance. "I'll let you get your fair licks, but I ain't gonna hold him while you beat his head in."

"Let me go, you damn ..."

Terrance put his face close to Dave's. "Damn *what*?"

The waiter seemed to consider what he could get away with. "Dishwasher," he said finally.

Terrance laughed. "Ain't been a dishwasher for three years now. Not since that guy you just clobbered hired me to work the grill."

Rickey took another step, hesitated, then dropped the board, spun, and stumbled. G-man caught him by the waistband of his pants and held him as he doubled over and threw up on the side of one of the Dumpsters.

Approaching sirens split the heat of the day. Terrance met G-man's eyes and sighed. "Ain't this some kinda fuckarow," he said.

III. RICKEY CALLS THE WRONG PLAY

These sounds, even in the haze:

The familiar engine of G-man's old Mercury, chugging steadily. Apparently he or somebody else had convinced G-man to dispense with the ambulance.

(*what ambulance?*)

The streetcar, rattling along its track; from its proximity, he could tell it was the St. Charles line, not the new one on Canal.

A hollow ringing in his head that seemed to emanate from the very spot where the board had hit him.

(*what board?!*)

G-man's voice, cutting through the fog. "Dude, we're here. C'mon, can you stand up? Just hang onto my arm. Jeez, he really got you good. I can't wait to put his ass in jail."

"G … I was just taking out the trash … I must've fell and hit my head …"

"*Somebody* hit your head, awright. C'mon, look, be careful on these stairs." G-man's strong arm encircled his waist and practically boosted him up a small flight of stairs.

"Where are we? We gotta get back to the restaurant, dude, we got two-fifty on the books."

"I know it," G-man said grimly, but he kept hustling Rickey along, through a door and up another flight of stairs. At the top of that flight was a big, airy room where Rickey was allowed to sit down again. He grayed back out for a while.

The next thing he knew, a searchlight was probing his left eye. "He's pretty groggy," said the voice of God. Rickey didn't believe in God, but he knew G-man did. Were they in church? They'd better not be, if G-man knew what was good for him. It didn't make sense anyway; why would G-man make him go to church when his head was hurting so bad?

"Yeah," said G-man. "What about all that blood?"

"Oh, that's nothing. Scalp wounds bleed like a bastard."

Would God say "bleed like a bastard," if he were real? Rickey didn't think so, but he wasn't sure.

"I'll get the nurse to clean it up and put some Dermabond on it. Nothing to worry about."

"Who are you?" he managed.

A face resolved itself in his vision, old and bearded but not enough of either to be God. "Dr. Herbst. Your friend Lenny Duveteaux called me, asked me to squeeze you in so you wouldn't have to go to the emergency room. I owe Lenny a couple favors."

"Everybody owes Lenny a couple favors."

"See," the doctor told G-man, "he's starting to make sense."

The doctor had that Uptown New Orleans drawl that tried to sound Southern and didn't quite make it. He'd never say "awright" for "all right" or "axe" for "ask"; that was for lower-class downtowners like Rickey and G-man. They'd moved up to Marengo Street in the Irish Channel years ago, well within the boundaries of Uptown, but their Brooklynese speech would forever mark them as Lower Ninth Warders.

"Any blurred vision?" The doctor held up a newspaper in front of Rickey's face. "What's the headline say?"

"'ANOTHER NEAR MISS.'" A category-5 hurricane in the Gulf had jagged northeast and gone to Florida last week.

"What's the caption?"

"Some shit about morons buying bottled water and plywood."

"I really think he's OK," the doctor told G-man. "Cracked his coconut pretty good, but as long as he rests in bed for a couple days, he'll be fine."

Rickey's eyes met G-man's. G-man was still wearing his customary shades, but Rickey could see the alarm behind them.

"Can't rest," Rickey said. "We got two-fifty on the books."

"Excuse me?"

"Reservations," G-man explained. "Two hundred fifty customers." He took a deep breath, then said bravely, "But it doesn't matter, Rickey. You gotta go home and rest."

"Yeah, right, and you gotta bite my crank. I'm working tonight. If I keel over, you can drag me off the line and dump me in the walk-in to cool down. I'm not laying on my ass at home while y'all get slammed."

He stared at Herbst, expecting an argument, but the doctor just shrugged. "It's your head. You've got a concussion, but if you think you can work, you probably can. Might want to keep a bucket nearby—you'll likely make yourself sick."

"A concussion!" said G-man.

"It's no big deal," Rickey said. "Remember that Saints game in '89, when they played Tampa Bay? Bobby Hebert got a real bad concussion, but then the backup quarterback got hurt too and Bobby went back in. Played the rest of the game. He was a fucking iron man."

"Did they win?"

"Well, no. And he called a couple wrong plays, plays he had in college. But he didn't, like, die or anything."

G-man frowned but offered no further argument. *If you can stand, you can work* was part of the cooks' gospel.

The cops had wanted Rickey to come to the police station and make a statement about the attack, but he managed to convince them he didn't want to press charges. As far as he was concerned, the beef was between him and Dave Hammond: he'd smacked the waiter on the back of the head, the waiter had smacked him back a little harder. If he ever saw Dave again, Rickey would probably take him down, but whining to cops and judges was for sissies. Even so, dinner service had already begun by the time they got back to Liquor. G-man came around to help Rickey out of the car, and Rickey gripped G-man's shoulder, steadying himself.

"You sure you gonna be OK?"

"I better be, huh?" Rickey touched the swollen lump on the back of his head and grimaced. "I'm just embarrassed that a fucking *waiter* got the drop on me, that's all. It was a fair fight, I'd a kicked his ass into the middle of next week."

"Course you would. Like you even need to tell me that."

They entered the restaurant through the back door and walked into the kitchen. The crew was already busy with the first wave of early diners, but as soon as they saw Rickey, they all stopped whatever they were doing, put down their knives and spatulas, and broke into applause.

"Aw, now, what the fuck?" said Rickey, but he was grinning.

"Thickest skull in New Orleans!" Terrance hollered.

"You wanna get the drop on Rickey, you gotta sneak up behind him and hit him with a damn *plank*!" This from Tanker, their pastry guy.

"Plank, hell," said Devonte. "That was the whole *tree*!"

"And Rickey was still ready to kick his ass!" That was Marquis, who'd been the freshest meat in the kitchen before they hired Devonte and loved to lord it over the poor kid.

"OK, OK." Rickey held up his hands. "Yeah, I'm ready to work, but I feel kinda wobbly on my feet. Y'all gotta help me out tonight, keep an eye on what I do, let me know if I fuck something up. OK?"

"We're always ready to let you know if you fuck something up," said Tanker. "Not that you ever admit it when you do."

Rickey took his customary place at the expediting station. The expediter stood at the front of the kitchen, called out orders to the various stations as the tickets came out of the printer, and put the finishing touches on plates just before they went out to the dining room. In automotive terms, he was both the kitchen's driver and its steering column. G-man, at the sauté station, was the carburetor; taking raw materials and turning them into finished dishes, he produced the majority of the food that came out of this kitchen. Marquis wasn't yet seasoned enough to work sauté by himself, but he was assisting G-man tonight, a sort of booster fuel. Terrance at the grill, Tanker in his dessert nook, and Devonte at the cold-appetizer station were wheels; while their role wasn't as close to the heart of kitchen as G-man's, the car wouldn't go anywhere without them. And the diners were the network of streets upon which the car traveled; they weren't central to the design of the vehicle, but without them, it would have nowhere to go.

(The front of the house, as far as Rickey was concerned, was the old coot who drove twenty miles an hour right in front of you on a road with no passing lane. Today's events had not improved his view of this unavoidable but highly irksome facet of restaurant life.)

The night went smoothly enough at first. Dr. Herbst had given Rickey a vitamin shot, which didn't have much to do with his head but had pepped him up a little. As it wore off, the tickets seemed to proliferate and blur before his eyes. He could still read them, but he had to squint to keep the letters from jiggling wildly all over the little slips of paper. He had to stop and think about how to finish each plate, normally an automatic process: did the chervil sprigs go on the redfish or the softshell crab? Was it the pork or the mackerel that got a dash of chili oil from the squeeze bottle? Several dishes needed more than one final touch, and that increased his confusion. The kitchen was very hot, very bright, very loud. He began to feel nauseous, but stepped on that in a hurry: he could get sick later. Instead he pulled another ticket from the printer and scowled at it. The words sizzled and danced, but he thought he could make them out. "G," he called, "ordering one Indian lamb shank, two lobster with fried spinach, one stuffed quail."

The kitchen sucked in its collective breath. The cooks were too busy to really stop what they were doing, but there was a slight, hushed pause that would have been undetectable to anyone not familiar with their rhythms.

"Dude," G-man said at last, "those aren't dishes we have. Those are *Peychaud Grill* dishes."

The Peychaud Grill was where Rickey and G-man had earned their chops. They'd worked in a bunch of restaurants before that, but the Peychaud Grill and its chef, Paco Valdeon, turned them from half-assed hot-line meat into formidable cooks. The Peychaud had gone down in flames and been closed for years now, with Paco variously reported to be cooking on the beach in Mexico, running cocaine in South America, or dead. Whatever had become of him, he would always be Rickey's first real chef, the one who had not just given him permission to be serious about food, but shown him that there was no acceptable alternative.

Evidently Paco's dishes were hardwired into some reptilian part of Rickey's brain, accessible even when his own creations had begun to fail him. He wondered if he might actually have some kind of brain damage, but tried to brush the thought aside; there was no time to worry about that right now and anyway he had never been MENSA material. Instead he made a monumental effort to collect himself, and then G-man was there beside him, gripping the meaty part of his arm: "Dude, what do you need? I think I better stay on sauté, you don't have the energy for that, but I could put Devonte on desserts and let you take his station, and Tanker could expedite, or—"

"No. I'm fine. I can do it."

"You're *not* fine. Look, I'm not mad, I'm just worried, but you're calling out orders from ten years ago. That's not fine and you know it."

"Yeah, I know it. But let me just get my shit together, G. Anything else happens, I'll go be a pantry bitch."

"You sure?"

"Yeah."

"OK." G-man's eyes were doubtful, but Rickey knew he couldn't afford to hang around discussing it. "I better go get my own shit together, then, before everything crashes and burns."

Rickey wanted nothing more than to hook an arm around G-man's neck and let G-man lead him out of the overbright, pulsing hell his own kitchen had become, but instead he just said, "Sure. Go on."

As G-man walked back to the sauté station—limping slightly, Rickey noticed; damn, but they were a gimpy crew tonight—a young waiter named Tommy peered through the pass. "Hey, Chef?"

"Yeah?" Rickey scowled at him, expecting an earful of woe about how long his tables had been waiting for their entrees or the like.

Instead, Tommy stuck his arm through the pass. Cupped in the palm of his hand was a tiny pocket mirror, and on the mirror's surface were a cut-down drinking straw and a short line of cocaine. "I know you're having a rough night because of what Dave did," the waiter said. "I just wanted you to know that some of us are on your side."

Rickey gave him a long look, then bent over, picked up the straw, and snorted the coke without taking the mirror from Tommy's hand. "Thanks," he said. "How they looking out there?"

"Oh, drunk. They'll be all right."

Rickey's vision seemed to miraculously clear as he looked at the row of fresh tickets. He hadn't had cocaine in years, wasn't a big fan of the stuff, but right now it was hitting the spot. *Just what the doctor ordered*, Rickey thought, and laughed aloud to think of the useless Dr. Herbst prescribing it. *Take one bump and call me in the morning.* Maybe he could get through this night after all.

IV. GALL AND WORMWOOD

G-man saw Tommy at the pass with something shiny in his hand, saw Rickey bend over the waiter's outstretched arm, shiver a little, then straighten his shoulders and scan the tickets in front of him with renewed confidence. He guessed what Rickey was doing and rolled his eyes, but he couldn't get too worked up about it. After all, Paco Valdeon had been quite the coke fiend. Maybe Rickey needed to get into Paco mode to survive this shift.

"Yo, G," said Terrance from his spot behind the grill.

"Yo, T."

"What you call this veal bone sauce again?"

"Um, avocadomeno."

"AVGOLEMONO," Rickey shouted. "Jesus Christ! It doesn't have anything to do with avocadoes. It's a classic Greek egg-lemon sauce, except ours has Citron vodka. Morons."

It's the coke talking, G-man silently reminded himself. He looked forward to the time when the coke would shut up, but as long as Rickey could expedite in a way that made some kind of sense, he didn't particularly care if Rickey acted like an asshole. He hoped the drug wouldn't interact badly with the knock on the head Rickey had taken, but as long as Rickey didn't keel over dead, things could hardly get worse than having your expediter call out dishes that weren't on the menu.

"And we serving it with ouzo, right?" said Terrance, tipping G-man a wink.

"ORZO!" Rickey bellowed, unable to see that Terrance was messing with him. "Orzo pasta. Jesus fucking *Christ*!"

It was a long slog of a night. In the end, G-man could find nothing in it to be proud of except that nobody had walked out and only two diners had sent their food back. One of those was a steak Rickey had called out mid-rare when the diner had ordered it mid-well, and people who ordered their steaks mid-well often took a perverse delight in sending them back to be further incinerated, so that wasn't too terrible. The other was worse: an entrée Rickey had simply forgotten to order, one of a six-top. The other five diners had gotten their food while the poor woman sat and stewed. The kitchen made her duck special on the fly, but by the time the waiter got it to the table, she was drunk and belligerent and simply refused to eat it. "I guess she showed *us*!" the waiter had cackled, cramming the succulent slices of duck breast into his mouth, but G-man felt bad about it: that woman would have unpleasant memories of Liquor forever, would tell anyone who'd listen about her deplorable evening there. The flawless appetizer she'd eaten would become gall and wormwood in her memory. The free drinks the waiter had plied her with would only haze her anguish a little.

The coke had long since worn off by the time they broke down the kitchen, and G-man was able to get Rickey home without much trouble. They sat slumped at their kitchen table, Rickey gingerly feeling the goose egg on the back of his skull, G-man just staring at the white ceramic tabletop because anything more stimulating would overtax his mind. "You sure you're OK?" he asked Rickey finally.

"Yeah, man, I'm fine."

G-man made a fist. "How many fingers I'm holding up?"

Rickey laughed, reached across the table for G-man's hand, brought it to his lips, and kissed one of the many fine white scars on the knuckles. "For real, I'm fine," he said. "I got a head too hard for any goddamn waiter to crack."

"I guess you do."

The sheets on their bed sometimes got a funky smell from too many nights of coming home and falling into them without showering off the kitchen grime, but Rickey had changed them the day before and they were still crisp and clean. G-man expected to be asleep as soon as his head hit the pillow, but instead he lay awake for a long time, listening to Rickey's even breathing and wondering what he would have done if the guy had seriously hurt Rickey. All at once he was engulfed in a white-hot, pounding rage almost completely foreign to him. He felt as if he'd just taken a punch to the chest, had to work to catch his breath.

Jesus. Rickey talked about being pissed off all the time. Was this how he felt? G-man didn't see how anybody could stand it.

He closed his eyes, folded his hands across his chest, and muttered under his breath, "OurFatherwhoartinheaven-hallowedbethynamethykingdomcomethywillbedone—" After years of being estranged from the Church of his childhood, he had started to come back to it a little. Not the endless dogma and rigmarole, but the deep quiet place he was able find inside himself on the rare occasions when he went to Mass. He wasn't entirely comfortable with this renewed faith, attraction, reprogramming, or whatever it was, and Rickey, who took certain of the Church's positions as personal affronts, loathed it. Still, after all that had happened today, he couldn't help but offer up his thanks for Rickey's extraordinarily thick skull.

Without warning or logic, G-man found himself thinking of their first kiss. They'd been sixteen, in Rickey's bedroom, Rickey's mother away for the weekend. G-man had simultaneously known and not known it was going to happen; it seemed both inconceivable and inevitable. When Rickey finally did lean over and kiss him, G-man's hand had risen as if of its own accord to cup the back of Rickey's head, not wanting him to draw away. He realized as his fingers twined in it that he had never touched Rickey's hair before. It was silky but slightly tangled, as Rickey and his hairbrush had only the most passing of acquaintances. That hadn't changed in all these years.

The details, the memories, the automatic gestures and associations incomprehensible to anyone outside the hermetic twosome of the relationship—these were the things G-man could not imagine losing when something, against his will, made him contemplate losing Rickey. No one else in the world would remember that kiss, how scary it had been and yet how the world had opened wide around them, infinite with possibilities that hadn't existed the instant before. Where would all that go if one of *them* were gone?

No. Better to hope, at least, that there could be some kind of permanence, some link that survived. And that, G-man's sister Rosalie had once told him, was one of the reasons why you kept saying the prayers even when you weren't sure you believed in them.

He said another Our Father, more slowly this time, really thinking about the words. He could forgive those who trespassed against him; he'd never been able to hold much of a grudge. But those who trespassed against Rickey? That was harder, that was the test.

Suddenly he wanted to wake Rickey up, wanted Rickey wrapped around him, on top of him, inside him as intensely as he ever had. His gut clenched with an atavistic, purely sexual desire; his heart cried for Rickey, craving the physical and emotional engulfment of this man who was the center of his life. He moved toward Rickey, stopped, made himself roll over on his back again. What was he doing? You didn't wake up a concussion victim who'd just had a night from hell because you were horny.

He reached down and cupped his balls with one hand, grabbed his dick with the other and squeezed the head so hard that he gave an involuntary little grunt of pain.

"G, what are you doing?"

"Nothing."

"You jerking off?"

"Kinda."

"Is there some particular reason you'd lay there yanking your crank instead of just waking me up?"

"Well ... I figured you needed your rest."

Rickey snorted. "I couldn't sleep anyway with all that whispering, you old Holy Joe."

"Sorry. I just couldn't quit thinking—"

Rickey stopped his mouth with a kiss, palmed his dick and stroked, squeezed, stroked, mustering the expertise and affection G-man had been unable to summon. G-man wrapped his arms around Rickey's neck, careful to keep away from the knot on the back of Rickey's head.

And just like that, life was good again. There was no pall of fear, no blinding rage. He felt effortless tears on his cheeks. Rickey wasn't bothered; he just rubbed his face against G-man's, wetting them both further. One of Rickey's unspoken erotic mottoes was *the more bodily fluids, the better*; he loved the taste and feel of come, sweat, spit, tears.

He also liked to talk a lot; they both did, the meaningless call and response of love: *you like that, you want some more, yeah, oh, give me it, please give me it.* Their tastes were simple and similar and, sixteen years after that first kiss, as happily pedestrian as those of any old married couple.

Sex had almost always been able to fix things for them, whether tension between themselves or the depredations of the world at large. It was never complicated, never something they used as a tool or a bargaining chip, nor lost the knack of even on the rare occasions when something else was off-kilter between them. G-man didn't know if other couples were this lucky, but for their sake, he hoped so. The inextricable blend of friendship, passion, and soul-deep comfort with Rickey was by far the sweetest gift the world had ever given him. He couldn't imagine what life would be like without it; he suspected that without it there might well be no life.

V. SHAKE MOVES UP IN THE WORLD

Shake Vojtaskovic was deeply and secretly ashamed of the fact that when he got promoted to head chef of La Pharmacie, his first thought was *This is really gonna put the piss in Rickey's cornflakes.*

There was no reason for such a flash of pettiness. He'd worked with Rickey for more than a decade, off and on. Rickey wasn't always easy to get along with—hell, let's face it, Rickey wasn't *usually* easy to get along with—but Shake genuinely liked the guy. He was funny, insanely talented, basically good-hearted. There was just something about him that set your nerves on edge, that put tinfoil between your teeth, that made you think about pissing in his cornflakes.

Of course there was also the fact that Rickey had originally worked under him—Shake had been sous chef at the Peychaud Grill when Rickey and G-man were raw line cooks—and he had ended up working under Rickey, but that was no big deal. Rickey had hit the jackpot three years ago with one genius idea (a menu based entirely on booze) and financial backing from celebrity chef Lenny Duveteaux. Shake was more of a journeyman cook, fast and solid but not long on ambition. Though he'd been cooking since he was seventeen, this was the first head chef job he'd ever held, and he had only gotten it by way of a horrible accident.

Chef Götz LaVey took inordinate pride in his long, luxurious blond hair; he claimed it was a chick magnet equivalent to if not greater than a badass car, a fat bank account, or a huge dick (which he also claimed to possess, not that anybody wanted to know about that). He wore it pulled back in a ponytail when he was cooking, of course, but that hadn't helped him on the day the automatic meat slicer jammed while cutting the beef daube glace. If anything, the 'do had made it easier for the machine to yank his face into the gleaming machinery when the thing kicked back on as he was examining it. Individual strands of hair might have ripped out of his scalp, but the ponytail reeled him in like a bull redfish. During his twenty-one years in restaurant kitchens, Shake had grated his knuckles, sliced through his nails, amputated his fingertips, worked with hangovers and the stomach flu, and smelled chicken that had been rotting in a powerless walk-in cooler for two weeks, but he was proud of the fact that he'd never puked on the job ... until the day of the daube glace. There was no shame in it, though; everybody in the kitchen had puked that day.

Chef Götz wasn't incapacitated for long, but he would need plastic surgery and skin grafts. Worse, he'd turned blade-shy; word was he couldn't even touch a paring knife. The head chef job was Shake's by default, starting that night.

La Pharmacie achieved its trendiness by unearthing ancient Creole dishes and replicating them with a twist, often an ill-advised one; Götz had been planning to serve the daube glace with pineapple-Tabasco crème fraiche and Indian frybread. After he rode off in the ambulance, Shake pried the big jellied hunk of beef and aspic out of the slicer, washed off the blood, pared away the portions that had come in closest contact with Götz's rearranged physiognomy, and sliced it by hand. It didn't come out as paper-thin as it would have in the slicer, but then again, Shake still had both cheekbones and all of his nose. He trashed the crème fraiche and Indian frybread, sent the pantry bitch out for several boxes of Melba toast, and served the daube with a garlic horseradish cream. It was the bestselling app they'd had in weeks. La Pharmacie's owners started thinking maybe Götz should have made an appointment with the meat slicer ages ago.

Today, with Götz's mishap a few weeks in the past, *Big Easy* magazine had sent a photographer over to take Shake's picture for a feature on new chefs at old restaurants. Less than a year in business, La Pharmacie didn't qualify as an "old" restaurant by any standards, let alone New Orleans ones whereby any restaurant open for under two decades was considered a young upstart. Shake guessed there hadn't been much top-end turnover at Antoine's, Arnaud's, or Broussard's lately. He didn't mind having his picture made, but the photographer had left him a few back issues of the magazine, and as Shake flipped through it while eating his staff meal, he reflected that he didn't think he had ever seen an issue of *Big Easy* without a picture of Rickey in it. If it was possible to receive blowjobs from a magazine, *Big Easy* would put G-man out of business. Rickey had been on the cover twice already, once when they'd named him Chef of the Year and once when Liquor had won a James Beard award. Not that he didn't deserve it—he'd blown away most of his competition for the local honor, and a Beard award was a huge deal in the food world—but Shake couldn't help wondering whether Rickey would have made the cover both times if he'd looked like, say, Danny DeVito. Maybe so; God knew Lenny Duveteaux was no looker, and he'd probably been on more *Big Easy* covers than any other chef in history.

The picture Shake was looking at now showed both of Liquor's co-chefs at the top of a story about The New Cocktail Culture, whatever the hell that was. Both were dressed in their whites. Rickey sat at a table holding a glass of what could have been any kind of whiskey, but Shake knew it was Wild Turkey. That and beer were about the only things Rickey ever drank. His hair was a lot shorter than it had been the last time Shake had seen him, almost buzzed. His vivid eyes, more turquoise than strictly blue, blazed out of the photograph. Rickey was not a skinny guy by anybody's standards, but there was a sharp, nervous cast to his features that the camera loved. G-man stood behind him, tall and rangy, arms folded across his chest. He had removed his shades for the photograph, but Shake thought he should have kept them on; his squint and his long, blunt nose gave him a moleish look.

"Cocktails are a way of celebrating different cultures," Rickey was quoted as saying. "Look at how the Sazerac symbolizes New Orleans, how the daiquiri makes you think of pre-Communist Cuba. It's a little bit of somebody's world, right there in your glass." Shake knew Rickey loathed Sazeracs and thought any mixed drink with more than two ingredients was "floofy." He wondered if he, too, would have to become fluent in Media Bullshit now that he was a head chef. Maybe he should call Rickey, get some pointers.

He thought he'd done all right, though. He wondered if he'd hear from Rickey when the issue featuring him came out. Shake had always believed in giving credit where credit was due, and this interview had been no exception.

VI. STANK-ASS MOTHERFUCKER

G-man could usually tell whether or not it was going to be a good mail day by the look on Karl's face when he handed over the mail. Karl was the maitre d', and he knew Rickey's moods as well as anyone in the front of the house. Bills were neutral, a fact of life. Personal letters were bad, as they usually indicated a customer who'd been unhappy enough with some aspect of his meal to pen an impassioned screed about it. Food and trade magazines could go either way—Rickey liked looking at them, but generally found something in them to piss him off. Today's mail looked iffy: a hand-addressed letter from something called Ducks Unlimited, probably a financial solicitation, and the new issue of *Big Easy*.

Rickey was in the office making out next week's schedule. G-man dropped the letter on his desk and started paging through the copy of *Big Easy*. This didn't look good. A feature on new chefs at old restaurants quoted Shake Vojtaskovic, late of Liquor and currently of La Pharmacie, saying, "If I've learned anything from my last few jobs, it's to avoid the gimmick. Don't go for a cute trick or any easy sell. Just make good, simple food—that's what diners really want."

G-man must have made some small sound in his throat, because Rickey looked up, saw the expression on his face, and snatched the magazine out of his hands. He read silently, his lips moving. For a moment G-man dared to think maybe there wouldn't be an explosion. Then it came: "GIMMICK? GIMMICK? I'LL GIVE HIM 'AVOID THE GIMMICK'!" Rickey grabbed the phone. G-man hoped Shake wouldn't be at the restaurant, but it was no good; Rickey knew Shake's cell number.

A torrent of invective such as G-man had seldom heard, even from his notoriously foul-mouthed partner, came pouring out as soon as Shake picked up. "Gimmick? GIMMICK? You stank-ass motherfucker! You shit-sucking bitch, I'll give you a gimmick right up your wide tan track! You got such a problem with my gimmick, how come I never heard nothing about it when you was working here, making goddamn good money too, you motherfucking bitch-ass cracker—" At his angriest, Rickey tended to revert to a Lower Ninth Ward street patois that was somewhere between black and yat.

"Rickey," G-man could hear Shake saying on the other end. "Rickey, listen."

"Yeah, listen to my ass in your face, you fucking shitstain—"

"Rickey—"

"Give him a chance," G-man murmured.

"What," Rickey said finally. It was not a question; nor was there any hint of open-mindedness in it. Rickey was sensitive about his gimmick, always had been.

"Look," said Shake, and G-man reached across Rickey to punch the button that would put him on speakerphone; he wanted to hear this. "I know it sounds like I was talking about Liquor, but I swear to God, they took my shit out of context. I was talking about the stupid-ass gimmicks of the guy who was chef here before me. You know he was gonna serve beef daube glace with pineapple-Tabasco crème fraiche?"

Rickey was stunned into silence, but only for a moment. Then he glanced back down at the article and said, "Yeah, so what's this shit about your *last few jobs*? Seems to me working here was one of your *last few jobs*."

"Well ..."

"Yeah. That's pretty much what I thought."

"It was just the damn liquor all the time!" Shake cried, real desperation in his voice. "I think you're a hell of a chef, Rickey, and Liquor's a great restaurant. But god-DAMN, don't you ever get tired of having to find a way to stick booze in everything?"

"Booze set me free," Rickey said, and now his voice was not ghetto-raw, but icy. "Booze gave me a way to have my own restaurant with G, and cook the food I want to cook, and you better fucking believe I'm not sick of it. What I'm sick of is cooks who make their reputations here, then get a job in some trendy shithole and take a dump on us the first chance they get."

"Hey, I didn't make my *reputation* at Liquor. In case you forgot, I was sous chef at the Peychaud when you were one of Paco's little line bitches."

"Oh, right, and the name Shake Vojtaskovic was on the lips of culinary New Orleans. I guess I did forget. You know damn well the only cook that mattered at the Peychaud was Paco himself."

"Yeah, yeah, Paco Valdeon, a.k.a. God. I hadn't known Paco better, I'd a thought maybe you and him had a thing going on, the way you talk about him."

"WHAT? LISTEN, YOU CAN SUCK MY HAIRY NUTSACK, YOU FUCKING WAD OF FUCKJUICE—"

G-man plucked the receiver out of Rickey's hand, leaving Rickey to gawp at him in utter, frozen surprise. He put the phone to his own ear and said, "You know what, Shake? That was low even for you. But guess what? We forgive you, because you got no idea what you're getting into taking over that place, and the shit you'll be dealing with is gonna be worse than your wildest dreams."

Gently, he replaced the receiver in its cradle. For a minute he and Rickey just stared at each other. Then Rickey said, "Well, I think you handled that better than I did."

G-man laughed. After a moment, reluctantly, Rickey did too.

"Fuck him," said G-man. "It's his first head chef job, he thinks he's hot shit, that's all. He'll be Flavor of the Month for a little while and then everybody'll move on to some other trendy joint. People might laugh at our gimmick, but we got staying power."

"Yeah, cause New Orleanians like to get drunk."

"It's not just that and you know it. Here, open the rest of your mail."

"Just junk," Rickey muttered. He picked up the envelope from Ducks Unlimited and slit it open with an old paring knife. As he read, his eyes grew wide and the scowl left his face. When he had finished, he handed the letter to G-man.

Dear Chef John Rickey:

I am writing to you as a representative of Ducks Unlimited. As you may know, we are a major conservation organization dedicated to the preservation of wetlands and other waterfowl habitats. We are currently planning our annual banquet for 300 members to be held on December 14 at the Delta Grand, a historic theater in downtown Opelousas, which has a banquet space and a full cafeteria-style kitchen. We will have a number of guest speakers including our Guest of Honor, avid sportsman, bona fide Cajun, and former New Orleans Saints quarterback Bobby Hebert. We are interested in having you and your crew prepare the banquet as we want to do something a little different this year. We plan to have every course feature wild duck shot in Louisiana, and we understand that you are an expert at planning gourmet menus based around one ingredient. If interested, please contact me with a quote for the meal.

Sincerely yours,

Aristide "Tee" Fontenot
President, Ducks Unlimited, St. Landry Parish Chapter

VII. SEPTEMBER 14, 1986

John Randolph Rickey had turned thirteen eight days ago, and everybody knew thirteen was the age when you were really, for true, no-bullshit grown up. Even his mother agreed with him: convinced that pro football games were venues of peril and iniquity, Brenda had banned her son, a rabid Saints fan, from ever attending one. When he argued—which he frequently did—she laid the blame on his father. "If Oskar was here, babe, he could take you. That's a father's place. That Dome ain't no place for me."

"But Gary's dad could take us, or Little Elmer, Carl . . ." There was a variety of Stubbs sons old enough to accompany a pair of kids to a football game.

"No, I ain't gonna impose on them for your mortal responsibility. You over there enough as it is. Poor Mary Rose probably thinks she got her seven kids instead of six."

In fact, Mary Rose Stubbs had welcomed Rickey into her home since the boys had become inseparable at nine. Rickey wondered whether she'd keep doing so if she knew some of the weird thoughts he'd been having about her youngest son lately; she was a pretty strict Catholic. He doubted, though, that she would have any qualms about assuming his "mortal responsibility" for a couple of hours.

But none of that was at issue now. What mattered to Rickey was that, for reasons known only to herself, his mother had decided that thirteen was old enough for a boy—a young man, she'd called him—to attend a football game in the presence of someone other than his father. She had even bought his ticket, or at least arranged it somehow with Elmer Stubbs, who knew a guy in the ticket office. Rickey had been watching the Saints on TV ever since he could remember, but today he would see them in person, playing the Green Bay Packers.

The Saints really stank. Rickey wasn't a big enough fan to deny that; some of the longtime fans almost seemed to take a perverse pride in it. In 1980, they had won a single game and lost fifteen. Local

TV sportscaster Buddy Diliberto started wearing a paper bag over his head on the air, and fans followed suit. The next couple of seasons weren't much better. In 1983 they finally went 8–8, tying their previous record. The next two seasons slid downhill again, but this year the owner had hired a new coach, and last year's rookie quarterback had looked good in the preseason. The fans were hopeful in their fatalistic way.

Rickey had particular hopes for the quarterback, Bobby Hebert. He was a Louisiana boy: an actual Cajun from Cut Off, a wide spot on the bayou two hours south of New Orleans. Rickey had followed Hebert's career since his college days at Northwestern Louisiana, where he'd been a record-setter and got drafted into the USFL after his senior year. He'd hoped to go right into the NFL, but with a wife, a baby daughter, and food stamps buying the groceries, he couldn't afford to wait around and see if the more glamorous league would give him a whirl. He signed with the Michigan Panthers, made a nice chunk of change, and earned the nickname "The Cajun Cannon" with eighty-one touchdowns, more than 3500 yards per season, and two trips to the USFL championships.

In 1985, he became a free agent and it was a given that he'd enter the NFL. Everyone expected him to sign with the Seahawks until a senator in Cajun country decided that if a native son was going to play in the *real* pros, he should do it on Louisiana soil. The senator called the governor, Edwin Edwards, who was a Cajun too. The governor called the quarterback and said, "Hey, coonass, how come you tryin to go to Seattle? I hear it rains all the time out there and they got no food you'd wanna eat." And then Edwards set up a meeting with Saints owner Tom Benson, and Bobby Hebert came home to play.

Rickey loved this story. He'd grown up with poor kids who dreamed of making their fortunes as sports stars; it was his generation's version of a fairy tale. Even more than that, it was the food stamps. He and Brenda were no strangers to the envelope in the purse, the non-food items sorted into a separate pile on the conveyer belt, the occasional roll of the eyes from a wealthier shopper who'd made a pit stop at the ghetto Schwegmann's. Sure, Bobby Hebert was rich now ... but even so, it must have taken guts to say right out loud to a newspaper reporter that he'd had to feed his family with food stamps.

Also, he was pretty good-looking. Rickey didn't give that more weight than it deserved, but it didn't hurt, either.

Gary Francis Stubbs—not yet known as G-man; that badge of honor would be awarded him six years later by the most foul-mouthed chef he ever worked under—had turned thirteen in July and didn't think it was such a big deal. Rickey was an only child. When you had five brothers and sisters all older than you, thirteen didn't seem like such a lofty age; there was always somebody around to remind you that you didn't know anything yet. He'd also been to several Saints games. But this was the first one he'd ever been to with Rickey, and he was excited about that. His weird thoughts about Rickey lately had been very much like the ones Rickey had had about him, though, still fairly deep in the thrall of the Church, Gary hadn't given these thoughts free rein or even truly allowed them into his conscious mind. More than that, he simply *enjoyed* Rickey, always had. Everything was a lot more fun and interesting with Rickey around. To Gary, whose lifelong bad vision frequently caused him to think in optic terms, it was as if Rickey brought things into focus.

"You boys want a hot dog or anything?" said Elmer Stubbs. He was a lanky, sweet-natured man who closely resembled his son in looks and demeanor. They already had drinks, a vast beer for Elmer, another discreetly poured into two empty cups for the boys. Rickey had known how to drink beer for a couple of years and was just beginning to dabble in liquor, with mixed results. Gary, like most children of Sicilian blood, had been drinking red wine with dinner since he was weaned. Besides, Elmer said a man couldn't watch a football game without a beer to drink; to hear him tell it, such a thing was practically illegal.

"Nah, Daddy, let's get to our seats. We can grab something at the half."

They followed an usher's pointing hand, descended a short

flight of concrete steps, and emerged into the most amazing space Rickey had ever seen. He'd known the Superdome was big. You could see that much from the outside, and he knew the stats, of course: it covered fifty-two acres; it was the largest domed building in the world. But that didn't communicate an iota of what happened to your brain when you entered the part of the building that held the seats, the field, the tremendous overarching dome itself. Rickey had never been in any of the world's great cathedrals save St. Louis in Jackson Square, and then only on a school field trip where he'd idly wondered whether God would strike him dead if he palmed the five-dollar bill he could see poking out of the metal box where tourists stuck them before lighting candles. (Ultimately, more out of loyalty to Mary Rose than God, he hadn't.) Because he was not subject to religious awe, it was doubtful that any cathedral could have affected him as did this mind-assaulting expanse of bleachers and rafters and great translucent roof, ersatz sky glowing like neither day nor night. He felt a little dizzy. With the hand that was not holding his half-cup of beer, he grabbed a railing and wrapped his fingers tightly around it. For a moment it seemed to be all that tethered him to the concrete floor, that kept him from falling up, somehow, into the infinite moonscape of the Dome. Then he got a grip on himself and was fine.

"Don't worry," Elmer said. "We don't got sideline seats or nothing, but we ain't in the nosebleed section either. It's just down this way a little."

To Rickey, the seats seemed very close to the field, and he was enraptured from the coin toss on. The Saints scored a touchdown just a minute and a half into the game, and on the next drive, Bobby Hebert threw an eighty-four-yard pass to wide receiver Eric Martin. Rickey had understood the nickname "Cajun Cannon" in a theoretical way, but when he saw that ball leave Hebert's grasp and sail more than half the length of the field, moving so hard and fast that it seemed to bludgeon its way through the air, he realized for the first time that some people were simply designed to do a thing well. If they got to do it, then the world was a little better. It was the closest he had ever come to believing in any form of divine creation.

Hebert's bomb took the ball to the Packers' seven-yard line and set up an easy field goal for kicker Morten Anderson. Things sort of went downhill after that—the offense fell apart as it was apt to do, Bobby Hebert threw a couple of interceptions, and the defense had to mop up the mess—but the Saints won the game 24–10. By the time they filed out of the Dome, ascending those impossible levels among crowds of grinning, chattering fans dressed in black and gold, Rickey was euphoric, a little drunk on his second half-beer, and completely hooked. If someone had told him then and there that he'd just inherited a million dollars, his first splurge would have been a pair of season tickets. No, a trio, so Elmer could buy them beer. Elmer was absolutely right about the beer.

On the way home, in the backseat of Elmer's old rattletrap Pontiac, Rickey wondered if he would ever do anything as well as Bobby Hebert had thrown that eighty-four-yard bomb. He must have been put on earth to do something; certainly he had never felt purposeless. But what was his purpose? What talent lay buried in him that he didn't know about yet? Because he was not a reflective person by nature, this line of thought made him vaguely uneasy. He wished the talent would hurry up and show itself. On the heels of that thought, he wondered what Mary Rose was cooking tonight; he had been invited to stay for dinner and she was a wonderful cook.

"Hey, Daddy, I think Rickey's drunk," Gary said.

"Now don't you go telling your momma I bought you boys beer."

"Look at him, he's falling asleep. You damn waste case."

"Language," Elmer said automatically, but it was just something Mary Rose had drilled into him; he didn't really care if they cussed.

"I'm not drunk," Rickey said. "I'm thinking about the game."

"You're wasted on one beer. You got red eyes like a old stewbum."

Rickey roused himself from his daze to crawl across the seat and knuckle Gary's head, and Gary grabbed his arm, and they wrestled in the vast backseat while Elmer piloted them safely home. The beer was still pleasantly muzzy in his head, the sensation of his best friend's skin on his own was delicious in a presexual way, and all in all, Rickey reflected then and later—even years later—that had probably been one of the finest days of his life.

VIII. DUCK

Of course, his purpose and his talent turned out to be cooking. He'd started to realize that a year or so later, when he began to experiment with recipes from the cookbooks his mother bought but seldom used. When they were fifteen, he and G-man had gotten their first restaurant jobs as dishwashers at a Lower Ninth Ward greasy spoon, where Rickey eventually pestered the owner into letting them work the grill.

The thought that he might now design an elaborate meal for Bobby Hebert, who had first put into his head the whole idea of purposes and talents, overwhelmed him completely. The quarterback had long since retired and was now hosting a local sports talk radio show, but as far as Rickey was concerned, he was the biggest star Louisiana had ever produced. Still good-looking, too—better, probably, with a wash of silver in his black hair and perfect new teeth to replace the ones knocked out in Tampa Bay and all the other smashmouth games. The Cannon hadn't been one of those quarterbacks who danced around the action; he had always played hard, hard.

G-man saw all this going through Rickey's head and pointed at the letter. "Look. See there? Banquet for three hundred. That means steam-table splooge. Quit picturing yourself swanning around some cute little private dining room serving perfect dishes to Bobby Hebert."

"It wouldn't have to be splooge. We could find a way to do it right."

"We can find a way to do something they'll love, sure. I'm not saying we shouldn't do it. I just want you to give up the idea of being Bobby Hebert's personal chef."

"I'm not ..." For the first time since he'd opened it, Rickey looked up from the letter, saw G-man's face and G-man's absolute knowledge of him. Suddenly embarrassed, he laid the letter facedown on the desk. "Hell. I dunno. Maybe we shouldn't do it. Liquor, beef, now duck—I'm sick of people thinking I'm some kinda one-trick whore."

"Pony."

"Pony, hell. People get the idea you do one thing well and ask you to do it over and over again, they think you're a whore, not a damn pony."

Looking at Rickey, G-man remembered a dream he'd had a few nights ago. In it, he was the same broke-ass Lower Ninth Ward boy he'd always been, but Rickey was the scion of some rich family, the kind of kid who might have been an escort at the Rex ball. Oddly, this vast imaginary gulf in their social status had made their budding relationship not more difficult but easier; no one suspected, whereas in real life their folks had pegged it almost immediately because the two families lived just a few blocks apart and saw each other all the time. (Despite this proximity, Rickey *could* have put on airs about his neighborhood if he'd wanted to. He had grown up in the subsection closer to the river known as Holy Cross, while the Stubbses lived on the other side of St. Claude Avenue and were plain old Lower Ninth Warders.) They had thought they were being terribly secretive, but it's hard to be secretive when you are sixteen and in the throes of either true love or desperate lust; the combination makes it wholly impossible. In G-man's dream, rather than their hungry bouts of after-school sex where and when they could get them, they had been able to spend entire greedy nights in Rickey's huge Uptown house, in his bedroom far away from the rest of his sketchy dream-family, wallowing in it the way they really had done when they first moved in together. Nineteen, with nothing but a few crappy pots and pans and an old double bed G-man's sister Rosalie had given them. They'd worn out the bed within a year, though it had had to serve them two more.

G-man wondered now whether the dream could have had something to do with how their life had actually turned out. Rickey wasn't an old-family scion, but his ideas and his ability to seduce people's palates had brought them, if not exactly fame and fortune, then at least a lot more attention and cash than they'd ever expected to have. More than G-man had expected, anyway. He sometimes wondered if Rickey hadn't known all along, at the bottom of his mind, that he was going to build an interesting life for the two of them. They had a better bed, if not quite as much time as they'd like to wallow in it. And, of course, they did live Uptown now. People they knew from the Lower Ninth Ward still made a certain face sometimes upon learning of it, a kind of contemptuous wince. In the minds of some lifelong downtowners, anyone who lived Uptown was white, rich, racist, and probably a crook.

Without Rickey, G-man knew perfectly well, he would be a rock-solid line cook or sous chef in somebody else's restaurant. He would never have been head chef—would have deliberately avoided it—and he might not have started cooking at all, might have gotten a job at the candy factory where his father and his brother Henry worked. Now, because of Rickey, they got their pictures in magazines. They had been on TV once, interviewed by the lady from *Steppin' Out*. And, G-man had known as soon as he read the letter, now they would get a chance to travel. Opelousas was just three hours away, but to G-man, who had only gone farther than the Mississippi Gulf coast thrice in his life, it seemed a whole different world. It was the hometown of Louisiana's first celebrity chef, Paul Prudhomme, who had invented a dish so popular that it endangered an entire species of fish. There were black people there who played zydeco music on accordions and washboards. The police chief was always making the news for conducting war games (he called them "Homeland Security drills") without warning anybody first. G-man couldn't imagine what kind of place it would be, but he could hardly wait to get a look at it.

He occasionally wished Rickey liked to travel more. They could have gone to food shows and guest-chef appearances in Chicago, Napa, even France—all sorts of places, but Rickey said they wouldn't have a chance to see anything because they'd be too busy acting like trained seals. That might or might not be true, but G-man knew the real reason they hadn't accepted any of the invitations was because Rickey purely hated to leave New Orleans. He was like a little old man already, the way he had to be pried out of his natural element. He wouldn't even be considering the Ducks Unlimited gig if not for the promised presence of Bobby Hebert.

"You're not a one-trick pony or a whore either," he said. "You're a damn good chef who knows what Louisiana people like. We got people come from all over the state to eat at Liquor. We'll just take it to them for a change. Hell, you know what? Bobby Hebert's probably *already* eaten here."

"No he hasn't."

"How do you know?"

Rickey looked back down at the desk, and G-man thought he was blushing a little. "Cause when he took the WWL gig, I told Karl to come tell me right away if he ever came in, and if it was our night off, to call me."

"Oh." G-man thought about this for a moment, but it didn't really surprise him. "Well, anyway, come on, be serious. Of course we're gonna do it. How many cooks ever get the chance to cook a whole dinner using wild ducks?"

"What're we gonna do for the dessert?"

They looked at each other and suddenly grinned, because it was such a silly question. Tanker would take great pleasure in concocting a dessert that involved duck cracklins or a triangle of candied duck skin or some other crazy thing. It would sound disgusting and be delicious. Those were the kinds of dishes he lived for.

"You know what else?" Rickey said.

"What?"

"This'll put a fucking knot in Shake's panties."

Privately, G-man wondered: even with Bobby Hebert and a semi-famous chef, how much press was a Ducks Unlimited banquet in Opelousas likely to get here in New Orleans? If Rickey wanted to think so, though, there was no reason to argue. Some of Rickey's best ideas came as the result of vendettas.

IX. LIKE A RAT IN THE WALL

The thing was—and Rickey hadn't even figured this out completely in his own mind, let alone spoken of it to G-man—that he was sick of being the kind of person who thrived on rages and vendettas. It was the cliché of the temperamental chef, the fat tyrant screaming in the kitchen. He wasn't much of a screamer, but plenty of his employees were scared of him and all were cautious around him. That part he liked; you couldn't run a restaurant right if your employees weren't a little scared of getting reamed out by you. It was the effect on the rest of his life that he didn't like so much. Last year, during a bout of back trouble, he'd had his first physical in years and learned that his blood pressure was high. Not dangerously high, but high for a guy thirty-two years old who got a lot of physical activity. He didn't put much faith in doctors and only thought of it at odd moments, but he wondered if it was something he *should* be worried about.

Worse than the mystifying prognostications of doctors was the gnawing he felt inside himself, every day, almost every single minute of his life. It was like a rat gnawing in the wall of an old house, scraping ceaselessly at the punky wood until you thought the noise would drive you crazy and you started pounding on the wall. Lower Ninth Ward rats didn't always run away when you pounded, either. Rickey knew those rats well, and it seemed that one had moved Uptown with him, had taken up residence in his head, always there, doing its thing. The only times he didn't feel it were when he was sleeping, drunk, or having sex. G-man could ease it by talking to him sometimes, but even G-man couldn't make it entirely go away.

The conversation with Shake had woken the rat up good; it was fairly spinning in there. He'd think about it all night during service, replaying it in his mind, imagining how he could have given it to Shake even worse. God, he was so sick of that. He wanted to find a peaceful place within himself, the kind of place that G-man just seemed to have naturally. He'd asked G-man about it many times, but G-man didn't really know why he was the way he was; couldn't know; it was like asking him why he had chestnut-brown eyes when all his brothers' and sisters' were nearly black. At best, he might say something about the steadiness of his favorite basketball players, Kareem Abdul-Jabbar, Karl Malone, Michael Jordan or some other mighty, unflappable hoopster. He drew strength from these things, and from whatever his belief in God meant to him. Rickey could not profit from such things. But maybe, if he were to cook a great meal for Bobby Hebert, who in a way had helped show him his purpose …

Christ, he was putting too much into the thing. At this rate he'd give himself a nervous breakdown before he even figured out the amuse-bouche.

So he pulled himself together and finished his prep work, and thankfully it was a busy night and he was able to lose himself in the rush during service. The next morning he got up early, called Aristide "Tee" Fontenot, talked over the details of the event, and offered a price that Fontenot accepted immediately. Rickey wondered if he should have gone higher, but he didn't really care; the price he'd named would net them a decent profit, and the presence of Bobby Hebert would be an immeasurable bonus.

With hours left before he had to be at the restaurant, he started going through his cookbook collection. It had gotten a lot bigger over the past few years, since he'd had a little money, but for this he went to his old, well-thumbed, stained standards: Richard Olney, Elizabeth David, M.F.K. Fisher. Olney's *French Menu Cookbook* was his favorite cookery volume of all time, but it was no help here. Olney only dealt in foie gras, which of course they wouldn't have unless "Tee" Fontenot was willing to somehow catch a flock of wild ducks alive, keep them in a pen, and force-feed them twice a day until the banquet. His Elizabeth David omnibus was more useful. She had a great-sounding duck dish with cherries that Rickey was amused to realize his old friend and nemesis, the late celebrity chef Cooper Stark, had blatantly ripped off for his own cookbook. She also had duck in daube, which could be prepared ahead. In his mind's eye, Rickey saw it on a plain white plate—none of this holed, weird-colored, boomerang-shaped business for him—the translucent golden-brown aspic glistening, the duck meat subtly flecked with red and black pepper. Old-school. Confit could be done ahead, too, another good classic dish. They'd do both of those for sure.

Prepared ahead. Rickey scowled. How was that going to work? He picked up the phone and called Fontenot back. "Listen, Mr. Fontenot—"

"Aw, now none a' that. I awready told you, you gotta call me Tee."

"Tee," Rickey said with a little difficulty; in his mind it was a woman's name, one he associated with the old-line New Orleans restaurant Commander's Palace and the Brennan family. "Listen, what if I had some dishes I wanted to make ahead? Would you be able to get me some ducks in advance?"

"Like how many?"

Rickey thought about it. He could bone out the bodies and use them for the daube, keeping the wings and legs for the confit. He'd have to buy some duck fat—wild ducks were way too lean to make confit on their own—but that was OK. Two legs and two wings per duck, three hundred people ... the servings would be small, of course. "Fifty?" he said.

Fontenot whistled. "Well, the season opens November 10. Birds runnin good, we might could get you fifty by the first of December. Some teal, pins, gadwalls, maybe a few dos gris if they early. Fly 'em into the city so they'll be nice and fresh. On a plane, I mean—their flyin days gonna be over!" Fontenot laughed heartily at his own joke.

Rickey thought about it. He'd been mostly lost after "teal," but had scrawled down phonetic approximations of the other names and would look them up on the Internet later. What mattered was the timing. Thirteen days, if the ducks arrived on time; a day to cut them up and do the preserving, so call it twelve; that would be just enough time for the confit to get good and seasoned. "I can work with that," he said.

"Good boy, good boy. Anything else I can help you with?" This was pronounced *Anyting else I kin help yoo wit?*; there was no *–th* sound in the Cajun accent.

"Not right now. I'll probably call you back about fifty times, though."

"You do that." *You doo dat.*

So: a cold amuse-bouche of duck en daube; then the confit with a nice vinaigrette salad, maybe arugula and frisée, sharp greens to cut the richness of the duck fat. But lots of people didn't like frisée. It could be tough, and it looked so ugly if it was even a little bit old. Bobby Hebert might not like it. Rickey had a nightmare vision of the Cajun Cannon fussily picking frisée out of his salad and setting it on the side of his plate. Red-leaf lettuce? It was tasteless, but it would look good with the dark green arugula. No! He had it: radicchio, slightly wilted in a little of the duck fat! It would be gorgeous *and* delicious.

So there was one, no, two dishes. Then a soup. They'd have to do a gumbo, of course; this crowd would probably string up the chef if they didn't get a gumbo. He didn't need a recipe for that; if he couldn't make a damn good duck and sausage gumbo after seventeen years in New Orleans kitchens, he might as well hang up his toque. He'd order some andouille from Poche's in Breaux Bridge …

But what if a damn good duck and sausage gumbo in New Orleans was only a mediocre one in Opelousas? Cajuns took their gumbo very seriously; their entire Mardi Gras celebration was based around it, or so Rickey, who'd never spent a Fat Tuesday outside of New Orleans, believed. Shit, he'd better do some research on that too.

G-man came into the kitchen rubbing his eyes, dressed in a pair of boxer shorts and a faded Utah Jazz T-shirt. "You're up early," he said.

"Ain't no jazz in Utah," Rickey answered. It was something he always said when he saw G-man wearing that particular T-shirt, and G-man paid it no more mind than he would if Rickey had said, "It's hot today." He wandered to the coffeemaker, poured himself a cup of the brew Rickey had fixed hours ago, tasted it, grimaced, and set about making a new pot.

When G-man finally had a cup of coffee in front of him, Rickey turned around the yellow legal pad he'd been making notes on and slid it across the table. G-man read his notes, frowning at the list of odd duck names—TEAL, PINS, GATWOLLS, DO GREE. "Aren't these dishes kinda labor-intensive for three hundred? I thought we'd just do your basic salad, gumbo, main course, dessert."

"Well, you thought wrong. I'm not doing some boring-ass banquet menu for these people. This is gonna be restaurant-quality food."

"You're not doing some boring-ass banquet menu for Bobby Hebert, you mean."

"No, I don't!" Rickey pulled his notebook back across the table. "Quit fucking teasing me about Bobby Hebert for one second. I'm not cranking out boring-ass banquet food for *anybody*. These people are paying good money and they want a fancy meal, the kinda shit they think we eat all the time in New Orleans. I'm damn well gonna give it to them."

"OK, OK." G-man's eyes suddenly looked more naked than usual, and Rickey felt bad for snapping at him.

"Sorry. I didn't mean to yell at you. I been up for hours—I probably need some more coffee." Rickey got up and poured himself a cup. "But seriously, G, I want to do this thing right. I'm not making splooge because I don't think that's what they want. I'm thinking more like a tasting menu, at least seven or eight courses."

"Fine. But where are you gonna get the crew?"

"We'll just close the restaurant for a couple days. Take the crew up there with us the day before the dinner, stay overnight, get into the hall early the next day and do all our prep."

G-man was shaking his head. "Rickey, what the fuck? We can't close the restaurant on a weekend right before Christmas. You know we're always busy then."

"This gig's paying well enough we can afford it. Hell, we could afford to stay over an extra night in Opelousas, see the sights."

"But you gotta consider the bad will it'll create. Walk-ins want dinner after they just spent all day Christmas shopping, find out we're closed—bang, they're pissed off, they're gonna cry and whine and tell the whole world about it."

"Fuck 'em," Rickey said stubbornly. "Let 'em go eat at La Pharmacie. That's the hot new place anyway, right?"

"Might not be by Christmas."

Rickey smiled, then scowled again. "Well, I don't care. That's what I was gonna do. If you really don't think we can close, we'll leave Terrance in charge of the kitchen with Marquis and Devonte. You, me, Tanker, and Jacolvy, we can knock out the dinner. I'm not one of these pussies who needs a crew of fifteen."

"Jacolvy? He doesn't know shit." Jacolvy was an eighteen-year-old Rickey had hired through a juvenile offenders' job training program. As a kid, he'd specialized in home burglaries and car robberies, and Rickey still kept a close eye on him around the kitchen equipment. He worked harder than any raw recruit Rickey had ever hired, though, and they had a soft spot for him because he'd grown up in the heart of the Lower Ninth Ward, on Tennessee Street right by the Industrial Canal levee.

"He'll be our prep bitch. Plus, by then, he'll know two more months' worth of shit than he does now."

G-man finished his coffee and got some more. On his face was a hangdog look that annoyed Rickey deeply. Finally he said, "What if I didn't do the dinner? You take everybody else with you. I'll stay and run the kitchen here by myself. I can do it for a couple nights if I had to, or maybe Lenny could lend me a cook."

"Fucking A! Run the kitchen by yourself, right. I thought if there was one person I never had to get into a dick-measuring contest with, it was you."

"I'm not trying to get into a dick-measuring contest. I just don't think we should close the restaurant and I don't think four cooks is enough to do a seven-course tasting menu for three hundred."

"Seven or eight courses," Rickey insisted. "A lot of the shit'll be prepped in advance—all we'll have to do is plate it up. I'd just as soon do this dinner without my knives as try to do it without you, and besides, I know you want to go to Opelousas."

It was true; Rickey could see it in G-man's face. *I never take him anywhere*, Rickey thought. But why *go* anywhere, when you got right down to it? Opelousas was fine; they could be back in New Orleans in three hours if need be. The thought of being more than three hours from New Orleans or unable to return to the city immediately for any reason filled Rickey with a deep and nameless dread. He supposed he wasn't very adventurous in some ways, but adventure outside of New Orleans had never worked out all that well for him. *Outside the city limits, the true heart of darkness begins.*

This adventure would work out well, though; he intended to make sure of it. He wasn't heading into the heart of darkness. He was cooking for Bobby Goddamn Hebert, and he'd be goddamned if G-man was going to kill his buzz.

Rickey turned to a fresh sheet of paper and dove back into his pile of cookbooks. G-man watched him for a moment, still worried but unable to keep himself from grinning a little. This fancy tasting-course plan sounded like the height of folly to him, but if Rickey was determined to make it happen, he probably would. After all, he had a winning track record.

X. NOT TO HAVE FIRE IS TO BE A SKIN THAT SHRILLS

Shake finished leaving another irate message for his produce guy and hung up shaking his head. It was like people didn't hear what you told them, or simply didn't care. He had ordered pea tendrils and Sultan's Ruby heirloom tomatoes, specifically mentioning that he planned to combine them in a salad. It would have been an easy-ass dish for which he could charge $12 without anyone batting an eye. Unfortunately, he hadn't been here to inspect the order when it arrived yesterday, and the pea tendrils had made it but the tomatoes had not. Now the produce guy wouldn't return his calls. If he got the heirlooms today, he could still make the salad. After that, the pea tendrils would be past their prime and he'd have to use them in another dish. Maybe some sautéed Gulf fish with a vinaigrette sauce, like he'd seen Cole Parker doing over at Poivre.

Shake didn't have a lot of experience designing specials and was a little dismayed at the constant temptation to rip off other chefs, chefs who seemed to have their fingers on the pulse of the fine-dining crowd more firmly than he did. Well, if he paired the pea tendrils with the fish, he'd use morels instead of the oyster mushrooms Cole Parker was doing. *White* morels, if he could get them. Nobody in New Orleans was doing white morels.

"Hey, Shake?" said the manager, leaning familiarly through the pass. That was another problem—two, actually: nobody in the place called him Chef, and the front-of-the-house people felt far too comfortable in his kitchen. He'd never thought he would care about the former issue, but it turned out that when even the greenest pantry bitches forgot to address you as Chef, it affected the entire restaurant's perception of you. As for the latter, no chef wanted front people in his kitchen unless they were good-looking waitresses impressed by a white coat. Not that there had been much of that at Liquor, not under that tyrannical turquoise eye.

"Yeah, what?"

"The people from *Cornet* are here. They said you were supposed to do an interview and get your picture made for the fall dining guide."

"Aw, crap."

He'd begun to understand why Rickey sometimes seemed to have extreme tunnel vision: if you didn't tune out the distractions, you'd never get anything done. Publicity begat publicity, and there was always somebody wanting to take your picture, get a quote, jack you off. The only good part was that sometimes the handjobs were literal rather than figurative. Plenty of women really *did* lubricate at the sight of a white coat; he'd always taken advantage of that, but it was a lot easier to do so when you were the head chef.

That wouldn't be happening today, though, he reflected as the pair from the local freebie paper entered the kitchen. The writer was a plump little man with a long, snuffling nose and an unfortunate mustache. The photographer was a broad-shouldered woman with a buzz cut, an earring in the shape of a pink triangle, and a T-shirt that said WHAT WAS YOUR FIRST CLUE?

"Humphrey Wildblood," said the writer, extending a short-fingered hand. "We don't have much space—I've got to accommodate all the restaurants that advertise in *Cornet*—so I'll need you to boil down your philosophy of cooking to a sentence or two."

The photographer glanced around the kitchen. Her gaze settled on the six-burner flattop and the big sauté pans hanging above it. "Say," she said, "do you think you could set something on fire?"

"Uh, I'm not really cooking anything yet."

"Yes, but it would *look cool in the picture*," she told him patiently, as if addressing an infant or someone who'd maybe won a silver medal in the Special Olympics.

"I don't know, Dymphna," said Humphrey Wildblood. "I always like those pictures where the chef's sitting at a table with a nice glass of wine."

Dymphna? thought Shake, but he knew when he was beaten. If his choices were the dreaded Wineglass Shot or setting something on fire, he'd take the option that made him look like a macho idiot over the one that made him look like a preening pussy.

As he poured cheap bourbon into an empty pan and tilted it so that the flames caught the liquor and billowed up like a special effect at a Kiss concert, Shake prayed that Rickey wouldn't see this picture. He knew there was little chance of getting his wish—every cook, waiter, and foodie in New Orleans looked at *Cornet*'s fall dining guide, if only to snark at Humphrey Wildblood's alternately acidic and ass-kissing descriptions—but every now and then the gods smiled. He had thought they were doing so when they dragged Götz into the meat slicer and gave him this job, but he was already beginning to wonder.

XI. THE HELPING HAND

"What the hell is this thing?" G-man asked Jacolvy for the third time.

He'd entered the walk-in to find the kid rummaging surreptitiously among boxes and bins. At first he'd just hung back and watched, wondering if Jacolvy was going to steal a couple of steaks or a bag of shrimp. He hated thinking that way about his employees, but he and Rickey didn't have any prior experience with the juvenile offenders training program and didn't know what to expect from an eighteen-year-old who'd already wreaked more havoc in the world than the two of them combined. However, it soon became apparent that Jacolvy was intent not on removing anything but on concealing something. That was when G-man cleared his throat and stepped forward. He wasn't entirely opposed to drugs on the premises, but if they were going to be there, he was damn sure going to know about them.

"Chef! I was just, uh, uh …"

G-man reached up and grabbed the item he'd seen Jacolvy drop behind a row of empty stock containers. It wasn't a dime bag of pot or a crack rock like he'd figured, but a small packet of black cloth wrapped in white thread. It gritted between his fingers as if some very dry, stemmy pot might be inside, but somehow he didn't think this was about drugs after all: there was something ceremonial-looking, even elegant about the little packet. "What is it?" he asked.

Jacolvy dodged the question. G-man asked him again, and he obfuscated. The third time G-man asked, though, the kid's shoulders sagged and he seemed to give up. "It's a toby. A helping hand. My momma give it to me. She made me promise to hide it here in the restaurant so I could keep my job."

"Keep your … ?" A tingle ran through G-man's fingers. "Is this some kinda voodoo thing? I thought you were Catholic." G-man glanced down at Jacolvy's right forearm, thin but beginning to be ropy with the muscles you got from sautéing; there was a spark of talent in him, and they'd been letting him make a bunch of staff meals. "You got a rosary tattoo."

"I ain't nothin one way or the other. That's for my momma. See, it got her initials in the middle, DRT—Drylean Renee Turner. She's Spiritual."

"Spiritual?" Now G-man was completely baffled; as far as he knew, that was a kind of song people sang in black churches, but not a whole religion.

"African Spiritual church. She go to St. Anthony of Padua on Almonaster."

"Sounds Catholic to me."

"They like all them Catholic saints awright, and they pray to Jesus and say the rosary. It ain't no voodoo church like people think. They just do a little root work, little candle burnin. My momma, she take me to the Reverend, say she fraid I gonna get fired cause I missed one little old parole meetin. Reverend wrote my name a buncha times on a piece of paper, wrote the name of this restaurant, y'all's names."

"Me and Rickey?"

"Yeah. Then he taped 'em to the bottoms of candles and made me say prayers and eat pecan pie while he burned 'em."

"Pecan *pie?*" G-man was sure he couldn't have heard that last part right.

"Yeah. It wasn't as good as my grammaw's, but it was tollable." Now that G-man had made him start this story, Jacolvy seemed determined to finish it. "Then the Rev, he give me that there helping hand, say I gotta hide it here in the restaurant. Say I ain't gonna get fired long as I do my job and nobody find that thing."

"You're not gonna get fired if you do your job *anyway*," G-man said. "You really believe this stuff?"

"I dunno, man." Jacolvy looked miserable, but defiant. "I heard Chef sayin you went to Mass one day. You really believe them priests turn wine into blood and all?"

"I don't take Communion anymore." But G-man saw the kid's point. "I don't know. I was raised with all that stuff."

"Well, you know how it is then." Jacolvy's thin face was miserable; G-man saw that his eyes, which had always had a hooded, closed-off look, now sparkled with ill-concealed tears. "Mostly I just done it for my momma. She so desperate to see me do right, keep a job, and I done messed up so much ..." He shrugged helplessly. "I just thought maybe it make her believe in me, make her get some peace in her heart about me."

G-man felt a lump in his throat. If he didn't watch it, he was going to be back here bawling in the cooler with their young felon. He handed the little packet back to Jacolvy. "Just stick it up there on the shelf," he said. "Get it back in there good. We clean these lower shelves twice a month, but nobody ever cleans way back there." G-man started to turn away.

"Thanks, Chef." A pause, then: "Please don't tell Chef. He'd fire me for sure, I know it."

G-man looked back at him, more perplexed than ever. "Rickey wouldn't fire you for this. How come you think he would?"

"Cause he hates any kinda religious shit. I could tell by the way he said you went to Mass. I mean, he wasn't talkin trash about you or nothin, don't get the wrong idea, but ..."

Jacolvy shrugged his thin shoulders expressively. With his slight build, huge brown eyes, and veneer of thuggishness over the soul of a man willing to get tattoos and do weird religious ceremonies for his momma, he was beginning to remind G-man of Allen Iverson, the NBA shooting guard who seemed to have ten pounds of heart for every pound of his body weight. Despite his scrapes with the law—hell, Iverson had had them too—G-man suddenly felt sure that Jacolvy was going to be a roller once he really learned his way around the kitchen.

"Well, Rickey isn't a big fan of organized religion, but he's not gonna fire you over it. That'd be illegal, for one thing."

"It would?" Jacolvy looked as amazed as if G-man had just told him he'd be expediting tonight.

"Sure, man. Didn't all those juvie courts and lawyers teach you anything?"

"Shhyeah. Taught me you better have a lotta fuckin money or the system gonna grind you down to a nub. I never met nobody in charge, black or white, who thought I was anything but trash till I got in the job trainin program."

"Shit. Well, I ..." Now G-man was embarrassed, but he wasn't sure why. The awkward moment was broken by the sound of loud, maniacal laughter coming from the direction of Rickey's office.

"Jeez, I better go see what he's up to. Say, you wanna work an off-site banquet with us in December? You'd have to stay over a couple nights in Opelousas."

"I gotta check in with my PO, but yeah, sure, if she say I can."

"Let me know if you need us to talk to her," G-man said, and left Jacolvy to hide his helping hand in peace. As he hurried down the hall, he could hear Rickey pounding his fists on the desk, still laughing insanely.

"Dude. You finally just lost it, huh? I gotta stop what I'm doing and drive you down to the mental ward at Charity?"

Rickey looked up. The fall dining issue of *Cornet* was spread out on the desk before him. Wordlessly, he pointed to a picture. G-man walked around the desk and stood behind Rickey, leaning over to see what he'd gotten so worked up about. The picture showed a rather grim-looking Shake in chef's whites, his face almost obscured by the more photogenic tongues of fire shooting up from his pan. Beneath it, the caption read, "SNAKE VOJTASKOVIC of La Pharmacie is a flamer extraordinaire."

"Oh, *no*," whispered G-man, almost in awe. "They *didn't*."

"They ... they ..." Rickey gulped, wiped his eyes. "They did."

"*Flamer extraordinaire?*" G-man bit the inside of his cheek, trying to maintain some sort of composure. His mother had taught him not to laugh at the misfortune of others.

"Snake," Rickey said, and set himself off again.

G-man couldn't help it; he started laughing. By the time he got himself under control, Rickey had picked up the phone and was dialing.

"Oh, you're not gonna—"

"Yeah, is this Chef Snake?" Rickey didn't pause to hear an answer, but plowed ahead. "I'm proud of you for finally taking one for the side. Look, you know I'm not really into the whole gay pride thing, but I think I got a rainbow flag around here somewhere. You can have it if you want to, you know, represent."

Rickey didn't have the speakerphone on this time, but G-man could still hear the resounding "FUCK YOU, RICKEY" and click of Shake ending the call.

G-man leaned against the wall, laughing so hard his stomach hurt. He slid slowly to the floor, grabbed a stray napkin from atop a nearby pile of cookbooks and magazines, and waved it in the air, surrendering. "Stop. I'm gonna die."

"So's Shake. I mean, Snake." In the worst faux-queeny voice G-man had ever heard, Rickey said, "Giiiiirrrrl, he's just gonna *die* of embarrassment."

G-man dropped the napkin and fell over on his side, legs kicking weakly in the air. If he didn't stop laughing soon, he thought he might actually pee himself.

"Rickey?" It was Tanker, standing at the office door. "Hey, Rickey, I need to—Jesus, what are you clowns *doing*?"

Rickey showed him the picture.

"Oh, no way," said Tanker. He looked again, laughed, and shook his head. "No fucking way. What, you got Humphrey Wildblood in your pocket now?"

"Course not," Rickey said with dignity. "I just got a pure heart and a damn good menu, and old Snake's starting to reap what the world owes him."

"You got a damn good menu," G-man said. "I don't know about the pure heart."

"Well, *you* got one anyway."

"Don't fuck with Chef Goodmenu and Chef Pureheart," said Tanker, rolling his eyes. "Instant karma gonna get you, gonna knock you off your feet."

"What feet? He crawls on his belly like a *rrrrreptile*."

"Yeah, when he's not busy being a flamer extraordinaire."

"Oh my God," said G-man, picking up the napkin again and mopping his face with it. "Oh, jeez, please stop, I'm begging you."

By the beginning of service that night, the item had been cut out of the *Cornet*, taped carefully on the wall beside the expediting station, and pointed out to everyone who entered the kitchen. He might or might not make his proud mark on the world at large, but here at Liquor, Shake Vojtaskovic would never again be known by any other name than Snake the Flamer.

XII. THE WINE, THE MOONLIGHT, THE PROSCIUTTO

After closing the restaurant one night, Rickey and G-man drove out to a spot they liked on the shore of Lake Pontchartrain. They brought a bottle of wine—neither of them was much of a oenophile, but G-man was slowly working his way through the Italian reds, learning about better versions of what had always been on his family table—and sat on the seawall passing it back and forth, legs dangling above the surf, not talking much, watching the moonlight ripple on the dark unquiet water. It was October now, often one of the most beautiful months in New Orleans, but this had been a hot one and the breeze from the lake felt good on their slightly kitchen-baked faces.

As the level in the wine bottle decreased, they began to lean against each other. Eventually Rickey was leaning a little more, and G-man slipped an arm around his shoulders. They weren't much given to public displays of affection, but there was nobody else out here to see. Rickey let his head nestle into the curve of G-man's neck. His hair stank of sweat and grease, his skin was sticky, and there was a crusty stain on the sleeve of his T-shirt, but to G-man he felt wonderful.

"G?" Rickey said sleepily.

"Yeah, sweetheart?"

"You think fourteen days is enough to make a good duck prosciutto?"

G-man sighed.

"What?"

"Nothing. I just never thought I'd be jealous of a hundred ducks."

"Fifty ducks. Fifty is all we're getting in advance. Then around a hundred more when we get there, depending on how the season goes."

"Half a duck per person, huh?"

"Maybe a little more for Bobby Hebert."

"Can't we round it out with some city ducks?"

"Mr. Fontenot says they don't want any city ducks. What was it he called 'em? ... Oh yeah. Marshmallows."

G-man laughed, then turned his head and put his lips against the soft hollow behind Rickey's ear.

"Mmmm ... hey, listen ..."

"Wha?" said G-man, muffled.

"What if we *wrapped* duck breasts in the prosciutto and ... OW! Goddammit, G! Jesus Christ, you fucking *bit* me on the fucking *earlobe*! I can't believe it!"

"Sorry. I didn't mean to bite down like that."

"Do you want to go home or something?"

"I guess we can talk about ducks just as well here as there."

"We don't have to talk about ducks."

"You sure you can stop for five minutes?"

"I been a little single-minded, huh?"

"Yeah, like the Saints are having a little bit of a losing season ... Aw, don't worry about it," he said to Rickey's wounded expression. "I know you gotta be single-minded about stuff like this. It's just, you know, it's only October."

"Exactly! It's way too early to say they're having a losing season. They could still go twelve and four."

"Sure they could, Mr. Who Dat, but I was talking about the banquet. You can't spend your every waking minute between now and December thinking about it. You still got a restaurant to run."

"Course I got a restaurant to run. But I *know* how to do that. I don't know how to do this banquet."

"We worked banquets before, back at Reilly's. And you done 'em at Escargot's."

"Yeah, but I never *planned* any. And besides, those were garbage. This one has to be perfect."

"Yeah, I know." It was no use reminding Rickey that things would inevitably fall short of perfection. Rickey knew that, but he still felt like a slacker if he didn't strive for perfection all the time and achieve it at least ninety percent of the time. It made him exhausting to work for. G-man didn't mind, as he was naturally a hard worker and found it easier to do things right than to go through the stress of fucking them up, but he admired the cooks who were able to remain a part of their crew for any length of time. Rickey really took it out of them, yet even the treacherous Shake had hung in there for three years. G-man knew Rickey was one of those head chefs who made the rest of the kitchen want to rise to his level. He also knew he could never have been such a chef himself; he had the talent and stamina, but not the drive or the ability to simultaneously terrify and inspire.

"Well, you wanna go home?"

"What for?" G-man said a bit sullenly.

"I don't know. Maybe take a shower, then get in bed and mess around?"

"I thought you didn't want to."

"Sure I want to. I'm just a little slow on the uptake."

"Well," said G-man. "Maybe." He wasn't really hedging; he just hoped Rickey would talk a little more about what they might do when they got home.

"Course, we don't have to wait till we get in bed to start messing around. Shower's big enough for two."

"Uh huh …"

"I just gotta look up this one duck galantine recipe first."

G-man had already knuckled the top of Rickey's head quite savagely before he saw that Rickey was laughing.

XIII. PARENTAL GUIDANCE SUGGESTED

Shake knew his family was coming in for dinner, but he hadn't expected their arrival to be heralded by his father's loud and unmelodious voice singing the jingle that had advertised the family's pest control business since 1953. "Don't let termites cave your WALL IN! Dial five two two six thousand, DAWLIN!"

A few minutes later the hostess ducked into the kitchen, a haunted look in her eye. "My God, Shake, your dad—I just asked him where I'd heard your family name before, because it's so unusual, and he started, like, *bellowing* at me—"

"I know," said Shake. "He's a little hard of hearing. Just make sure Orlando takes good care of them, huh?" Orlando was the only server over thirty at La Pharmacie, a career guy who gave the impression that he should certainly be making his fortune at Antoine's or Galatoire's, but had consented to slum among the tables of this flash-in-the-pan Uptown bistro. He was a prime asshole, but he was also the only waiter Shake trusted to handle the food right.

"Oh, of course, of course," she said, retreating gracefully. Bitch. She couldn't have lived in New Orleans long; else she'd know Vojtaskovic wasn't a particularly unusual name. A student, probably, studying business or pre-law or some damn thing. She was a bony creature with cropped hair, the kind of girl whose hipbones would bruise you as you fucked her, but she always looked at him as if certain he was dying to get into her tiny pink Capri pants. *Maybe if you stood in the pantry and dropped 'em,* Shake thought, *but I sure wouldn't go to any trouble over it.*

That was a terrible way to think about a woman, he knew, especially right before he went out to greet his own mother. Oh, God. What would she be wearing? He realized it had been at least ten years since he had seen her in anything besides the shapeless snap-fronted garments women her age called "house dresses." Trying to picture her sitting at one of La Pharmacie's sleek-varnished black tables in such a garment—maybe one with floral sprigs—he closed his eyes and shuddered a little.

He knew what his father would be wearing, anyway: a short-sleeved Oxford shirt, either solid blue or white with a blue stripe, and khaki pants hitched up a little too high. Since it was still warm, he would not be wearing his Saints windbreaker over the ensemble. Johnny Vojtaskovic hated the Saints now, but he had bought the jacket thirty years ago and was too cheap to buy another one as long as there was some life left in it.

He palmed sweat off his face, wiped his hands on a side towel, and went out to greet them. As he approached the table, he saw hopelessly that, although Lydia wasn't wearing one of her house dresses, the outfit she had chosen was almost as bad: some kind of brown skirt suit with a huge, pink, flagrantly artificial flower pinned smack in the center of the bosom. *Well, fuck it,* he thought as he bent down to kiss her, *just because I work in this fancy-ass joint now doesn't mean I gotta be ashamed of how my mom dresses.* He saw the hostess staring at them and gave her a look hard enough to make her busy herself among the menu folders.

"That girl didn't know who we were!" his father announced. "I hadda sing her the termite song!"

"I know, Dad. She's just a kid." Over his parents' heads, Shake met the eyes of his brother Rob, who'd come with his wife. Rob held down an administrative position at the Chalmette Refinery, an occupation Johnny Vojtaskovic found much more respectable than cooking. Right now Rob looked amused and slightly embarrassed at Shake's whites, as if his little brother had come to the table in a gorilla suit.

"Richard!" His mother's voice wasn't as loud as Johnny's, but it was more insistent. "Richard, babe!"

Outside his family, Shake hadn't answered to that name for a couple of decades. "Yeah, Momma?"

"You ain't gonna give us nothing too fancy to eat, are you? Because you know your father won't like it, and he gets the indigestion."

"No, Momma. I got a real nice meal planned for y'all. Nothing too fancy."

"I want to try the foie gras in chocolate sauce," Rob's wife, Suzy, piped up. Rob had e-mailed Shake to warn him that Suzy hung out on the local Internet dining boards and considered herself some kind of serious foodie, which struck nearly as much terror in Shake's heart as the presence of his blood relatives. He was proud of his foie gras au chocolat, though; he'd send it out for her and Rob while the old folks had his most popular app, the oysters and bacon with melted leeks on a crisp crouton. He'd been toying with the idea of renaming it Oysters La Pharmacie, making it his signature dish.

"Foie gras!" his father hollered. "What the hell is that?"

Rob smirked. "It's liver, Dad. You don't want any."

"I like a nice plate of liver and onions!"

"It's not calves' liver," Suzy said. "It's the liver of a duck force-fed to make it get great big and fat." She spoke deliberately and, Shake thought, a little sadistically—but he supposed being Johnny Vojtaskovic's daughter-in-law might well make one sadistic. She turned wide eyes on Shake. "Do you sear it or make a torchon?"

"Torchon," he said. Everybody who'd ever cooked at the Peychaud Grill knew how to make a perfect foie gras torchon. Paco Valdeon had drilled it into their heads that the connective tissue must be removed on an almost cellular level, and if a charcuterie plate ever came back with a microscopic shred of tissue on it, God help the cook who'd made the torchon that week.

"I think that's so much more original. *All* the chefs sear it these days."

It was true, but Shake couldn't help a small, inward eye-roll. Goddamn foodies were never content to just enjoy their meals; they always had to show you how *knowledgeable* they were.

"You can try the foie, Dad," he said. "I don't think you'll like it too much, though. I got some nice oysters for you and Momma."

"Plaquemines ersters, I hope!" The Vojtaskovic family had been working oyster beds in Plaquemines Parish since 1922. Upon his parents' retirement, Johnny had promptly sold his share of the beds, moved to the city, and bought the pest control business, but he still considered himself an oyster expert bar none.

"I wouldn't dare serve you any other kind. Look, I better go get started on your first courses. I'll check back with you in a little while."

Thank God they didn't read *Cornet*, he thought as he headed back to the kitchen. Suzy had probably seen his picture and the awful caption, but he hoped she was kind enough not to mention it to the others.

Suzy pulled the clipping out of her purse when they were halfway through the second course, a dark, rich squab and andouille gumbo. "Mr. V, Miz V, you saw this?"

"Aw, Suze, I told you not to show 'em that damn thing," said Rob, but his heart was not in the words.

Lydia Vojtaskovic took the little square of newsprint, squinted at it, and smiled, perceiving only that her son had appeared in print again. She had the *Big Easy* write-up framed and hanging in her kitchen. Suzy didn't like that much; even though Rob's work was much more important, managers from the Chalmette Refinery seldom got their pictures in *Big Easy*.

Lydia passed the clipping to Johnny, who brought it close to his eyes, then held it at arm's length, then scowled at it. "That's what they got him doing back there? Setting things on fire?"

He handed the clipping back to Lydia, who tried to return it to Suzy. "Oh, you can have it," Suzy said irritably. It hadn't had quite the damping effect she'd hoped; the elder Vojtaskovics addressed their sons by their Christian names and probably had no idea whether Richard's nickname was Shake or Snake, and the homosexual reference had gone over their heads entirely. She pursed her lips as the third course was set before them. "Oh, look, Robby," she said, "carpaccio."

"What the hell is that?" bellowed Johnny Vojtaskovic.

Dutifully, Shake never let two courses go by without checking on his family. He heard his father's opinion on the waiter ("He looks like a bum. What is he, Serbian?"), the décor ("I guess they got some Uptown fruit in here to do it"), the beautiful Jamaican bartender ("Who wants to look at some nappy-haired gal with an earring in her nose while they trying to drink their Scotch?"), and Shake's choice of shellfish in the ragout of clams and chorizo with garlic confit ("Well, they ain't ersters, that's for sure"). All of these *bon mots* were delivered at top volume, and by the time Orlando served dessert to the table—setting the plates down with a touch more force than was strictly necessary—Shake couldn't go anywhere in the restaurant without sensing mental laser beams of hostility aimed straight between his eyes.

He had thought they'd head home early. His parents had to drive all the way back to Slidell, where they'd moved a couple of years ago. Nevertheless, they remained at the table past closing time, adding wine and booze to his tab. "I'm going to start vacuuming around their feet," the hostess threatened the second time she came in the kitchen.

"Just let me finish breaking down. I'll get rid of 'em."

He hurried through his closing tasks, then went out to the dining room. Suzy was drinking a twenty-seven-dollar glass of ice wine. Everybody else had Scotch—not the well brand, Shake was betting. Johnny produced a cigarillo and would have lit it off the candle had Lydia not deftly plucked it from his fingers. "Gimme that!" shouted Johnny, stricken.

"There's no smoking in these fancy restaurants, Mr. V," Suzy said viciously. "It's not good for the *palate*." She flashed Shake a commiserating yet somehow superior little smile.

In the end, Shake had to sit with them for fifteen minutes and drop several increasingly broad hints before he finally got them to finish up their drinks and start moving toward the door. "I really hope y'all liked it," he said as he waited with them for the valet.

"It wasn't too bad," Johnny admitted. "But next time, let us relax a little after dinner—you don't gotta rush us out!"

Shake watched them drive away, hoping half-heartedly that they wouldn't plunge off the Twin Spans. He wouldn't mind so much if

Rob and Suzy hit an open drawbridge on their way back to Arabi, but he'd never heard of that happening except in the movies. When both cars were out of sight, he went back into the restaurant, lowered his aching carcass onto a barstool, and dropped his head into his hands. Before he could order a drink, Orlando swooped down upon him to report further disgraces: "They didn't leave a *tip*."

Shake dug out his wallet and handed over two twenties. He'd been planning to grab lunch up the street at Casamento's the next day, but there went his fried oyster loaf and dozen on the half shell; he guessed he'd be eating cereal instead.

Orlando looked at Shake as if he'd have preferred arguing to getting the money, but Shake stared him down, and finally the waiter took himself off to do whatever career waiters did when they got off work—get drunk and practice insulting each other, maybe. "Can I please have some of that Scotch my folks were drinking?" Shake asked the bartender.

"Get it yourself," she told him. "This *nappy-haired gal's* going home."

XIV. THE GADWALL HAS LANDED

In the early 1930s, the Levee Board built a V-shaped seawall in Lake Pontchartrain and filled the V with six million cubic yards of mud from the lake bottom. These were (and remain) the sort of labors required to create land above sea level in New Orleans. Once they had the land, they built a state-of-the-art airport on it. Huey Long caused the airport to be named for Levee Board president Abraham Shushan, a longtime cog in his political machine. Its grand opening the weekend before Mardi Gras 1934 was heralded by a crashing thunderstorm that drove sodden dignitaries into the hangars. Not too long after that, Long was assassinated and Shushan was accused (though never convicted) of laundering money for his campaign. The new governor—a reform man, in name anyway—insisted that thirty-two hundred imprints of Shushan's name be removed from the airport. Glass was scraped clean, ashtrays painted, door handles filed down. The place was unimaginatively renamed the New Orleans Lakefront Airport.

Rickey learned some of this from posters in the terminal lobby. He also learned that Mr. Shushan had eventually died in a plane crash, which seemed a gratuitously cruel twist of fate. Though he hadn't known the history of the airport and had never had occasion to fly out of it—Lakefront mostly handled private and charter flights these days—Rickey had been coming here since he was almost a baby. He remembered sitting on the observation deck with his parents, watching the planes land and take off. They couldn't have come as close to the terminal as he remembered, but the noise had been thrilling and a little scary. On one wondrous occasion, the Goodyear Blimp was tethered in the field between runways, its elephantine bulk trembling in the lake breeze. Or so he recalled; probably it had been tied down too tightly to move at all.

He'd gotten here early today because he wanted a look at the place, and was gratified to see that aside from the disappearance of the observation deck—a casualty of Homeland Security, he guessed—Lakefront Airport hadn't changed a bit since he'd last seen it twenty-odd years ago. The terminal was still an art deco fantasy of glossy colored marble and brass. The little restaurant still served reconstituted Sysco soups and odd sandwiches. You could still fold yourself into an old-fashioned phone booth and make a call, though it cost fifty cents now. Rickey had two quarters in his pocket, so he parked his butt on the deeply scratched but highly polished little wooden ledge and called home. "Hey, man."

"Hey, man." It was their day off, and Rickey could hear a TiVo'd basketball game in the background. "Ducks on the ground yet?"

"No, but the flight's on time. Listen, you want to meet me over at the restaurant after I get 'em?"

"What for?"

"I thought maybe we ought to break one down, cook a breast and a leg in some real simple way. You know, get a feel for the meat. I never had wild duck before, did you?"

"I don't think so, but it can't be all that different, huh?"

"G, you know what happens when you *assume*? You make an *ass*—"

"I know, I know. But why don't you just bring one home? I don't want to spend our day off at the restaurant."

"Well, I kinda thought we might go ahead and start on some stuff. You know, like the confit and the prosciutto."

The sound G-man made was not precisely a whimper, but Rickey wasn't sure what else to call it.

"You just want to lay around and watch hoops, huh?"

"Well ..."

"C'mon, G, the season's hardly even started yet."

"Yeah, but that's the best time, because anything's still possible."

"Uh huh, and when it's midseason you'll say *that's* the best time because it's just starting to get exciting, and when they playoffs start you'll say *that's* the best time because *dude, it's the playoffs*."

G-man laughed at the accurate imitation of his voice, then grew serious. "I know, dude, but I got that bone in my foot again. It was killing me all last night. I really wanted to rest today."

"OK, OK," Rickey said, knowing when he was beaten. G-man wasn't a complainer. If he said he wanted to rest, he probably needed to. Rickey would do him the favor of pretending Steve Nash and Amare Stoudemire were just added bonuses.

They hung up, and within five minutes, the plane Rickey was waiting for taxied down the runway. Tee Fontenot had told him, "Look for the guy with no tie," and sure enough, everybody who disembarked had a tie on except for one barrel-shaped, silver-haired man.

"Mr. Schexnaydre?" Rickey was pretty sure he'd mangled the name. Apparently it was a common one in Cajun country, but he'd never heard it until his phone conversation with Fontenot a couple of days ago.

"Chef!" The guy seized his hand, gave it three hard pumps. "Got your ducks, yeah! They're coming off the plane in a minute—let's see if we can't get somebody to help us load 'em in your car."

"I got it."

"You sure? It's twelve big coolers, pretty heavy."

"We can make several trips." In truth, Rickey wouldn't have minded help, but he pictured Schexnaydre snapping his fingers at some random black person—*Say, boy!* He knew the rest of Louisiana wasn't the unmitigated hotbed of race-baiting fundamentalism some New Orleanians tried to pretend it was, but old suspicions died hard.

In the end, Rickey borrowed a dolly from the baggage handlers and dealt with most of the load himself while Schexnaydre tagged along behind talking about the golf courses, fishing areas, and hunting grounds he planned to visit on this trip, none of which was actually in New Orleans. The ducks were packed in Styrofoam coolers with the names of species scrawled on the outsides: TEAL, GADWALL, DOS GRIS. "Tee said to let you know you'll get some of the late arrivals at the banquet," Schexnaydre said.

"Diners?"

"Ducks. These are the ones that come through early in the season."

"OK."

"You don't hunt?"

Rickey thought of the one time he'd fired a real gun: a friend's uncle's nine-millimeter. The friend, a Lower Ninth Ward kid who'd since been in and out of Orleans Parish Prison and would probably graduate to Angola eventually, had swiped the gun from a drawer and carried it to a vacant lot near the river for the other kids to gawk at. They'd taken turns firing at a telephone pole, scattering like droplets of water in a hot skillet at the first sound of police sirens. He'd rather enjoyed the feel of all that firepower in his hand, but with the possible exception of a few bosses he'd had, he couldn't see himself firing it at anything alive. "Nope," he said. "Don't get out of the city much."

Schexnaydre made a face. "Never heard of that stopping some of these … people. You can have New Orleans. Don't know how you stand it."

"I like it," Rickey said in a tone of voice that actually shut the man up for a couple of minutes.

They were wedging the last cooler into the backseat of Rickey's Plymouth when Schexnaydre said, "I'm the one who recommended you to Ducks Unlimited, you know."

Rickey looked up at him. "Thought you said you hated New Orleans."

"What can I say? I'm not a city boy. Appreciate a good meal, though. I've eaten at your restaurant three or four times now. Think you got most of the famous places beat all to hell."

The famous *places?* Rickey decided he was about ready for this guy to get on with his golfing, fishing, and hunting. "Well, thanks for the good word."

"Sure thing." Schexnaydre winked. "You gonna take care of me next time I come in, huh?"

"You know it."

And Rickey would. Schexnaydre might be a bit of an asshole, but if he was telling the truth, he'd done them a favor. In the restaurant business, you took care of people you knew, people who'd done you favors, people who claimed to have done you favors. Even if you didn't particularly like them, you made sure they had a good waiter, sent out an extra course, comped their drinks or desserts. If you didn't, you could be sure everybody they knew would hear about it. It was just the way things worked.

Nonetheless, he was happy to take his leave of the great white hunter and head back into town, his car laden with ducks. He couldn't wait to see how they handled. Rickey was a little too old to like work above all else, but he still felt an unparalleled excitement when he got his hands on something he'd never cooked before.

At the restaurant, he unloaded the twelve coolers and stashed them in the walk-in. Though his back had begun to ache, he felt the strong rush of well-being he always experienced when he was alone in the restaurant. No other cooks to fuck things up, no waiters to nag him, no customers to bitch and moan and expect special treatment. Of course he needed the cooks and waiters and customers, but once in a while it was nice to have the place all to himself. He sat in the dining room for a few minutes, not trying to imagine it from a customer's perspective, not thinking about the kitchen or wanting a drink, just enjoying the good place he had created.

His research suggested that teal was a good training duck, so after a little while he walked back through the kitchen, opened the cooler marked BW TEAL, and selected a plastic-wrapped package that felt heavier than it looked. He hummed "Born Free" under his breath as he carried it out to the car.

As he entered the house, G-man hollered "Duck!" and threw a Nerf basketball at him. Rickey bobbled the ball, then caught it in the hand that wasn't holding the bagged bird.

"What? You been sitting here planning that the whole time I was gone?"

"Pretty much. Game's a total blowout."

"Well, c'mon in the kitchen and help me see about this bird."

G-man got up and limped after him.

"Your foot still fucked up?"

"Aw, it's not too bad. How's your back?"

Rickey shrugged.

"Couple old geezers," G-man said ruefully.

"I know it, Gramps. You feel like taking a whack at the butchering?

You always been better at cutting things up."

"Sure, hand me that Wüsthof ..." G-man set the knife on the countertop, reached into the bag Rickey had brought home. "Aagh!"

"What? Jeez, dude, what is it?"

"Feathers!"

"You're fucking kidding me."

G-man pulled the duck out of the bag and brandished it at Rickey, his hand wrapped its neck. From the top of his fist emerged a tiny, slit-eyed, unmistakably duck-billed head. From the bottom hung a brown, blue, and white body that had been gutted, but not deprived of its feathers or its webby feet. The ooze from a small perforation stained its delicately dappled breast.

"Jesus Christ."

"Least we know it's fresh."

"Goddammit, you mean we gotta pull the feathers off fifty ducks?"

"*We* don't." G-man gazed at Rickey over the tops of his shades. "Jacolvy and Marquis do. Or the dishwashers, even."

"Whatever. We still lose two pair of hands. And I don't want the dishwashers doing it—they might tear the skin." Rickey stewed for a minute, then got over it; the ducks had come the way they had come and there was no point in agonizing. "Give it here. I'll pull the goddamn feathers out."

"You want me to cut off the head and feet first?"

"No ... oh, shit, G, I don't know. This is fucking gross."

"No it's not. It's the same thing you cook with every day—this is just what it really looks like. Probably good for us to deal with real animals once in a while instead of getting all our meat in cute little packages."

"I cut down a pork leg just last week. I don't think a whole pork leg is a *cute little package*."

"Maybe not, but it sure ain't a pig." G-man took a cleaver out of the drawer, slapped the teal on the cutting board, and lopped off its head with one neat stroke. Two more strokes and the legs fell into the sink. Although he knew G-man was right, Rickey still felt a little nauseous; he was pretty sure nobody had ever been decapitated in his kitchen before.

They sat at the table with the sad little body between them, pinching feathers and yanking them out. It was hard at first, but grew easier once they got the hang of it. Rickey was no longer particularly grossed out, but he felt a little sad at first. They used premium meats at the restaurant—Niman Ranch pork, free-range chickens, no hormone-pumped beef—but he didn't kid himself into thinking most of the animals whose flesh he cooked had led wonderful lives. If you were a farm animal, even on a high-end farm, you were pretty much screwed from the moment of birth (or hatching). This bird, though, had lived free in the Louisiana marsh, some of the most fragile and beautiful land in the world. Rickey hadn't spent much time out there, but even driving one of the narrow roads through the wetlands would imprint them on your heart forever. He pictured the duck and its mate flying over the marsh at dusk, moss-fraught cypress trees and grass hummocks black against the sky, water reflecting the smeary oranges, pinks, and grays of the sunset. The birds coasted in and landed, seeming to run across the surface of the water as their wings scooped the air, iridescent baffles.

Then he shrugged. At least they'd had some pleasure in their lives. Unless you were going to become a vegetarian, which he sure as hell wasn't, he guessed you ought to be able to think about stuff like this and deal with the meat anyway. G-man was right as usual.

When they had all but the pinfeathers off, Rickey singed the skin with his crème brulée torch, burning away the fuzz and stubble that remained. A smell somewhere between burning hair and melting plastic filled the kitchen. Rickey consulted his notes as G-man cut the bird into pieces and put the carcass in a big pot to cook down for stock. From his cookbooks and some game websites, he'd gathered that wild ducks varied dramatically in their fat content depending on the breed, the season, and where they'd been shot. They started out plump up north, but by the time they got all the way down to Louisiana, they could be pretty lean.

G-man handed him a breast. Rickey palpated it thoughtfully, cooking it ten different ways in his mind before he applied any actual heat. It was smaller, denser, and way darker than a domestic duck breast, and didn't seem to have much of a fat layer between the skin and the muscle. The kind of meat that would overcook in a heartbeat. Rickey decided he'd brine both breasts, wrap this one in bacon and leave the other one plain, sauté them both, compare the results. Normally you'd brine a whole bird, but since this one was already cut up, he'd leave the breasts in saltwater for only ninety minutes or so—long enough to keep them juicy (he hoped) without too much salt getting into the meat. In the meantime, he'd experiment with the legs.

Thirty minutes later they sat down to their first taste of wild duck: a single small thigh sautéed in olive oil with turnips, onions, and whole cloves of garlic. Rickey had cooked it just until the skin was crisp, but he had been able to feel the muscle fibers shrinking when he prodded the meat in the pan, ands sure enough, the first bite was tough and dry.

"Don't worry about it," G-man said when he saw Rickey's discouraged expression. "You said yourself we're mostly gonna be doing confit with the legs. That won't be dry. Taste these vegetables—the flavor's great."

Rickey forked up a turnip cube and chewed it slowly. There hadn't been much fat to flavor them, but they were still permeated with a dark, rich essence, salty and complex, a little bloody. Rickey supposed this was the taste people called "gamy" and wrinkled their noses at. Well, the Ducks Unlimited people wouldn't be wrinkling their noses. Neither would Bobby Hebert, who in true Cajun fashion talked on the radio about eating snapping turtle (*cowan*) and oyster drills (*bigarneau*) during his youth in South Lafourche Parish. A little gaminess wouldn't faze them; Rickey just had to cook the goddamn shit right. The thought heartened him. He didn't quite know how to do it yet, but he'd figure it out.

They cooked the breasts mid-rare and sauced them very simply with a mushroom demiglace G-man found in the freezer. The plain breast was even drier and tougher than the thigh had been, but the bacon-wrapped one was exquisitely moist. "We're getting there," said G-man, tucking a thick slice into his mouth.

"One down, forty-nine to go."

XV. BIG NIGHT

Amuse of Gadwall en Daube Glacé

Gumbo of Pintail and Poche's Andouille Sausage

Confit of Dos Gris with Arugula, Radicchio, Cracklins, and Satsuma-Bacon Vinaigrette

Butter-Poached Drum Wrapped in Wood Duck Prosciutto with Porcini-Garlic Jam

Braised Teal with Dried Cherries and Kirsch

Savory Bread Pudding with Greenhead, Chestnuts, and Green Apples

Palate Cleanser of Juniper Sorbet

Crème Brûlée Flavored with Dos Gris Fat, Served with a Triangle of Crispy Duck Skin

Rickey seldom felt constrained by the liquor gimmick, but he was glad to get a break from it. Still, he hadn't been able to resist adding a little kirsch to the Elizabeth David recipe. His restaurant deserved a nod, at least.

"Pretty jiggy fish dish," G-man said when Rickey showed him the rough menu.

"I think it'll be real good."

"Hey, jiggy's a compliment. I like the juniper sorbet, too. Carries out the game theme."

"That's what I thought," Rickey said modestly.

There had been a certain amount of angst regarding the dessert course. Tanker wanted to do a caramel wonton filled with shredded duck confit. He'd served a similar wonton at Liquor with a foie gras mousse filling and it had been spectacularly good, but the dish just wasn't plausible for three hundred. "I can't have you fucking around with hot caramel half the evening," Rickey said. "We need you on the line. The dessert's gotta be pretty simple, something you can prep up in advance."

As well, Rickey also wasn't crazy about the idea of trotting the duck confit back out for an encore performance, but he didn't tell Tanker that; he knew Tanker would just suggest that he do something else for his salad course.

"Simple!" Tanker groused. "*You* get to do all the fancy shit in the world, but desserts gotta be simple. Desserts get no respect."

"You'll thank me when you're slamming out crème brûlées instead of folding up three hundred fiddly little wontons," Rickey said. "I saw you making those things, remember? You were cussing balls-out and burning your fingers, and you only had to do about fifty."

Against G-man's wishes, Rickey had gone ahead with his plan to close Liquor the weekend of the banquet. He wasn't crazy about it himself, but there was just no way to stretch the crew thinly enough to cover the restaurant and the Ducks Unlimited dinner without sacrificing quality at one place, probably both. Of all the things that made Rickey crazy, the idea of willingly sacrificing an iota of quality gnawed at him the most ferociously. Closing would cut into their profits a little, but not as much as regular customers getting bad meals ultimately would. People never forgot that shit, they never forgave you for it, and most times they never came back—just told all their friends and Internet cronies how you'd fallen off.

It wasn't just the potential loss of revenue that gnawed at him, though; he simply couldn't stomach the idea of serving a dish that was less than the best he and his crew could make. He supposed that was one of the things that had kept him in business this long even though he'd never headed a kitchen before opening his own restaurant. It also made him a royal pain in the ass to work for, he knew, but that couldn't be helped.

So the crew was going to caravan to Opelousas in three vehicles: Rickey, G-man, and most of the food in one car; Tanker, Terrance, Marquis, and the rest of the food in a second; Devonte, Jacolvy, and the two dishwashers in a third. They planned to get there the afternoon before the banquet, spend part of that night and all the next day setting up. Everybody would stay over two nights in the motel rooms Tee Fontenot had booked for them. The day after the banquet, the younger cooks and dishwashers would drive back to New Orleans. Rickey and G-man would stay over an extra night to check out the town and maybe eat some boudin. Tanker and Terrance could do whatever they liked.

That was the basic plan. Rickey wasn't naïve enough to think it would go exactly as he'd laid it out, but he hoped for no major deviations.

The drive was an easy three hours on the I–10. G-man took the first turn driving. Actually, Rickey would be happy if G-man decided to take *all* the turns driving; it wasn't one of his favorite things. They had soaped the legend D*U*C*K on the rear windshields of all three cars, as if they were a caravan of culinary surgeons hurrying to administer good taste to some war-torn region. D*U*C*K didn't actually stand for anything, but Rickey figured nobody would give a shit.

Past Baton Rouge, the interstate turned into a long bridge over the Atchafalaya Basin. Living and dead cypress trunks rose from an eternity of duckweed, swamp water, pale reflected sky. A faint clean aroma of duck fat emanated from the sealed containers in the backseat. They'd both been quiet for about fifteen miles, each lost in his own thoughts, when G-man said, "It's a really great menu."

"I know." It was a conceited thing to say, but Rickey *did* think it was a great menu, and G-man didn't expect false modesty from him.

"I didn't even spend all that much time on it. When I went to write it down, it was like it just came to me."

"Cause you'd been thinking about it since September. It was forming in … you know … your subconscious mind."

"I guess."

"See, that's why you're a genius."

Rickey's first response to the word "genius" was not pleasure, but a mixture of embarrassment and alarm. "I'm not—" He realized it was meant as a compliment. "Well, goddamn, I don't know about all that. I got a little talent. It might've helped me design the menu, but it's not gonna get me through tonight."

"That's why we got a good crew."

"Yeah," Rickey said. He stared out the window. That *genius* still nagged at him. What had made G-man say such a thing? Once, when he was still reading the online dining forums, he'd seen himself described as a "culinary savant." When he looked up *savant* in the dictionary, the first definition was *A person of profound or extensive learning*; the second was *One who performs by rote or instinct rather than great intelligence; idiot savant.* He'd decided he didn't want to know which definition the person on the message board had meant.

He hung on for twenty more miles, almost to their turnoff onto I-49, before he could stand it no longer. "What the hell did you have to say that for?"

"Say what?"

"What you said I was."

"A genius?" G-man glanced over at Rickey, who was slumped against the passenger door. "I don't know. It's what I think. I meant it in a nice way."

"I just don't like you setting me apart like that. It makes me feel weird. I'm not some kinda egghead. I'm the same as you."

"Rickey, if you were the same as me, we'd still be on the line in somebody else's restaurant. Don't give me that bullshit. There's nothing wrong with being a genius—you're probably the only person in the world who thinks it's an insult. Now quit leaning against that door before you fly out."

This last was something G-man's mother had often said to them when they rode in her car as kids, and Rickey was surprised into a laugh. He couldn't quite leave the matter alone, though: "Well, I don't like it."

G-man lifted his hands a couple of inches off the steering wheel. "I'm sorry. I'm sorry. I promise I'll never do it again." Five more miles of quiet. They passed a big yellow billboard advertising a Cajun meat market. A grinning pig in a chef's hat offered steaming boudin links, boudin balls, andouille, cracklins. All the savory products of the boucherie, the Acadian tradition that turned every part of the pig into something irresistible. Rickey realized he hadn't eaten since early the evening before. He'd just begun to wonder why he wasn't hungry, even in the face of such temptation, when G-man said, "You nervous about meeting Bobby?"

"Seems like if I was, you wouldn't want to get me started thinking about it."

"I rather you think about it now, talk about it now, get it over with. You're not gonna have time to be nervous tomorrow."

"Well, that's just it. I'm a little nervous now, but tomorrow night I'll be in the zone. Bobby's gonna be just another mouth to me." He saw G-man's look. "Well, an *important* mouth. But he's a team leader, you know? He's not gonna be impressed unless he sees us get *everybody's* meal right."

"I guess you got a point there."

"Course I do. Anyway, aren't *you* nervous?"

G-man shrugged. "I was always more of a Rickey Jackson man."

"Figures," Rickey said. "Protect the quarterback. Dome Patrol. Hell, G, you're my Kitchen Patrol."

"I never had the bulk to be a linebacker."

"Yeah, but if kitchen chops were muscle, you'd have the bulk of four guys."

"Aw, jeez." G-man shook his head as he made the turn onto 49. "Now you're just getting back at me for calling you a genius."

☛

The Delta Grand wasn't what Rickey had expected. From Tee Fontenot's description of a "historic theatre," he'd envisioned something posh and elegant, maybe in an art deco style. Instead their venue was an average-looking building in the heart of Opelousas' small, old-fashioned downtown, across the street from the courthouse square and right next to the jail. The lobby was decorated with posters for teen dances and hip-hop shows. Fontenot had said he and a bunch of the banquet organizers would be hunting today, and no one was there to greet Rickey and G-man when they arrived, but the door was unlocked and they started carrying stuff inside.

The kitchen was no French Laundry, but it would do: a large, high-ceilinged industrial space with a long hot line, four big stovetops, and a half-dozen rolling steam tables that Rickey planned to push out of the way. Tanker, Terrance, and Marquis arrived about twenty minutes later in Terrance's Oldsmobile, carrying the rest of the food. They went to work putting things away, rearranging, scoping things out. Rickey found the rest of his ducks in one of the tall reach-in coolers, but he couldn't put Devonte and Jacolvy to work plucking feathers, because they weren't here yet.

He pulled out his cell phone and called Devonte. The younger man answered after six rings. In the background, Rickey could hear a thumping bass—not Devonte's considerable car stereo, because there was also muffled laughter and the sound of an announcer saying, "Give it up for TAMIKA!"

"Where the hell are you?"

"Oh! Uh … Chef?"

Rickey closed his eyes, breathed deeply, and reminded himself that wherever Devonte and Jacolvy were, they had his only dishwashers with them. "Yeah, D," he said. "This is Chef. Standing here in the kitchen of the goddamn banquet hall"—his voice started to rise, but he got control of it—"just wondering where my pantry guys are."

"Uh, well, we just stopped off for a drink. Got thirsty drivin. We on our way right now."

"That's right," Rickey heard Jacolvy say, or maybe it was one of the dishwashers.

"Fine, but where *are* you? As in geographically?"

"Where we at?" Devonte asked somebody on his end. There was a lot of whispering, then: "Say someplace called Bayou Goula."

"Bayou *Goula*?" That was not only way the hell south of the interstate, but on the opposite side of the river from where they should have been. "How the fuck did you get there?"

"We got off in Baton Rouge lookin for a place to get a drink. Got lost."

"And found yourselves at the nearest strip club, huh?" Devonte started to speak, but Rickey cut him off. "Forget it. I don't want to hear about it right now. What I *want* is for you to still have a *job* tomorrow, and for Jacolvy not to violate his *parole* by being *underage* in a fucking *titty bar*. And in order to make that *happen*, D, you need to stand up right now, wipe that stupid fucking smirk off your face, get the rest of my crew out of there, get directions back to the interstate, and drive due west until you hit Lafayette. At that point you need to turn north onto I-49 and proceed directly to Opelousas. Don't stop for another drink. Don't stop to pee. Don't stop to wipe your *dick* on some hoochie momma's *G-string*. You understand what I'm telling you?"

"Yeah, Chef. Sorry."

"And if you got that kid drunk, you can goddamn well dump him off at the motel and pluck all these goddamn birds yourself."

"Awright, Chef."

"You *heard* me?"

"Yeah, Chef."

Rickey snapped his phone shut, more mad at himself for allowing that bunch to ride together than anything else. Jacolvy was nineteen, Devonte twenty-two, the dishwashers not much older. None of them had ever been out of New Orleans before; it was hardly surprising that they'd be tempted to go off looking for trouble. He should have made Marquis ride with them—no, Terrance. Marquis might have gone right along to the titty bar, but Terrance wouldn't have put up with it. Rickey wondered what other missteps he'd made in his planning, what other errors lurked ahead like rakes in tall grass just waiting for him to step on them.

The youngsters arrived a couple of hours later, shamefaced, ready to work, smelling only a little of beer and scarcely at all of weed. It wasn't long before they were sitting on opposite sides of a big plastic trashcan, exclaiming with disgust as they plunged their fingers into refrigerator-chilled feathers.

They were busy setting up and prepping until almost midnight. Probably some of the stuff could have waited until tomorrow, but as Rickey announced to the crew, "We need to get our ducks in a row." It wasn't until they started groaning and booing him that he realized what he'd said.

He and G-man wanted a drink. They strolled through the square and along the streets certain they'd find something open—this was still south Louisiana, after all—but the downtown was deserted. The central block seemed to have been bombed out entirely. Most of it had been occupied by a big department store that still bore traces of bygone elegance—gold lettering on the doors, colored tile mosaics in the entryways—but standing on those mosaics and peering through those doors, they could see burned beams, holes in the ceiling with moonlight streaming through, black mold and eerily verdant ferns swarming up the walls. Merchandise still lay scattered here and there, men's ties and ladies' blouses thirty years out of date, an easy chair rotting in a display window.

The rest of the downtown was similar: an old Rexall drugstore with blinded windows, a defunct dollar-and-dime store, something called the Archway Lounge that gave them hope at first, but turned out to be just a scorched and gutted brick space full of weeds, trash, and empty pints of liquors they'd never heard of. Crystal Palace gin, Barking Colonel bourbon. There were still scattered businesses trying to make a go of it, and obviously there was some money in the town, but something had struck a blow to the heart of it. G-man shivered. "Let's just get in the car," he said. "Maybe we'll find something if we drive."

They drove around the entire town twice and couldn't find

anywhere that seemed to be open except a couple of ramshackle lounges with pickup trucks and motorcycles parked outside. "I don't feel like dealing with some big zydeco scene," Rickey said. "Everybody in there's gonna be dancing, playing washboards, wrestling alligators with their bare hands."

"Yeah, and there's always a Mardi Gras parade going on in New Orleans and we all drink Hurricanes on Bourbon Street all the time."

"What?"

"Stereotypes."

Rickey shrugged. "I just don't feel like socializing. We'll have to do enough of that tomorrow night."

They drove on to the motel, a low structure built in an L shape around a patch of asphalt. A pall of roasting pork aroma hung over the downtown area. "They must leave it to slow-cook all night, then make boudin in the morning," Rickey said.

"Wish I had some boudin right now."

"Day after tomorrow. We get this dinner done, then we get to be tourists."

In the motel office, a bedraggled parrot in a cage eyed them, then said quietly, "Bugger." They were forced to endure its scrutiny for ten minutes before they could raise anyone to check them in. Rickey dug out a pint of Wild Turkey he kept in the car for emergencies and sat on the edge of the hard mattress sipping straight from the bottle. The room was marginally clean and aggressively threadbare. The only amenity was a piece of soap the size of a postage stamp in the shower stall, which was visible from the bed. Somebody cursed audibly on the other side of the wall, then fell silent. All things considered, Rickey felt more comfortable here than in the gilded Dallas hotel he'd once been booked into.

G-man stretched out on the bed and flexed his foot, trying to pop the bones in his toes. After another two swigs of Wild Turkey, Rickey scooted back on the bed, lifted G-man's sore foot onto his lap, and started rubbing the sole. It was really the top of his foot that gave G-man misery, but Rickey's thumbs felt so good on his instep that he decided not to say anything.

"I don't know if I'm ready for this," Rickey said.

"You can quit if it stinks."

Rickey pinched G-man's big toe. "No, asshole, I mean the dinner. I'm freaking out a little."

"How come? We're in good shape with the prep and we got a great menu. What's to freak out about?"

"I don't know." Abruptly, Rickey pushed G-man's foot away, stood, and went to the door. He opened it and stood looking out over the parking lot. The night was clear and warm for December. After a couple of minutes, a greasy-looking little man came wandering along the breezeway, saw Rickey standing there, and said, "Hey, bro, where you from? Got a dollar?"

The guy stood looking expectantly up at Rickey, who didn't appear to have heard him. Gradually the panhandler's expression changed from lazy anticipation to confusion to alarm, and he hurried away. Rickey shut the door and stood in the middle of the room staring around as if he'd forgotten where he was. He had a wild look in his eye that G-man didn't like at all. It was easy to see why the greasy-looking guy had gotten nervous.

"I just got a bad feeling. We forgot something, or something's gonna happen out of our control. Something's gonna go wrong."

"Rickey!" G-man said sharply.

"We never should've agreed to do this, what the fuck do we know about doing banquets, we're just gonna embarrass ourselves in front of Bobby Hebert and everybody, Ducks Unlimited is gonna ask for their money back—"

G-man sighed, heaved himself up off the bed. His foot felt a little better from resting and being rubbed, and he managed to make it across the room without limping, though of course "across the room" only entailed about three steps. He gripped Rickey's shoulders and gave him a little shake. "Rickey!"

"*What?*"

"Quit it! What are you, some whining little pantry bitch? Get ahold of yourself!"

"But G—"

"But nothing. We're not having that. Now, come here. Lay down." G-man didn't particularly enjoy talking to the love of his life the way he'd address a trained dog, but that was just the way it had to be sometimes. There was no real rhyme or reason to it. The night before they opened the restaurant, Rickey had been as cool as a spearmint snowball, but he'd had a total meltdown about two weeks later: bawling his head off, saying he didn't know what he was doing, wanting to go sit on a beach somewhere, the whole nine yards. Once that was over with, he'd gotten on with the business of running the restaurant. You never knew with Rickey. Just when you expected him to get hysterical, he'd likely as not stare down the situation and do what needed to be done. Other times, the least little mishap could send him down the pike.

G-man wasn't letting him go down the pike this time, though. There was too much at stake, not just for the restaurant but for Rickey personally. If he worked himself into a frenzy tonight and his work tomorrow suffered as a result, he'd never forgive himself. G-man pushed him gently onto the bed and lay down beside him, one hand on his chest, the other stroking the back of his neck. Gradually, Rickey's fists unclenched and his breathing slowed.

"You gonna be OK?"

"Yeah, I think so."

"You ready for this dinner?"

"Yeah."

"What are we gonna do if something goes wrong?"

"We're gonna handle it."

"There you go."

Rickey leaned over to the nightstand, got the Wild Turkey and swigged again, lay back down.

"If I make you come, do you think you could go to sleep?" G-man said.

"I don't want to fuck in this room. The bed's too hard and the walls are too thin."

"We don't have to fuck. We can just mess around."

"I don't know. I think I got too much on my mind."

G-man waited. Just to amuse himself, he started counting in his head. He'd gotten halfway to a hundred when Rickey said, "Mess around how?"

By morning, the weather had turned gray and leaden. It still wasn't cold, but it was getting there. This change made Rickey happy: he had designed a seasonal menu and people would enjoy his food more if it felt something like winter outside. The pall of pork was gone. They woke up the rest of the crew, found coffee, headed en masse to the Delta Grand, and began the day-long prep regimen that would take them right up to the banquet at seven this evening. Rickey was glad they still had a lot to do. He didn't want any downtime to think about possible mishaps. He was stirring the roux for the gumbo, waiting for the vast batch of oil and flour to turn from light golden-brown to the nut-brown that would give it a dark, rich flavor, when Schexnaydre walked into the kitchen with another man. "Chef! Good to see you again. I'd like to introduce our president, Tee Fontenot."

Rickey turned away from the stove. When he saw Fontenot, his jaw dropped, and he immediately felt bad; an instant later he realized it couldn't matter. There were no dark glasses, no white cane, but it was immediately evident from the milkiness of his eyes and the tilt of his head that Fontenot was blind.

He either didn't notice that Rickey had missed a beat or was polite enough to ignore it. His grip on Rickey's hand was surprisingly strong, but why should that be surprising? Losing your sight didn't mean your muscles atrophied. "Good to finally meet you," he said in that musical Cajun accent. "Sure does smell fine in here. Those ducks cooking up nice?"

"Real nice. Took me a little while to figure things out, but now I really like cooking with them. They're beautiful."

"They better be. I shot some of 'em myself."

A smile creased Fontenot's leathery face, and Rickey had time to wonder if he was being fucked with. Then Schexnaydre said, "Tee, we better get out of here and let these boys do their thing."

"Yeah, otherwise we won't get nothing to eat tonight. Ain't that right, Chef?"

"Yessir."

Fontenot cackled as if Rickey had made a witticism and turned away. Schexnaydre's fingers barely touched his elbow, guiding but not leading him; he seemed to navigate pretty well. Surely he couldn't really shoot ducks on the wing, though?

"Bobby Hebert in town yet?" Rickey called after them.

Fontenot half-turned toward the sound of his voice. "Nope! Duck hunting down in Lafourche! He's coming in this afternoon—on a helicopter!"

"You flying the helicopter, too?" said G-man. Rickey stared at him, and G-man looked horrified at himself, as if the words had popped out of his mouth before he could stop them. Even Schexnaydre was taken aback, but Fontenot slapped his leg and whooped.

"Flying the helicopter, me! That's a good one! You heard that, Schex? Flying the helicopter! I oughta ride along and get the pilot to let me take the controls for a minute! See old Bobby's face! Oh, Lord!"

The volume of these comments dwindled as Schexnaydre led Fontenot out of the kitchen, but they could hear him going right up until he climbed into Schexnaydre's quad cab in the rear parking lot.

"You think he really shot some of these ducks?" Terrance said.

"Who knows." Rickey shook his head. "We're in another world, man."

"You got that right."

Rickey unpacked his hotel pans of confit. He scraped away the top layer of melted fat that had covered the meat for two weeks, sealing in its juices and permeating it with flavor. He didn't keep confit on the menu all the time, but customers raved about it when he ran it as a special, said it was the best in town. His big secret was replacing a quarter of the duck fat with pork lard, which deepened the taste without overwhelming the duck. Most people couldn't identify the magic ingredient; they just knew it was bone-gnawingly good confit. This time he'd had to augment the wild duck fat with store-bought, and nobody would be gnawing the bones since he was shredding the meat off of them to serve in little haystacks on the salad. Still a decent batch, though, he confirmed by popping a dark, oily chunk of thigh into his mouth. Thoroughly laced with fat, it all but melted on his tongue.

By four o'clock, everything was as prepped as it could be for the moment. Glistening mounds of daube glace nestled in endive leaves in the fridge, perfect little bites waiting to amuse hungry mouths. Salad greens chilled on plates, ready for a dollop of confit and a ladle of satsuma-bacon vinaigrette. Pots of gumbo warmed gently in water baths. Bread puddings were assembled, waiting to go into ovens. Three hundred perfect balls of juniper sorbet sat in three hundred Chinese soup spoons. Rickey had thought the white sorbet would look nice in the white spoons. When he prepared a sample dish, though, he didn't like the monochrome effect. He'd been momentarily frustrated: using artificial colors seemed pointless and dishonest, but anything natural—beet juice, saffron—would alter the juniper flavor. Tanker had saved the day by showing him how to make liquid chlorophyll out of pureed spinach strained through several thicknesses of cheesecloth. It had a clean, slightly grassy taste that went well with the juniper, and the mint-green balls looked really good in the spoons. Like something from the cover of a glossy food magazine, Rickey thought, though not even torture could have made him say it out loud.

Banquet service differed radically from the way they usually ran their kitchen. Instead of cooks working different stations, all seven of them would work on each course in a kind of assembly-line procedure: two three-man teams plus one guy running around making sure everything was going smoothly. To prepare the braised teal, for instance, G-man would warm up the already cooked duck breasts in the ovens and get the warmed plates from the dishwashers. Meanwhile, Rickey, Terrance, and Jacolvy would break the plating sequence into three steps. Jacolvy would start the plate with a circle of potato-parsnip puree and a half-ladle of sauce. Terrance would lay down the meat. Rickey would finish the plate with more sauce, a scatter of kirsch-plumped cherries, and the side veg—in this case, a small heap of garlic-sautéed kale—and top it with a metal hat that would keep the food hot and allow the waiters to stack plates three high on their big trays. On the other side, Tanker, Marquis, and Devonte would be doing the exact same thing. If the plates went out in ten rounds of thirty, Rickey figured they could serve each course in about seven minutes. You didn't want to have some people still waiting for a course while the guest of honor's table was taking the last bite.

"We're good to go," Rickey announced. He pulled two six-packs of beer out of one of the fridges and handed the frosty bottles around. He didn't actually want cooks working drunk, but because he'd come up with the idea for Liquor after he and G-man had been fired for drinking beer in the kitchen at a crappy French Quarter tourist joint, he made a point of doing this at important moments. It was part good-luck charm, part positive reinforcement: a way of saying *I trust you enough to buy you a beer* before *your shift, not just after.*

"I was just gonna do some burgers or something for staff meal," G-man said as they finished their beers, "but how about we go across the street instead? That diner over there looked good."

"What, the Palace Café?" Rickey nodded. "That place is famous. Calvin Trillin wrote about it, I think. Well, sure, long as we can get back here by five-thirty or so, we should be fine."

They walked into the banquet hall, where waiters had begun setting and decorating long tables, and through the lobby to the street. A young policeman stood outside the theater looking half scared, half mad. As the seven cooks emerged, he held up a hand. "No foot traffic on the street right now. We got us a situation here."

"A what?" Rickey said.

"A God-Damn clusterfuck!" Schexnaydre yelled. Rickey hadn't seen him come up, but here he was, baring his teeth and glowering at the young cop. The policeman tried to wave him back, but Schexnaydre barreled right past him. "Piss the hell off, you little pissant! We got a Ducks Unlimited banquet starting in three hours and no time for this bullshit!"

"Sir, this is a potential terrorist situation—"

"The fuck it is! This is another one of Harry Comeaux's goddamn war games. All I got to say is he better wrap it up *real* soon or he's gonna have the sportsmen of St. Landry Parish to answer to. Now get out of my way—I'm taking these gentlemen over to the Palace!"

"Sir—"

Schexnaydre actually growled at the cop, a low wordless sound, and the poor guy took a step backward. Like a row of baby ducklings, the cooks followed Schexnaydre across the street. Just as they got to the other side, an armored personnel carrier draped in American flags rounded the corner of the courthouse square and trundled right past them. A small gray-haired man with thick glasses sat atop it, holding a rifle and staring straight ahead. "Comeaux, you stupid piece of shit!" Schexnaydre hollered, shaking his fist, but the little man's steely gaze never wavered.

They entered the Palace Café—a dim, high-ceilinged place that looked as if it hadn't changed much since 1953 or so—and took two tables. Rickey ended up with G-man, Tanker, Marquis, and Schexnaydre. "What the hell's going on?"

"Our Chief of Police." Schexnaydre spat out the words as if they were drops of bile. "Another one of his damn Homeland Security drills. You probably read about 'em in the New Orleans papers—they love to print stuff that makes us look like a bunch of dumb coonasses. Comeaux gives 'em plenty of material. He wants to make sure we're up to snuff just in case Osama bin Laden ever decides to hit Opelousas."

"Y'all got a big Israeli population or something?" Tanker said.

"They got the Jew department store over in Eunice, but I don't know of any others. All the damn fool really wants to do is show off that tank of his. Last time he did this, he ran it into a brand-new police cruiser. Totaled it."

The cooks sneaked glances at each other as they scanned the menu. Finally Rickey said, "What about the banquet?"

"Well, all of us still gonna be there, of course, but right now Harry Asshole Comeaux's got the town airspace under no-fly orders. Lord only knows what time Bobby Hebert'll be able to get in, if he can make it at all."

Rickey's stomach rolled over. "I told you so," he whispered to G-man. "I knew something awful was going to happen."

"It hasn't happened yet," G-man murmured back. "Try to relax. Get you something to eat."

Rickey scanned the menu. It looked great, lots of old-fashioned Cajun, Creole, and diner-style dishes of the kind you either didn't see in New Orleans anymore or you saw costing $27 and tasting like crap. Here, the most expensive item on the menu was the "heavy beef T-bone" at $13.95. Just as he'd almost decided on the shrimp etouffée, he saw a red-faced man in a white bathrobe and an Arab headdress entering the restaurant. The guy looked about as embarrassed as anybody Rickey had ever laid eyes on. "Say, Miz Tina, you think I could get a glass of iced tea?" he asked the lady at the cash register.

The lady sighed. "Chief's doing one of his drills again, huh?"

"Yeah, and I'm supposed to say some kinda hummina-hummina and set off this damn—scuse me—this darn suicide bomb, but I'm awful thirsty."

Miz Tina signaled to one of the waitresses, who brought the guy a glass of tea. He drained it quickly and walked back across the street looking resigned.

"How's the etouffée?" Rickey asked the waitress.

"It's—" She tried not to turn her head as a loud bang and a series of pops came from the direction of the square. "It's real good. You get two vegetables with it, but we're out of the candied yams."

Somebody in the square was shouting through a bullhorn. Rickey couldn't make out the words. The waitress pressed her lips together so tight that all the color left them for a moment, then lifted her chin resolutely and smiled at the cooks. "And don't forget to save room for our baklava," she said. "We make it with fresh pecans."

The meal was superlative: the etouffée subtly spiced, the vegetables perfectly seasoned, the baklava rich with butter and brown sugar. Rickey grew further demoralized, as he always did when faced with a restaurant meal in which he couldn't pinpoint a single flaw. It wasn't that he wanted *bad* meals—well, not unless dining at the restaurant of a chef he secretly hated—but picking at tiny flaws in other people's cooking made him more secure in his own abilities. It wasn't a trait he was particularly proud of, but so far he'd been unable to conquer it.

G-man, who harbored what Rickey considered an unreasonable disdain for phyllo, bucked the baklava trend by ordering the chocolate cream pie. He was still scraping his fork over the plate when Rickey glanced at the clock on his cell phone and said, "OK, we gotta get back."

"Let's hope the damn streets are safe for human habitation," said Schexnaydre, who'd just had a cup of shrimp and okra gumbo. He'd be having gumbo again later, at the banquet, but that didn't seem to bother him any.

There was no further sign of the armored personnel carrier or the man in the Arab headdress. The courthouse square was eerily deserted, but maybe it always got like that after the downtown workers had gone home; most of Opelousas' nightlife seemed to take place on the outskirts. The pork smell had begun to settle over the town again. Back in the kitchen, Rickey reviewed everybody's mise-en-place, checked the plates, made sure the gumbo was hot but not scorching. He set up two big rondeaus of his butter-poaching liquid and, along with Tanker, began par-cooking the drum. Butter-poaching was a technique recently made trendy by California chef Thomas Keller. Unlike most trendy techniques, Rickey thought it had a lot of merit. Keller posited that cooking seafood too fast—"violently" was the word he used—caused it to seize up and fail to retain flavor. By poaching the seafood very slowly in an emulsion of butter, white wine, stock, and shallots, it was possible to retain a texture nearly as lush and silken as that of raw seafood. Rickey and Tanker cooked three hundred pieces of fish to just a hair below done, wrapped them in the duck prosciutto, and stored them in hotel pans. They'd crisp them off in the ovens later, just before it was time to serve the course.

The task took a fair amount of concentration. Rickey was glad, as it took his mind off the approaching evening. His heart was no longer in the event, but he knew he had to overcome that attitude.

Even if Bobby Hebert never showed up, there were 299 other guests who deserved a great meal.

He wanted another beer, but decided against it. He'd already had a second one over at the Palace, and he didn't need a third. His mind had to be absolutely clear for this event. Thirty minutes until the diners were seated. He held up a hand in front of his face to see if it was shaking. Nope, rock-steady. But where the hell was G-man? That was all he needed now, his key cook disappearing. Maybe he'd just gone to the bathroom or something. Here he came now, walking back into the kitchen with Tee Fontenot and ... who was that tall guy behind them? Rickey blinked, shook his head, looked again.

"Chef!" said Fontenot. "Where you at? Got somebody wants to meet you!"

G-man folded his arms across his chest and leaned against the counter looking pleased with himself, as if maybe he'd helped Fontenot fly the helicopter that had finally brought the guest of honor here.

"It's a pleasure to meet you," said Bobby Hebert, grasping Rickey's hand in both of his own. "Man, I don't know how you chefs do it, coming up with all these great recipes. Must be hard work, huh?"

Rickey looked up into those dark, slightly hollow eyes, shook the hand that had thrown the ball that had first made him think about his purpose in life, felt his knees weaken, tried to tamp down the huge, goofy grin that wanted to spread across his face. "Yeah, I guess it's pretty hard," he said. "No big deal. I been doing it all my life."

XVI. LE FER DANS LE LIT

It was going to be a long time before G-man let him forget that nonchalant *I guess it's pretty hard.* For weeks, months, possibly years, Rickey knew he'd be listening to variations of the line: *Ooooo, yeah, Bobby, it's pretty hard awright, especially when I look at youuuuuuu.* Rickey didn't care. He visited the head table three times during the course of the evening, listening to the Cajun Cannon rave about his menu.

"Man, I gotta tell you I never thought a New Orleans cook could make a great duck and sausage gumbo—that's a Cajun thing. You got it right, though. Tastes like you grew up on the bayou."

The other people at the table nodded, and Rickey breathed a small inward sigh of relief. He was confident about his other courses, but he hadn't been sure he was capable of making a gumbo that would wow this crowd.

A little later: "That's the best duck I ever had, that teal! It's a lean bird, how you got it so tender?"

Rickey leaned over, put his hand on Bobby's shoulder—trying not to notice the hard pad of muscle there, but he couldn't quite help it—and spoke his secret directly into Bobby's ear. "Wrapped it in bacon, then threw the bacon away. You like the cherries with it?"

"Yeah, yeah, yeah! I think I taste a little liquor in there—that's what y'all do, huh? I'm gonna have to check out your restaurant."

"You do that. We'll take real good care of you."

"So how you like the Saints this year, Chef?"

"I like 'em a lot." The team had been on a rare winning streak and was currently 11–4 with a good chance at a playoff berth.

G-man came out with him to help deliver the palate cleansers. Rickey didn't believe in chefs serving diners, had never done it even once in his career, but tonight he made an exception. They placed the soup spoons containing green sorbet balls in front of Bobby, Tee Fontenot, Schexnaydre, and another man they didn't know, and were just turning to go back to the kitchen when the entire crowd stood up and gave them a thunderous round of applause. Cries of "Speech! Speech!" and the sound of stomping feet rang through the hall.

G-man patted Rickey on the back. "Go on, you heard 'em. Share your genius, genius."

Rickey hunched his shoulders and made his way to the front of the hall, where a zydeco band was playing. The guitars and accordions trailed off and the singer relinquished the microphone.

"Uh, thanks," Rickey said. "I think this might be the only place I ever been where people like eating more than they do in New Orleans."

That was good for another prolonged round of applause. "*C'est si bon!*" somebody shouted.

"I wasn't gonna talk about this, but I got a little story I'd like to tell you. Just a real short one before you get your dessert. The month I turned thirteen, I went to my first Saints game in the New Orleans Superdome …"

The story went over well. Even with the bright stage lights in his face, Rickey could see Bobby Hebert's wide white smile when he finished it. Suddenly embarrassed, he hurried back to the kitchen door, where G-man was waiting for him.

"Why aren't you in there helping them set up the crème brûlées?"

"I wanted to hear what you had to say. You're a natural."

"Yeah, a natural dork. I was shit-scared."

"Dude, you sounded great and they loved it. I bet Bobby comes in to eat within the month."

Rickey braced his hands on the counter and let his shoulders droop. He realized he was exhausted. "You know what?" he said. "Except for the band, we're the only black people here."

"I hate to tell you this," said Terrance, "but y'all ain't black."

G-man waved a dismissive hand. "You know what your problem is, T? You're always getting caught up in the minor details."

"It's kinda weird, though, huh?" Rickey said. "Opelousas seems like a pretty black town, but we got an all-white crowd in here."

"Are Cajuns white?" Terrance asked. "I thought they got themselves declared a separate race or something."

"Look like a buncha crackers to me," Marquis volunteered.

"Just your basic crackers with boudin," Rickey said. It was a lame joke, but it struck him as funny, and suddenly he was howling with laughter.

"Oh my God, he's hysterical again," said G-man. "Go calm down somewhere, huh? Fantasize about Bobby Hebert. We got the desserts covered."

"Fuck that." Rickey caught his breath and resumed his place on the line. "I started this dinner, I'll finish it. Tanker, where's the damn duck skin triangles?"

After the desserts had gone out, Rickey tucked into a crème brulée he'd saved for himself. He didn't have much of a sweet tooth, but he wanted to see how these had turned out. The sweet cream was unctuous with the flavor of duck fat, smooth and golden-tasting on the tongue. In lesser hands than Tanker's it could easily have been a disgusting mess, but the ramekins were already beginning to come back into the kitchen scraped clean. Rickey closed his eyes. They had done it. In the great Liquor tradition, they hadn't known a damn thing about what they were getting into, and they had done it anyway.

The banquet was just enough of a success. The party afterward was way too much of one.

Rickey had always thought he could drink. No, screw that; he knew he could drink. These people, though, put him to shame. He never finished his first glass of Wild Turkey, because it was always refilled before he got more than halfway through. Bobby Hebert had already left, which was probably just as well. The last thing Rickey remembered was Tee Fontenot telling him a long, convoluted joke about a mother listening at the bedroom door on her daughter's wedding night. It seemed the daughter had chronic cold feet and liked to sleep with a hot iron in the bed. The joke was mostly in English, but its humor seemed to hinge upon the fact that the phrases "the iron" (*le fer*) and "do it" (*le faire*) sounded alike in French. The punchline was, "Well, if he doesn't want to do it in the bed, then do it on the floor!" Rickey knew he'd laughed himself nearly sick over this incomprehensibility, and he was pretty sure he'd countered with a joke about Superman drinking in a bar, but the rest of the evening was a bourbon-soaked blur.

He woke up the next morning in the motel bathroom, curled half on a very thin towel, half on the cold floor with the tiles imprinting themselves into his skin. For several minutes he was utterly unable to get up even though he knew water and aspirin would be attainable if he did. When he finally managed it, he caught sight of himself in the mirror and gave a little cry of anguish. Snarled hair, red eyes, stubble, thousand-yard stare. How far he had fallen since last night!

G-man was sprawled on the bed, fully clothed and snoring. Rickey lowered his head carefully onto a pillow. The motion woke G-man. "Oh, God," he whispered. "What did they *do* to us?"

"Just acted like themselves, I guess." Rickey's tongue was sticking to the roof of his mouth. He wished he had some more water, but couldn't bring himself to get back up.

"Never again."

"Drinking?"

"Drinking with Cajuns."

"Good idea." Rickey tried to roll over, but an astounding bolt of pain shot through his head and he abandoned the effort. "I bet they're not even hung over."

"Damn," said G-man.

"What?"

"This was supposed to be our touristy day. We were gonna eat boudin."

Rickey groaned.

"Maybe by tonight we'll be ready for a link or two."

Rickey fought his gorge, failed, leaned over the edge of the bed, and threw up on the carpet. He knew this was a disgraceful thing to do, but it was mostly drool, and the carpet clearly had previous acquaintance with such things.

By late afternoon, they felt almost human. It was Sunday and the Palace Café was closed, as was almost everything else in town. They finally found a meat market and sat outside in their car, drinking cold Cokes and squeezing boudin into their mouths. The pork, rice, and green onion filling whose very mention had made them ill this morning now tasted indescribably wonderful. They ate two links apiece and threw the rubbery casings out the window for a dog who was hanging around the parking lot. Rickey looked down at the shiny white paper spread across his lap, marked with cayenne-red grease spots and the scrawled price of the sausage. "I think I could eat another one," he said.

"Better not push your luck."

"How about we buy a cooler and take some home?"

"Sure, and some andouille too."

Rickey's heart lifted as they walked back into the market and scanned the porcine bounty in the display case: sausages, thick-cut bacon, Styrofoam bowls of hogshead cheese, the stuffed pigs' stomachs known variously as *chaudin* or *ponce*. He remembered shaking Bobby Hebert's hand (maybe hanging on a bit too long, but he didn't think the Cannon had noticed), remembered Bobby saying *I'm gonna have to check out your restaurant.* If you didn't consider a day-long hangover a real setback—which neither of them did—then the trip had been a great triumph.

XVII. JINGLE, JANGLE, JINGLE

On the night before the night before Christmas, Rickey and G-man decided to spend their evening off at Celebration in the Oaks, the big light show in City Park. Millions of colored lights were arranged in the shape of holiday scenes as well as things that seemed to have nothing to do with Christmas: circuses, dinosaurs, jazz bands. It was mostly a drive-through deal, but the best section was in the middle of the park, where you could leave your car and walk through the Botanical Garden and Storyland. Storyland was a fixture of every New Orleanian's childhood. It had a Tilt-A-Whirl and bumper cars and a merry-go-round the old folks called "flying horses," but what made it unique was the garden of brightly painted statues from fairy tales and nursery rhymes. The wolf from Little Red Riding Hood lurked in a playhouse, granny-capped and fearsomely befanged. A topless, slightly pornographic Little Mermaid sat on a rock in the middle of a small pond. Mother Goose swooped down from a low-hanging oak branch, looking as if she might snatch up a kid or two. There were things kids could climb and slide down and fall off of, and it was all just the tiniest bit macabre, as any great children's amusement should be.

The Saints had won their final game of the season the previous Sunday, beating the hated Atlanta Falcons, finishing with a 12–4 record, and securing a spot in the playoffs, something that was a big deal for any football team but a rare and shining moment for New Orleans. Rickey was ready to celebrate. The evening was cold, not painfully so but enough to feel like Christmas. He bought two cups of hot buttered rum that turned out to be nonalcoholic and foul, but he didn't care. Everything seemed magical.

Near the kiddie rollercoaster, they came upon another relic of their childhoods: a two-story sculpture of Mr. Bingle suspended from the branches of a live oak. Mr. Bingle had started life as a Christmas advertisement for the Maison Blanche department store downtown, but soon became a beloved New Orleans star. He was sort of an assistant to Santa, a little snowman with a red nose, an ice-cream-cone hat, and wings of holly. A flying snowman with holly wings didn't really make sense, but New Orleans kids had no idea what a snowman was supposed to look like. At the height of his popularity, he'd spawned dolls, a TV show, and a sparkly winter wonderland in the department store's display window.

This particular Mr. Bingle had made annual appearances flying high above Canal Street on the store façade, but fell into disrepair and obscurity when Maison Blanche sold out to a national chain. He'd spent the last several years in a warehouse somewhere in the Lower Ninth Ward. This year a group of Bingle lovers had taken up a collection to restore him and make him part of Celebration in the Oaks. The sound of the theme song pouring out of hidden speakers made Rickey's throat tighten. His memories of Mr. Bingle weren't entirely good—he remembered being five years old, sitting in the living room watching a Maison Blanche TV commercial while his parents fought in their bedroom—but, like every other New Orleans kid born between the fifties and the seventies, he felt a helpless, sentimental wave of nostalgia for the little snowman.

Jingle, jangle, jingle,
Here comes Mr. Bingle
With another message from Kris Kringle
Time to launch your Christmas season
Maison Blanche makes Christmas pleasin'
Gifts galore for you to see
Each a gem from ... MB!

As he stood blinking at the utter familiarity of the slightly mechanical ladies' voices—voices he hadn't heard in nearly thirty years—Rickey felt someone tap him on the shoulder. He turned and saw Shake Vojtaskovic arm in arm with a gorgeous, dreadlocked black girl.

"Hey, Snake," he said.

"Hey, Pudge."

"That what they're calling me now?"

"So I hear."

Rickey found that he didn't care. Shake had most likely made up the nickname, and even if he hadn't, nobody trusted a skinny chef. "Who's your friend?" he said.

"Oh … this is Lila. She tends bar at La Pharmacie. Lila, this is Rickey."

"Not Pudge?" the girl said in what sounded like a Jamaican accent.

Rickey shrugged. "Rickey, Pudge, dickhead, whatever you like."

Lila laughed, but not unkindly.

"You're in a good mood," Shake observed.

"Yeah. Things are going good." Rickey started to launch into a litany of boasts, then decided not to bother. What was the point? He knew what he'd done, and he no longer had anything to prove to Shake. "I hear good stuff about your place, too."

"Yeah. Some of 'em are probably even true. Things weren't all that great at first, but they're getting better." Shake glanced at Lila, who smiled back at him. "Plus I just got a great new sous chef who really knows what he's doing. Y'all ought to come in sometime. We'll do it up for you."

"I will," Rickey promised. Maybe he even would. He didn't expect much of La Pharmacie, but it would be nice to see an alumnus of his kitchen putting out good food. There was no point in making more enemies than you had to.

And whatever else he might do, he now felt certain that he could cook duck in more different and delicious ways than any other chef in the city. He was already planning a tasting menu that reprised the Ducks Unlimited banquet, with variations to accommodate domestic ducks and the boozy requirements of Liquor.

He and G-man talked to Shake and his new lady for a few minutes more, then continued on their way. As they walked into the Botanical Garden, an endless array of tiny lights seemed to stretch before them, multicolored and dazzling, repeated in the long reflecting pool. Stars were never visible in the night sky here, only the purple glow that hung over any brightly lit city, but this must be how they would look if you could see them. Things to count, even though counting them all was impossible. Things to wish on.

In the panoramic shimmer of lights, water, and sky, Rickey thought he could glimpse the future: true love, great food, Bobby Hebert coming to eat at his restaurant, the Saints winning the Super Bowl, the city of New Orleans standing whole, strong, beautiful forever.

Author's Note

The preceding pair of short novels spans nearly two decades in the lives, careers, and relationship of Chefs John Rickey and Gary "G-man" Stubbs. There are also three novels about the interim years, *Liquor, Prime,* and *Soul Kitchen* (Random House) as well as a double handful of short stories in my collections *The Devil You Know* and *Antediluvian Tales* (Subterranean Press). Sticklers for chronological detail may be interested to know that I wrote *Liquor* first, assuming it would be a one-off. It turned out I liked the characters enough to want to explore their earlier years in *The Value of X,* and their subsequent ones in the other stories.

In *D*U*C*K*'s original foreword, "Where the Storm Never Happened (For Now)," I noted, "I think of [*D*U*C*K*] as slightly alternate-universe fiction, a kind of fairy tale set in the same world of chefs and restaurants I've been writing about for several years now, but in which [Hurricane Katrina and the subsequent federal levee failure] didn't come to New Orleans. Maybe it took a different path (there's a slight hint of this in the story), maybe it never entered the Gulf at all . . . Just for now, I wanted to write a story where the bitch wasn't a factor." That's still how I see it, but I've been intrigued to learn that some readers interpreted the tale as a hallucination brought on by Rickey's head injury in Chapter One! Once the story passes out of the writer's hands, the reader is ultimately God, so you will have to decide for yourself.

Rickey, G-man, and their families have probably given me more joy than any other characters I've written about. I hope to write more about them one day, and I hope you enjoy them too.

—Poppy Z. Brite
June 15, 2009
New Orleans

Acknowledgments

As ever, thanks are due to my husband, Chef Chris DeBarr, without whom there would have been probably no Liquor stories and certainly no G-man. Check out his new restaurant, The Green Goddess, at www.greengoddessnola.com. Tips of the hat also go out to Henry Barber, Bob Brite, Connie Brite, The Boudin Link (www.boudinlink.com), Doug Brinkley, Gene Broussard, Cathy Campanella, the Culinary Institute of America, Stephen Ellison, Joel L. Fletcher, Gavin Grant, Dave Hammond, Kris LaMorte, Kelly Link, Kevin Maroney, Terry Maroney, the Palace Cafe of Opelousas, Greg & Saundra Peters, Bill Schafer, Ira Silverberg, Joseph & Gina Stebbins, and Carl Walker. For information on the New Orleans Lakefront Airport, I am indebted to Mark Grady for his May 5, 2005 article in *The Southern Aviator*.

About the Author

Poppy Z. Brite's fiction set in the New Orleans restaurant world includes *Prime*, *Liquor*, and *Soul Kitchen*. She has also published five other novels and three short story collections. She lives with her husband Chris, a chef, in New Orleans.

Printed in the USA
CPSIA information can be obtained
at www.ICGtesting.com
JSHW020935070224
56833JS00001B/2

9 781931 520607